I AM
THE
GHOST
IN YOUR
HOUSE

Books by Mar Romasco-Moore

Some Kind of Animal
I Am the Ghost in Your House

I AM THE GHOST IN YOUR HOUSE

MAR ROMASCO-MOORE

Delacorte Press

Text copyright © 2022 by Maria Romasco-Moore
Jacket art copyright © 2022 by Alex Garant
Interior illustrations copyright © Rumdecor/Shutterstock and
HiSunnySky/Shutterstock

All rights reserved. Published in the United States by Delacorte Press,
an imprint of Random House Children's Books, a division of
Penguin Random House LLC, New York.

Delacorte Press is a registered trademark and the colophon is a trademark of
Penguin Random House LLC.

Visit us on the web! GetUnderlined.com

Educators and librarians, for a variety of teaching tools,
visit us at RHTeachersLibrarians.com

Library of Congress Cataloging-in-Publication Data
Names: Romasco Moore, Mar, author.
Title: I am the ghost in your house / Mar Romasco-Moore.
Description: First edition. | New York : Delacorte Press, [2022] | Audience: Ages 14+. |
Audience: Grades 10–12. | Summary: Born invisible, seventeen-year-old Pie wants more
from life than lurking unseen in other people's houses, but when she finally reveals herself,
her mother disappears, and Pie begins to question everything she thought she knew.
Identifiers: LCCN 2021003897 (print) | LCCN 2021003898 (ebook) |
ISBN 978-0-593-17721-1 (hardcover) | ISBN 978-0-593-17723-5 (library binding) |
ISBN 978-0-593-17722-8 (ebook)
Subjects: CYAC: Invisibility—Fiction. | Loneliness—Fiction. | Lesbians—Fiction. |
Mothers and daugthers—Fiction.
Classification: LCC PZ7.1.R66834 Iah 2022 (print) | LCC PZ7.1.R66834 (ebook) |
DDC [Fic]—dc23

The text of this book is set in 12-point Bembo Book MT Pro.
Interior design by Andrea Lau

Printed in the United States of America
10 9 8 7 6 5 4 3 2 1
First Edition

I AM
THE
GHOST
IN YOUR
HOUSE

West Palm Beach, FL

My mother's greatest fear when she was pregnant with me was that I would come out normal.

She gave birth in the bathtub of some rich family's summer home in Palm Beach. The tub had a faux-gold faucet in the shape of an open-beaked swan, so that all the water flowing out of it was swan spit.

The family was gone for the season, the house deserted, my mother alone. Which meant that when the pain came, she could scream.

She said that was the first time she'd screamed aloud in years. She said it felt good. To let out the fear she'd been carrying all those months, nestled alongside me like a twin.

My mother had been to the hospital a few days before, but not as a patient. She'd walked in, unnoticed, helped herself to painkillers, disinfectant, latex gloves, drugs. She was prepared to cut the umbilical cord herself. She'd watched a video online.

When I finally came out, she held me up with gloved hands, exhausted. It was a relief, she told me, to see that I was breathing. And yet it was an even bigger relief to see, clearly visible through the skin of my stomach, the outline of the bathtub faucet behind me.

I was transparent, safe, that golden swan screaming silently inside me.

I was so happy, my mother told me, and maybe she was happy that I was invisible like her, happy that the pain of labor was over. But I don't believe for a second that she was happy to have me.

She named me Pietà, which is Italian for "pity."

1

The train to Pittsburgh was going backward, undoing all the distance we'd covered.

My mother had fallen asleep, head slumped against the window. Through her transparent body, I could see the landscape rushing past in reverse. Images flickered across her face: tree trunks, mountainside, sky. It made her seem restless.

"Mom," I whispered, nudging her.

The plan was to spend only one day and night in Pittsburgh, then catch a train for New York the next morning, so I was impatient to get there. Worried we never would. It wasn't as if we'd paid for tickets, at least. My mother and I don't need tickets.

We just need to be careful no one sits on us.

The sun was rising. Out the window, I recognized a river, which, half an hour before, had been indistinguishable from the night sky. Now it was a cloudy green, broken by red rocks trailing lacy veils of foam. Everything looked sharp in the morning sun, as if the train window were a movie screen. But the movie made no sense. Something arty, experimental. Short on plot.

Mother shifted and groaned softly in the seat beside me.

"We're going backward," I told her.

"Must be a freight train on the tracks." She waved a dismissive hand. "They have right-of-way."

In the seat behind us, a child started crying. I wanted to cry, too. It was silly and selfish, but I thought maybe the universe was conspiring to keep me away from Pittsburgh. The last time we'd been there, two years ago, things ended terribly. That was my fault, and Mom had told me in no uncertain terms that we were never, ever going back.

But I wanted to go back. I'd been wanting it every day for the last two years.

There was someone there I needed to see.

"I feel ill," my mother said, still curled up with her head against the train window. "Be a dear and fetch me a ginger ale."

"Okay," I said. "Of course, right away."

When Mom had finally given in and agreed to a brief Pittsburgh detour, it had seemed, perhaps, too good to be true.

Today, if the train ever started moving the right way again, we'd stop by the City of Bridges, and then tomorrow we'd go to New York City to celebrate my favorite day of the whole year. Not my birthday—that had already happened. Tomorrow was far better than my birthday, far better than Christmas.

Tomorrow was Halloween, the one day of the year that I could be seen.

Not because of magic or anything. Halloween is just the only day it's acceptable to wear a full-face mask without everyone assuming you are about to kill them. People could see the mask, but not my face.

I was born invisible.

Really invisible. Not just shy or overlooked. Not like a superhero, either. I couldn't turn it on or off.

Nobody in this world had ever seen my actual face, except for my mother, who was invisible, too. She saw me the same way I saw her, the same way I saw myself in mirrors. To her, and to myself, I looked like I was made of glass or water. Insubstantial. A girl who might break or wash away.

To anyone else, I looked like nothing.

I'd never had a job or a car or a friend. My mother and I roamed, taking what we needed, living in other people's houses like ghosts.

We had been formally exorcised, in fact, six times.

On the backward train, I stood and made my way down the aisle. We took trains because they have more space. Buses are like moving sardine tins. Airplanes, I imagine, are even worse.

I pressed my gloved hand against the automatic door panel at the end of the train car. We are invisible but not insubstantial. The door didn't know the difference between me and someone normal. One old Mennonite woman glanced up as the door rattled open for—from her perspective—no one, but this early, most passengers were asleep.

In the tiny metal no-man's-land between cars, the muted

rumble of the train became a clanking, wailing, whistling roar. On crowded trains, my mother and I were occasionally obliged to spend most of the trip in these thunderous spaces where the floor and the ceiling and the doors all rattle like wild. The wind wants to get in, wants to ride for a while.

In the café car, a conductor was sitting on one of the blue padded benches, eating a muffin. He frowned through me as I came in.

"Is that door broke?" he called to the café man, who shrugged.

The train shuddered to a stop, and I lost my balance, banging my hip against a booth. The conductor grumbled about the "goddamn freight trains" clogging the tracks.

I crept past him to the counter and pulled off one of my gloves. They were lilac silk with pearl buttons, lifted from a vintage shop in Chicago.

When the café man turned to wipe down the microwave, I hefted myself up onto the counter, reaching out with my bare hand for the stacked soda cans on the shelf behind it. The moment my fingers brushed against a can, it went filmy, translucent, as see-through as me. To the conductor and the café man, had they been looking, it would have disappeared.

That's how it works. That's why I always wear gloves. Anything that touches my bare skin turns invisible, too. For Halloween, I have to wear two masks, one on top of the other, because the first one will vanish.

My mother says that we are controlling this effect, on some level, but unconsciously. It's a reflex, like flinching when touched. Sometimes my mother can control it a tiny

6

bit if she concentrates super hard—can cause, for instance, only one small part of an object to become invisible—but I've never managed.

Ginger ale acquired, I slipped back out of the café car. Behind me, the conductor cursed "this run-down hunk of junk." We were still at a dead stop.

Mother was slumped forward in the seat when I reached her, head cradled in her hands.

"Mom?" I said quietly.

She glanced up, face pale, which is to say more see-through than usual. Out the window behind her, a hawk landed on a tree alongside the tracks, perched directly in line with her right eye.

We don't reflect any visible light, for the most part, though Mother says if we stood stock-still against a white wall, a close observer might spot a slight darkening of the air where our pupils are. But she and I can see a fraction of the spectrum that normal people can't. It means we see better in the dark, because there's a haze of infrared around anything living, anything warm. That's why I can see her, though faintly, and she can see me.

It's always been that way.

I tried to hand her the ginger ale, but she blanched, turned away, and clutched her stomach. I thought she was going to puke, but she didn't.

Instead, she disappeared.

A Small Town Somewhere Near Lake Michigan

Unlike me, my mother wasn't born invisible. It came on, like a condition, in adolescence. At ten, she told me, her invisibility first manifested, during a trip to the lake. She remembers standing at the edge of the water. Just a few feet away, her father yelled her name, but his eyes passed right over her. For a few wonderful moments, she was safe.

At first, her invisibility would come on unpredictably, last for a few hours, fade. The duration and frequency increased over the years until, by the time she was fourteen, it was permanent. Irreversible.

Not that she had any desire to reverse it.

My mother believes it was a defensive adaptation. Protective camouflage. Because already, by that age, she was being seen in ways she didn't want to be.

I have never met my grandparents and I never will. My mother doesn't like to talk about them. They weren't good parents, weren't good people.

At fourteen, as soon as she could hide from them, as soon as she could get away, she did. From then on, my mother took care of herself, haunting the houses of the rich, taking what she needed. She never finished high school, but she read voraciously, sat in on college classes. Learned all she could. Traveled. She was self-sufficient. Alone.

Not counting, of course, the five or so years she spent being an international art thief with my father.

She says she regrets those years now.

Never fall in love, she always tells me. *It isn't worth it.*

Well, too late.

2

I stared at the empty seat beside me on the train, which was supposed to be going to Pittsburgh but at that moment was going absolutely nowhere.

My mother is dead. That's the first thought that popped into my mind. It didn't make sense, but neither did what I'd just seen.

Maybe this was what happened when people like us died. I'd always assumed we died the same way as everyone else, but it wasn't like I had proof.

My mother had told me she didn't know if there were any other invisible people out there. We hadn't met any. It might just be the two of us. Alone in the world.

Except not entirely alone. We had each other, at least.

That was all we had.

Panicked, I clutched at the empty air where my mother had been. But it wasn't empty. My knuckles collided sharply with her shoulder.

She stuttered back into view.

"You hit me," she said, brows furrowed.

I gaped at her. A moment later, she doubled over and vomited onto the floor.

We always spoke quietly to each other on trains. The muted rush of air and clatter of wheels on tracks was usually enough to hide our words. But Mother's retching sounds were loud. A sharp acrid odor jammed itself up my nose.

"Aw, hell no," said the woman in the seat behind us. "Riley, you being sick over there?"

"Nuh-uh," called a kid from across the aisle.

I shoved the ginger ale into my backpack. My mother had figured out a system years ago: we cut slits in the shoulders of our shirts, then threaded the backpack straps through so they would touch our skin at all times and thus keep the packs (and everything in them) invisible.

My mother was wiping her mouth with a shaking hand. I waved urgently toward the far end of the train car. She nodded and followed me down the aisle into the larger of the two bathroom compartments. I slid the heavy door shut, latched it.

"What the hell is going on?" I asked her, trying to keep my voice level.

She leaned against the wall by the sink, eyes shut, one hand on her stomach. The train lurched back into motion beneath us. Going the right way this time, it felt like.

"Mom?"

Her eyes fluttered open. She reached toward the sink, cupped her hand under the faucet. "Turn it on for me, will you?"

I wanted to refuse, to yell at her for scaring me like that, but I knew that was a selfish, childish way to act. I was seventeen, nearly an adult now, so I reached forward, pressed the faucet button. Water dribbled out, gathering slowly in my mother's glassy palms. She rinsed her mouth. Rinsed it again.

"I'm sorry, baby," she said finally, straightening up. "I guess I got motion sick."

Which was bullshit. I'd been riding trains with her all my life, and she'd never gotten motion sick. We rode for days sometimes. Weeks.

"You disappeared," I said accusingly.

"Oh." A series of expressions ghosted briefly across her face. "I didn't realize."

I realized, though. Understood those flickers of emotion. She wasn't shocked, wasn't panicked. She knew. This wasn't the first time. I felt a flicker of rage.

"This has happened before?" I asked, far louder than usual. Loud enough that someone could have heard. I knew I wasn't being fair. She was sick, obviously. Something was wrong with her. I should be nice to her, not angry with her.

She frowned, seemed to consider lying, which was answer enough.

"When?" I demanded. "Why didn't you tell me?"

"Keep your voice down."

"You're the one who puked loud enough for the whole train car to hear."

She sighed and rubbed her eyes. Was she more translucent than usual? I wasn't sure. I could read the BE CONSIDERATE OF YOUR FELLOW PASSENGERS, DON'T LEAVE A MESS sign clearly through her left shoulder.

"What's wrong with you?" I asked.

"I'm fine," she said, another obvious lie. "I just need to rest."

We *had* been moving around a lot lately. But that wasn't unusual.

We are restless people by nature. We roam, from one house to another, one city to the next. There is a limit to how long we can stay somewhere before people start to notice. Even when we find an empty house, there is always the risk of the owners returning, or new buyers moving in, or (as happened exactly once) waking up to a wrecking ball smashing through the front window.

"You aren't fine," I told her. "That was scary." An understatement.

"Pie," she said, which is what I went by, since the name she gave me was too sad. "We can talk about this later." Her voice took on the hard edge of a maternal lecture, the same tone in which she had so often said, *We are never going back to that city, Pie, and you know why.* "Let's find a house as soon as we get in. I feel like I've barely had time to close my eyes the last few weeks."

I frowned at her. Three weeks ago had been my birthday, which we'd celebrated on the coast of California in a condemned beach house. My mother had gathered seventeen miniature cakes from various bakeries, and I'd taken a single bite out of each.

My birthday gift, she told me, was that I could choose where we went for a while. Which was unusual. I was used to my mother being in charge. Always following her where she wanted to go, following her many rules to keep us safe and undetected.

Do not wander off. Do not walk in snow or sand or gravel or mud or loose dirt. Do not exhale too much outside when the temperature is below freezing. Avoid walking in precipitation of any kind. Avoid smoke. Never get in a pool or other body of water in view of others. Do not sit on a soft surface unless alone. Never touch anything with an ungloved hand when someone is looking. Never move anything with a gloved hand when someone is looking. Do not take anything with a security tag. Do not take anything too personal or too ostentatious. Take only what you need. Be quiet, be quiet, be quiet. Never speak when someone can hear you. Never touch them. Never let anyone, in any way, know that you are there.

Somebody jiggled the bathroom door handle. My mother flinched. My anger died, guilt creeping in to fill the empty space. I'd been dragging us around the country at breakneck speed. Maybe this was all my fault.

"We'd better go wait between the cars," my mother said. She'd seemed normal the last few weeks. But maybe I hadn't been paying enough attention. Not a grown-up at all. Still just a silly selfish kid.

Probably the fact that she'd agreed to go back to Pittsburgh, even for a day, should have told me something was wrong.

Is that why she'd agreed? She was just too tired to argue?

It should have been enough that she still let me have Halloween, still let me bend the rules on that one day of the year. Pushing for Pittsburgh had been ungrateful.

Especially given what I'd been planning to do once we got there. What I was still planning to do.

"Okay," I said, deflated. "Yeah. Ready?"

My mother nodded. I took a breath, unlatched the bathroom door, slid it open. The Mennonite woman I'd noticed before was waiting just outside. She looked up, confused. I slipped past her, barely avoided brushing her arm.

The woman peered into the bathroom. "Hello?" she called.

I pressed the door panel at the end of the car, and my mother and I were lost to the screaming metal, the clanking floor, the rattling walls, the lonely wailing wind.

Anywhere with a Station

I've spent half my life on trains. Sometimes I wake up in a house and feel confused about why we aren't moving, why I can't hear the rattle of the tracks.

We once spent a whole month riding around the country in big loops, setting ourselves up in empty roomettes on double-decker sleeper car trains.

I learned to understand the world in terms of distance. *How far are we from New York?* I asked my mother once when I was young, pestering her when she wanted silence. *How far from California, from the moon?*

As an answer, she grabbed a jewel-handled hairbrush from the dressing table in the rich lady's bedroom where we were staying, plonked it at the upper-right corner of the four-poster bed. *New York City,* she said, pointing. A pill bottle placed on the lower-left corner became Los Angeles. A pair of silk panties retrieved from a drawer, the entire state of Florida. The Mississippi River she made from a robe tie. A pillow was the Rocky Mountains.

She kept adding more objects, naming them. It was magic to me. I studied that map for hours while my mother rested.

Drove a train made of an empty box of raisins from one end to the other, over and over.

I often thought of the country as a big bed when I was watching it rush past out a train window. The low rolling mountains of the East were a lumpy blanket. As the train moved west, the blanket was gradually ironed out, neatly pinstriped with rows of plants, until finally it grew so flat, the elevation so unceasingly even, that even a hill twenty feet high seemed like Mount Ararat, a miracle. If we kept going, the blanket crumpled up again, dotted with linty shrubs and then suddenly: mesas! buttes! The toes of giants sticking up beneath the covers. The craggy peaks of their knees. Their hips and shoulders, their faces. Active-volcano noses. And finally, the foot of the bed, untucked blanket trailing gently down to the ocean floor.

My mother and I have visited a lot of cities, sure, and even some smaller towns, but most of what I've seen of this country I've seen from the window of a train.

And what have I seen? Put into words, it doesn't seem like much. A sofa on the bank of a river. The sun setting against red cliffs. Watercolor skies reflected in flooded fields. A family of elk pausing beside a mountain lake, glancing up. A whole rodeo, for a moment. Children running in the streets, waving. Backyard pools sparkling turquoise. Two piebald horses standing side by side in opposite directions, so they looked like one creature with two heads. Wildfire smoke in the distance.

A whole lot of landscape, a whole lot of nothing. A lot of big empty land and wide lonely sky with nobody living in it, nobody even looking at it. Nobody but me.

3

The vestibules between train cars are mostly doors. One at each end, leading to the passenger cars. And then two exit doors on each side, leading out to the rushing landscape, to freedom/certain death. Out the dirty window on the way to Pittsburgh, I watched the river swish by a third time, glittering now with dappled sunlight.

My mother was sitting against the opposite door, hunched over, forehead resting on her knees, arms wrapped around herself.

I turned every few minutes to check that she was still there. It kept hitting me like little shock waves, that moment when she'd been gone. When I thought: *My mother is dead. I'm alone now. More alone than I've ever been.*

Which was saying something.

If there was a contest for the loneliest person in the whole world, I'd often thought I could win. You don't get much chance to socialize when no one but your mother can see you.

I am used to loneliness. I am good at it. It is a skill I have mastered. Loneliness is a part of who I am, a well so deep it could never be filled.

Occasionally people passed through the train vestibule on their way to or from the café car. If they'd reached out their arms, they could have touched us.

But, of course, they never did.

As we got closer to Pittsburgh, the scenery changed. Trees gave way to power lines, rivers to paved expanses, littered with brightly colored trucks and beams and shipping containers, brushed with rust, as if some giant child had left its toys out in the rain.

I rolled up one glove and checked my watch. It had a diamond for twelve o'clock, and Mother had been angry with me for taking it from the jewelry store in LA, because it set off an antitheft alarm on our way out and alarms give her headaches. Our train was running more than an hour and a half late. I told myself it didn't matter, not really. That it wasn't a sign, wasn't a judgment from the universe.

I wasn't usually impatient. You couldn't be if you rode trains. But in a way, I'd already been waiting for two whole years. Waiting to go back to Pittsburgh. Waiting to see her.

Tess.

Though, of course, she couldn't see me.

It was too loud to hear in the vestibule, so I leaned over and tapped my mother on the knee. We'd lived for several months, once, at a school for the Deaf. Since then, we'd kept up a study of American Sign Language. It was beautiful and useful.

"You okay?" I signed.

"I'm sorry," she signed back. "Let's find food, a house. I'll sleep. We can still go to that place you like. Tonight."

19

I hadn't told my mother the real reason I wanted to go back to Pittsburgh. I couldn't. My mother didn't even know about Tess. Didn't remember her name, probably. There'd be no reason to.

She was just a girl whose house we stayed in once.

Nothing more.

So I'd lied, told my mom I was absolutely dying to return to this museum, the Mattress Factory. The building used to be a warehouse, but now it housed experimental-art exhibits.

And look, it wasn't a total lie. I genuinely loved that museum. Last time my mother and I visited, it was featuring art made of light. In one of the galleries, I stood in the middle of a piece and the multicolored beams of light projected from the wall pierced my stomach, went right through me.

A train door hissed open, and I jumped back. The conductor strode through. My mother and I shuffled awkwardly around to avoid him as he peered out the window, speaking on his crackling radio to someone at the station.

The city came rushing up around us. It opened its mouth of tunnels and highway bridges and swallowed us whole.

The train groaned slowly to a halt in the station. When the conductor unlatched the door to the outside, we wriggled past him, hopped down to the platform, and hugged the far wall while passengers flowed off the train.

I've always loved the moment of disembarking, the excitement of entering a new city. Even when the city isn't *actually* new, somehow stepping off a train makes it feel that way.

This should have been exciting, returning to Pittsburgh, but I felt uneasy.

My mother took my hand, something she hadn't done since I was a child. I led her out of the station. She walked slowly, trailing me across the street beneath a highway bridge.

I tried to remember the layout of Pittsburgh as we walked. The main part of the city is basically shaped like a slice of pizza. Three rivers meet at the point of the slice.

The thought of pizza made me hungry. I should have grabbed something for myself from the café car.

We'd need to catch a bus as soon as possible, get away from downtown. Find some big old Victorian house in a rich part of the city. A house with more rooms than anyone could ever use. Baroque curtains. Plush cushions everywhere. Fainting couches. My mother loved a good fainting couch.

Maybe it was like fainting, the thing that had happened. Sure, in seventeen years I'd never seen anything like it, but what did I know? Not enough.

I turned to ask my mother what she thought about the fainting idea, but she wasn't there.

My heart turned over. I sucked in a breath too fast, nearly choked on it.

She *was* there, though, even though my eyes told me otherwise. I was holding her hand. I squeezed her palm. Hard. Harder. I could feel her, but I couldn't see her.

"Mom?"

"Yes?" she said, and like blinking, she was back.

My pulse didn't slow. I waited for her to say something,

anything, to acknowledge what had happened. Was she aware of it? She gave me a thin smile, said nothing.

Up ahead, a familiar neon sign glowed against the gray dawn sky.

"Are you hungry?" I asked. Maybe food would help.

"Sure," she said.

Sometimes we waited outside doors until someone opened them and we could slip in without drawing attention, but I was in a full panic, so I pushed right through the doors of the McDonald's. A few customers turned to look, but luckily most people would rather ignore unexplained phenomena. It's easier than admitting to themselves that the world makes no sense.

"I'll have fries," my mother said. "I need the restroom."

I watched her go, my heart still racing. Something was wrong and I didn't know what it was and I didn't know how to help and I didn't know why she was pretending it was fine.

I hurried past the line of customers to an empty stretch of counter, swung myself up, slid across, and hopped down on the other side.

Back in the humid kitchen, a boy who didn't look any older than me lifted a basket of fries from the fryer, scooped them into cardboard sleeves with a swift flick of the wrist, placed them onto a rack. I pulled off a glove, grabbed one.

I was only touching the cardboard, not the fries themselves, but it was enough to turn the whole carton shimmery. I couldn't control my power, not consciously, but it still relied on what I perceived as the boundaries of an object. That was why the backpacks worked. Or why, when I held a glass, the liquid didn't just appear to be floating uncontained in the air.

I snatched one fry out of the cardboard sleeve with my teeth and ate it, trying to concentrate on the taste instead of my fear. The salt buzzed on my tongue.

My mother and I had waltzed into five-star restaurants, lifted dishes from celebrity chefs. We'd had sous vide veal with white-truffle aioli. Mille-feuille brushed with gold leaf. People notice when a plate of duck confit or foie gras goes missing. At McDonald's, no one noticed some missing fries. Or if they did, they didn't care. They weren't being paid enough to care.

I sidled carefully but quickly through the cramped kitchen, reached out to the rack of freshly wrapped burgers between the kitchen and the counter area.

With my bare hand, I grabbed a burger—

And dropped it in surprise as a cashier on the other side of the rack screamed.

The instant I'd touched one wrapped burger, the whole rack had gone transparent. Only for a few seconds. But that was long enough.

"Jesus!" I heard the cashier saying. "You see that, Cheryl? Am I having a stroke?"

I was startled. But this, at least, I understood.

It had happened once before.

It was some side effect of stress and adrenaline. In my panic, the effect of my touch got stronger, less discriminating. I needed to be more careful, needed to slow down, to breathe, to focus. Not let things get out of hand.

23

The Cathedral

_____

Last time we stayed in Pittsburgh, things got out of hand.

I made something big disappear. Something so big that I shouldn't have been able to affect it at all. It was worse than a rack at McDonald's. Much worse.

A whole wall.

Not a garden wall, either. Not some minor divider. Not even the wall of a house.

The wall of a building forty-two stories tall.

I touched that broad stone expanse—well, slammed my hand against it, actually—and it melted away. Exposed all the rooms inside it like an overgrown ant farm sandwiched in glass.

People noticed, all right. Terrified ants. Some of them screamed or ran. Many more took pictures or videos on their phones. It lasted only a couple of seconds. I pulled my hand away quickly. But there were hundreds of people in that building, hundreds more outside. The building itself was tall enough to be seen for blocks, miles. All over the city.

The pictures and videos made their way onto social media. Local newspapers covered the event. A few national outlets even picked it up as a fluff piece. My mother was furious. My mother was scared. I showed her that people thought it was a trick. Something done with cameras, projections. They thought it was viral marketing or an episode of a yet-to-be-aired prank show.

She didn't care. She said we were never coming back to this city, no argument. She said I needed to be more careful. She asked me over and over: *What the hell were you thinking?*

What was I thinking?

When I'd touched that wall, I was angry, frustrated, hurt.

It wasn't really an accident. That's something I never told my mother. I'd wanted it to happen, in a way. Wanted the whole building to disappear. The whole world, even. I hadn't thought it would happen, of course, hadn't even known it was possible. But I touched the wall anyway, with my bare hand, without thinking, without being careful.

I did that because, despite my mother's warnings, I had fallen in love.

And the wall? It wasn't even the worst thing I did.

4

At the McDonald's, I slipped quickly out of the kitchen, burger abandoned, envelope of fries clutched in my teeth, both pearl-buttoned gloves jammed back on my hands. I vaulted over the counter, scanned the line of customers for people with their phones out. Which was most of them, of course. I hoped that no one got a picture. It was so quick.

"You saw that, right?" one of the cashiers was asking a businessman-looking guy at the front of the line. He shook his head.

"I saw it," said a lady behind him.

I ran to the bathroom, pushed open the door. A woman who was checking her makeup spun around. She must have seen the door swinging on its own in the mirror.

"Rebecca?" she asked. "Is that you?"

I didn't have time to worry about whether Rebecca was her friend or her long-dead sister. A faint shimmer was visible beneath the farthest stall.

"Mom?" I whispered when I reached the stall, but quietly, because the woman was still at the mirrors.

If I shifted my head back and forth, I could barely see through the crack between the stall partitions. My mother was kneeling on the dirty floor, hunched over, forehead resting on the rim of the toilet seat.

The woman at the sink finally left. I knocked on the stall door. My mother groaned and pushed herself up to her feet, unlatched the door.

"Here," I said, holding out the fries. Normally, I was more careful about holding something in a gloved hand—floating objects freaked people out—but I knew we were alone.

"No thanks," my mother said.

She took a step forward, wobbled, fell. As she was falling, she flickered out of sight again. I threw my hands out to where I thought she should be. The fries went flying, scattered across the tiles. My mother blinked back into view, leaning heavily against the wall.

"Mom!" I shouted.

"Keep your voice down," she said. "Someone might hear."

"What the hell is happening to you?" I asked.

"I'm not feeling well," she said. "I really need to rest."

"Okay," I said, "okay," though it was anything but that.

I couldn't take her to a hospital. I couldn't even ask anyone for help.

She let me grab her hand again and lead her out of the restaurant. I walked fast, hoping she wouldn't overhear any fuss from the counter. That was the last thing she needed, to know I'd fucked up again.

The sun had fully risen by now, lights clicking on inside storefronts. We passed three bus stops until I found one with people already waiting at it. A bus wouldn't stop for us, of course. I stood by the curb, gripping my mother's wrist.

The people waiting were restless. They shuffled about, checked their phones, craned their necks down the street, united in a brief community of shared misery. My mother and I waited, too, but apart.

Not one of them. Not really.

When the bus came, we darted on after the last person, just making it as the door hinged shut behind us. I steered my mother to the back. She settled in a window seat, gave me another weak smile before closing her eyes.

I pulled the ginger ale from my pack, opened it, overturned it on the empty seat beside her, let the liquid fizz into the cushion. Insurance. No one, I hoped, would try to sit next to a mysterious wet spot. I remained standing, scanning the passengers.

Usually my mother found us houses, but I would have to do it now.

Her typical tactic was to pick someone who looked rich or interesting and follow them home.

Nobody rich rode the bus, so the best I could hope for if I wanted a place quickly was someone who wasn't headed to work. Unless someone worked at an *actual* mattress factory, they were of no use to me.

There was a man I was considering. He wore a uniform— security guard, maybe, or janitor—beneath his jacket, and his head was slumped against the top of the seat. I had a hunch that he might have gotten off the night shift. I kept my eyes on him, ready to jump up and follow as soon as he moved to leave the bus.

We drove through downtown and into Oakland, the university neighborhood. Out the window, I glimpsed the towering Cathedral of Learning. All forty-two stories of it.

At the next stop, a few college students got on. Definitely a bad choice to follow. On their way to class, probably.

I glanced out the window, saw a girl in a black jacket leaning against the bus shelter, her back turned, smoking a cigarette. Something lurched in my chest, and before I quite knew what I was doing, I had pulled my mother to her feet. The bus was just starting to pull away when I shoved the back doors open. The bus driver slammed on the brakes. I jumped down to the pavement, my mother right behind me.

The girl in the black jacket turned around, and I saw my mistake.

For a moment, I'd been sure I knew her. Been sure she was someone else. Someone I'd known from two years ago.

Someone I'd thought about almost every day since.

The Heart

It felt like what I think being flayed must feel like. Being peeled. Having all your skin taken off, fast, and then having it grow back and get scraped away again. Slow this time. And then again. And again.

That's what it felt like to be in love.

5

"What's going on?" my mother asked. "Why did we get off the bus?"

I didn't know what to tell her. What the hell could I say?

I'd been wrong. Of course. I was an idiot. This wasn't Tess at all. This was a different girl. She was just dressed in a similar style. That enormous black jacket. Those big fuck-off boots, scuffed at the heels and toes.

This girl wore an orange knit cap pulled low, with stringy bleached-blond hair sticking out, the ends dyed a faded chlorine blue (Tess's hair was brown). Below the hat I could make out smudged black eyeshadow, lipstick in a shade of pink Tess would undoubtedly have despised. The girl wore thick foundation in a brownish taupe, darker than Tess's skin color.

The sun slipped out from behind a cloud and sparked off something beneath the girl's oversized jacket. Glitter, or maybe sequins. Her bony legs were bare, cold-looking. She certainly didn't seem like she was headed to class or to work, even as a barista or a record store attendant. She looked like she was dressed for nighttime, for going out, which might mean she hadn't made it home last night, was only heading back now. We'd passed by the big dorms already, so she probably didn't live in one of those.

"Let's follow her," I whispered to my mother, my voice camouflaged by the sound of passing traffic. "She's going home, I think."

"Okay." My mother sounded like she didn't care. She sank down on the bench seat of the bus shelter. I hoped no one would try to sit on her. Careful as we are, it has happened to both of us. It's an awful feeling, to be suddenly sat on.

That's one of those things normal people don't have to worry about.

I stiffened as a large group of students approached, talking and laughing. We were saved by the arrival of another bus. To my relief, the black-jacketed girl stubbed out her cigarette on the side of the bus shelter and boarded. I tugged my mother's sleeve, and we hurried after, took a seat right behind the girl.

As we rode, my mother's head slumped against her chest. When I reached out to shake her awake, she flickered again. One moment there, transparent but perfectly visible to me, the next second gone. A breath. Two. And she was back.

The bus shuddered to a stop. The girl stood.

"Come on." I helped my mother up and pulled her after the girl out the back door.

We trailed her down a street lined with apartment buildings and warehouses, her orange knit cap bobbing along in front of us like a buoy. Her jacket was studded with pins and patches. A rainbow. A knife. A fist.

I didn't turn around to look at my mother, didn't want to

see if she was disappearing or not, didn't want to think about what it meant.

A few blocks from the bus stop, we passed a three-story brick house with an ornately carved gable. The house was replicated almost exactly in a mural on the wall behind it. In the mural, the house was hit by a slant of sunlight, with white curtains billowing out the windows. A bride stood on the front steps, holding up her trailing gown.

The real house looked empty, with plywood in place of curtains. The sky was gray. I squeezed my mother's hand, almost as tight as she used to squeeze mine when I was little.

The girl we were following turned down a side street and approached a brick row house with a battered green plastic awning over the front door. My mother and I scuttled up behind her.

As the girl opened the door, a dark furry shape shot past her feet. It skidded to a stop half a foot away from my mother and me, tail puffed, back arched into a startled curve.

A black cat, its yellow eyes staring straight at me.

"Get back in here," said the girl, reaching for the cat.

I pulled my mother forward. We slipped into the front hallway. The girl followed a moment later, cat cradled in one arm. It hissed at us and jumped away.

It couldn't see us, either, but it could smell us. Sense us, maybe, in some mysterious animal way. We usually avoided houses with pets for this reason. Dogs would bark at us incessantly. Birds would squawk. Cats weren't quite as bad, since, as a species, they already had a reputation for staring intently at apparently empty space.

Maybe your cat has done this.

Maybe it was staring at me.

We stood in a dim entranceway facing a narrow staircase. To the left was a living room crowded with mismatched furniture. Wooden chairs around a small painted table. A mustard-colored couch. Books stacked on the floor to precarious heights.

"Neely?" came a voice from some other room at the back of the house. "Is that you?"

"Oh, hi, sorry!" the girl shouted as she walked into the living room. "I didn't think anyone would be home. Aren't you supposed to be at school?"

My mother let go of my hand and headed up the stairs. They creaked terribly, but hopefully anyone listening would blame it on the cat.

"Bathtub tried to escape, but I caught her," I heard the girl—Neely?—say below us as I followed my mother. "I think she knows it's almost Halloween. Acting all spooky and shit."

At the top of the stairs, there was another dark hallway, this one carpeted in a musty burgundy brown, and four doors, all shut except one. This wasn't an ideal situation, by any stretch of the imagination. It was a small house. Would there be any empty rooms, any quiet corners?

I peered through the open door—just a bathroom. My mother pushed past me, leaned over the sink, dry-heaved. I put my hand on her shoulder, but she shrugged it off.

I pushed the shower curtain to one side, intending to sit

on the edge of the tub, but stopped short. Lining the bottom of the bathtub was a thick layer of overlapping newspapers, and arranged on top were three skulls.

They looked like animal skulls. Not human, at least. They were almost definitely real. There was a distinct scent of bleach.

Behind me, my mother retched, vomited. I yanked the shower curtain shut.

"How long?" I asked my mother.

She ran the tap, rinsed out the sink and her mouth.

"How long what?" she asked without turning.

"How long has this been happening?"

"I started feeling sick this morning. Somewhere in Ohio." She moved over to the toilet, sat on the closed lid. I say "sat," but it was more like "sank." Collapsed. She was acting so calm, so blasé. It was for my benefit, I was sure, but it only made me mad.

"No," I said, moving over to lean against the sink myself, facing her. "I mean the other thing. The disappearing."

My mother squeezed her eyes shut, pinched the bridge of her nose. "A while," she said.

"Jesus."

"But it was only once or twice a week," she said. "Not like this. And I didn't know—I wasn't sure—"

"Why the hell didn't you say anything?" My voice was getting too high, too loud. This was so stupid. If moving around so much was making her sick, we could have stopped.

"I didn't want you to worry."

There was a creak from somewhere in the house, and we both froze. Waited. I could make out muffled voices from downstairs. No footsteps.

"What happens to you?" I whispered. "When you disappear?"

"I don't know."

"What does it feel like?"

"Everything just goes dark, okay? I'm sorry." She shot me a pained look. "I really need to lie down."

"Yeah," I said, "right, okay," though it still wasn't.

I slipped out into the hallway. There were no sounds from behind the closed doors, but that didn't guarantee that the rooms were empty. This house had a cat. I could use that.

I knelt in front of the nearest door and scratched insistently with my fingernails at roughly feline height. Scratched again, harder this time. When no one came to the door or shouted at Bathtub to knock it off, I figured I'd risk it. I turned the doorknob very slowly.

Light streamed into the room through sheer yellow curtains, dust motes swirling as thick as a swarm of summer gnats. A futon rested on the narrow wooden floorboards, the sheets rumpled into a grand rose-petal swirl. I took one step forward before something in the far corner caught my eye and my stomach dropped. I jumped back into the hallway.

A tall thin woman had been standing against the wall. Staring at me.

She was naked.

On her tiptoes.

Also, she had no arms.

I peered back in and relaxed. The woman was, as I should have realized immediately, a mannequin, propped against the wall. Feeling like an idiot, I took a step closer. The flat joint of the mannequin's arm socket had a perfectly round hole in it. Above the hole, in black Sharpie, someone had written what I presumed was her name: CINDY.

I ushered my mother into the room, eased the door shut behind us. She crawled onto the futon immediately, shoes and backpack and all. She clutched at the blanket, curled up, seemed to sink into herself. She hadn't taken off her gloves, so the blanket stayed solid, but the pillow where her cheek rested had gone transparent. Hopefully no one would come in and notice. Hopefully no one would come in at all.

I watched her, convinced she would flicker, or vanish entirely into the knot of sheets. She didn't, though. If anything, her outline grew more distinct. She looked as solid as a glass statue. Clear, but not like empty air. Clear like water, bending the light that passed through her.

For the first time in nearly an hour, it seemed, my pulse slowed. I breathed easy. Maybe my mother was fine. Maybe she was right: she just needed to rest.

I circled the room, running my gloved fingers lightly across the desk by the window. A long-lensed digital camera sat beside a laptop. To amuse myself, I picked the camera up and snapped a photo of my mother curled atop the futon. When I checked the viewscreen, the picture showed me what visible people would see. Just the futon. No Mom.

I deleted the picture, clicked through the others stored on the memory card. There were several shots of the little black cat sniffing curiously at the skulls I'd seen earlier. Then some street shots. A picture of the mural I noticed on our walk here. I'd clicked through to the first picture with a person in it—a Black girl with auburn hair and a faded maroon hoodie standing, unsmiling, in front of a brick wall—when I heard the unmistakable sound of feet pounding up the stairs. I scrambled to return the camera to how I'd found it, nearly dropping it in my hurry.

A moment later, the doorknob turned and the door swung open and I swore, much too loudly.

Tacoma, WA

When I was a baby, my mother often chose houses where other infants lived. It was mostly for camouflage—all those poor parents haunted by mysterious cries with no source—though it also meant she always had diapers within easy reach. As I grew, my mother found houses with children around my age whenever possible.

From the moment I spoke my first word, however, the rules were clear: I must never, under any circumstances, talk to anyone. Not to an adult, not to a child. We must stay hidden. If anyone became too suspicious of strange noises or missing food, we moved on.

When I was six, we stayed in a house outside Seattle. A girl named Christy, a year older than me, lived there. It was a waterfront property with a separate cottage, which is where we slept.

During the day, when the family was out, we'd sneak into the main house. I was playing with Christy's toys one day, building an elaborate Lego house, when she came bursting in. Maybe it had been a half day at school. Maybe she'd been sent home early. I don't know. I'd heard the door open but assumed it was my mother, who'd been out walking along the marina.

I jumped up, pressed my back against a wall.

The house I'd built sat in the middle of the floor. Christy stared curiously at it. I thought she might smash it, but instead she plopped down on the carpet and played with it, made her little plastic Lego people *clack* their way through the multicolored rooms. I was overcome with joy, watching her. It was almost like playing together.

I thought to myself: *She is my friend.*

From then on, every day when she went to school, I added to the house. A table. A bed. A clever yellow chandelier stuck to the ceiling of the tiny dining room. More rooms. A garden. A pond of blue bricks. I didn't tell my mother. It was my first secret. If Christy wondered who was building the house, she never said anything about it. She'd leave the plastic people in one room, and I'd move them to another. It was like talking. It was enough.

Until, of course, it wasn't.

One day, I added a smaller version of the Lego house inside one of the rooms. It was probably only three or four bricks, but I was proud of it. I put the only two girl mini figures she owned next to the miniature house, to represent me and Christy.

"What is that?" Christy said to herself, hours later, when she spotted the new addition. I sat a few feet away, watching. Even when I was young, I was good at being very still and quiet.

She frowned, picked the whole house up to get a closer look.

I don't quite know what possessed me.

"It's a dollhouse," I said.

"What?" She looked up very quickly, not quite at me but in my direction.

"It's a mini version of the house," I said.

"Who is it?" she said. "Who's talking?" She looked all around her room, eyes wide.

"It's me," I said. "I'm the one who built it."

She was staring away from me, at the door, as if she expected someone to appear there. I leaned forward and touched her arm. Very gently. I barely grazed it with my gloved fingers.

She dropped the house and screamed and screamed and kept on screaming until her parents came running from downstairs to hug her and smooth her hair and reassure her—as I stood silent and sorry—that it was only her imagination, there was no one there, no one in her room but them, and there never had been.

6

It was not the girl we'd followed off the bus who came into the room now. This person was taller and chubbier, and she heard me swear.

I could tell because she froze in the doorway. Steam rose from the coffee mug cradled in her hands and brushed against her brown cheeks before dissolving into her curls, which were black at the roots but exploded into bright blue and purple a few inches down. She peered into the room, eyes darting from the window to the desk to the futon. My heart hammered. My mother was right there, asleep. Invisible as ever, but still taking up space, a shape beneath the blanket.

That's the only way people "see" us. Our negative space. The absence we create. A place where the rain doesn't fall. Where the sofa cushions are compressed for no reason. Where sheets are held aloft by no body.

But the girl's eyes glanced right past the rumpled covers, the missing pillow. I gave thanks that the bed had been so messy to begin with.

The girl frowned, instead, at the corner where Cindy stood.

"Hello?" said the girl. Cindy remained motionless, the flat blue paint of her irises pointed straight ahead.

A breeze stirred the yellow curtains. The girl glanced toward the open window, and I could guess what she was thinking: *I must have just heard someone from outside. I'm being stupid. Mannequins don't talk.*

She walked into the room, the scent of coffee trailing after her, and headed right for me. I jumped up from the desk, shuffled backward until my shoulder blades hit the wall. As she approached, I got a closer look at her face and realized it was the girl from the photo I'd seen on the camera, though her hair was different. The girl sat where I had been a moment before and opened her laptop. I breathed out softly.

People react differently when confronted with evidence of our existence. We try to be careful, but it happens—an object vanishing or floating, doors opening on their own. Some people ignore it, but others freak out.

We are invisible but in no way invincible. I broke my ankle once jumping from a second-story window to get away from a woman who tried to trap me, believing I was a demon. We've been shot at only once, and luckily it's difficult to hit a target you can't see, but it was still terrifying.

While the girl was in the room, I'd have to be still and silent. She was fully dressed and drinking coffee, which gave me hope that she didn't plan to go back to bed, wouldn't stumble over my mother, who had not even stirred.

Which was unusual. My mother is a light sleeper.

From where I stood against the wall, I could see the girl's

laptop screen. She was scrolling through her Facebook feed. Craning my neck, I could just make out her name in the upper corner: Denise Crutchen.

On trains, I sometimes watched whole movies or shows this way, over the shoulders of strangers.

More footsteps came pounding up the stairs. I used the sound as an opportunity to push away from the wall and creep forward. A floorboard creaked loudly under my foot. Denise turned and I froze.

A voice from the doorway startled both of us.

"Is Jules skipping, too?" It was Neely. The girl from the bus.

"They are," said Denise, turning. "In fact, they're still in bed."

"I am shocked and appalled." Neely put a hand to her forehead, pretended to faint against the doorframe. "Left alone for a few days and suddenly you're a bunch of high school dropouts?"

"Oh, shut up." Denise rolled her eyes. "I'll go in at lunchtime. The morning classes are boring."

"Won't your aunt and uncle totally lose their shit when they get back?" Neely asked.

"They won't find out if nobody tells them. Right? Not a word, Neely. About any of this."

"Duh," Neely said. She sauntered into the room and perched on the windowsill. "Which reminds me: Do you have any more flyers for the party?"

"More?" Denise frowned. "I already gave you, like, thirty. This party is supposed to be small. You can't start inviting randos."

I had zero idea what anybody was talking about. My mother still hadn't stirred.

"I have a lot of friends," said Neely, a touch defensive. "Anyway, I thought I could invite Sam and Candace from that show last month. You remember them?"

"Not really."

A door opened, shut, and then the sink turned on in the next room. How many people lived here? With the noise as cover, I tiptoed the rest of the way to the futon and knelt beside it.

I touched my mother lightly on the arm. This near, I could see the ever-so-slight movement of her breathing. She was fine. She just needed rest. Right?

Denise was pulling a stack of papers out of a drawer in her desk. I could see a drawing of a bat at the top of one, some block-lettered words beneath that.

I leaned in real close to my mother, whispered as loud as I dared, which was not very loud, "Mom?"

Nothing.

"Hey," came another voice from the doorway. I turned. The person in the doorway had long tightly curled black hair, but only on top of their head, the sides shaved. A hint of stubble showed along their cheeks, which were a shade darker brown than Denise's. The robe they wore was short and floral, and a pink slip showed at the hem. Their fingers and toenails were painted pastel purple.

"Hey, Jules," Neely said. This room was getting crowded. We needed to leave.

I should never have brought us here in the first place.

45

Should never have followed the girl from the bus. Never have come back to Pittsburgh at all, probably.

And maybe I should have left my mother alone, let her sleep like she said she needed to. But I was worried she might roll over, give us away. And it was weird that she hadn't woken up yet, with all these people. I was scared.

Lonely.

I reached out and shook my mother by the shoulder.

She bolted upright as if she'd been burned, jostling some of the tangled blankets. The pillow popped back into full visibility. Her eyes flashed quickly from me to Denise, to Neely, to the door, where the new person—Jules—stood.

For a split second, I saw pure terror on my mother's face, and then she vanished.

"Shit," I said.

"What?" said Denise.

"I didn't say anything," said Jules.

I tried to touch my mother's arm again, but my hand went right through the space where she'd been only a moment before. There was nothing there. I patted the futon, frantic.

"What are you looking at?" asked Neely.

I saw that Denise was staring at the futon, frowning deeply, forehead creased.

"I don't know," she said. "Nothing, I guess."

In her peripheral vision, Denise must have seen the pillow reappearing, the blankets shifting, the surface of the bed moving oddly as I prodded it.

I froze. Inside my head: a steady scream.

Denise shook her head, as if disagreeing with her own thoughts. Her blue and purple curls bounced.

"Is it okay if I use your shower?" Neely asked. "I crashed at Ed's last night, and you know what his bathroom is like."

Denise blinked, snapped out of it. "Of course," she said. "We've just got to move the skulls."

I stayed as still as I could until they all filed out of the room. The instant I was alone, I whispered, "Mom?"

I held my arms out in front of me, moved them side to side, made my way slowly through the room, feeling the air.

"Mom?" I asked again, louder this time.

I patted down the bed again, spun around, knocked into Cindy, barely kept her from crashing to the floor. There was no sign of my mother. No sound, no movement.

I didn't understand how this could happen. Yesterday she had been absolutely fine, and now, somehow, she was just gone.

"Mom? Mom!"

I was practically shouting now. I couldn't bring myself to care if anyone heard.

Paradise Cove, CA

Maybe it was a lie to say that my mother had been fine just the day before.

She had been normal.

That much was true.

A little over three weeks ago, before my seventeenth birthday, in an empty mansion on the beach, my mother had spent a full day sitting out on the concrete roof balcony, wrapped in a stranger's pashmina shawl, staring at the ocean, silent.

It was a short silence, as her silences went, but an intense one.

I'd go up periodically, ask her if she needed anything, and she wouldn't respond. Wouldn't even look at me. I'd wanted to scream, to shake her by the shoulders.

But I knew better. I had tried that kind of thing when I was a kid, and it only ever made things worse. The best strategy was to wait out her silences, hope she snapped out of them quickly. I paced the empty halls of the abandoned house, kicked at rubble, traced the graffiti that covered ornate Middle Eastern–style tilework, and carved-wood panels of intertwined figures. The place was a mess of architectural styles, whoever had lived there so rich that they hadn't even bothered to stop paying for electricity when they left. I flicked a light switch on and off, sitting on the edge of a whirlpool tub filled with plaster dust, and seethed at my mother.

But I should have been thankful. That day of utter silence was a thousand times better than this.

At least she had been there, silent and see-through but perceivable, sitting in a brocade chair she'd dragged out onto the balcony, the upholstery no doubt growing mildew double-quick in the damp sea air. When I stood behind her, I could see the relentless pulsing of the ocean through the back of her head, through her chest, each wave like a heartbeat.

At least then I'd known for sure she was alive.

7

I circled Denise's room, circled it again, not thinking, a frantic animal panic overtaking my body, driving me to do something, anything. I ripped the blankets from the futon, tossed them aside. Stripped the sheets, as if maybe my mother had folded herself up flat, hidden beneath them. Idiotic. I pushed the whole futon aside.

Jules, the one with the purple toenails, stuck their head in the door, peered curiously at the chaos on the floor. They looked enough like Denise that I thought the two might be siblings. I was being too loud, too careless, but that could hardly matter if my mother was truly gone.

A door slammed downstairs. Still not thinking, I darted forward, ducked under Jules's arm, passing close enough that they felt it and jumped back. But I was already running down the hallway, down the stairs, gripped by the idea that my mother had just left, that I needed to catch her. I skidded toward the front door, flung it open, burst through.

But it had only been Denise. Her blue-purple curls caught the light as she walked away down the block. The little black cat shot through the open door behind me, skidded past my feet and onto the sidewalk.

"Hey! Get back here!"

I stepped aside just in time to avoid being bowled over by Jules, who ran past in pursuit of the cat. Denise turned.

"What the hell," she shouted. "Did Bathtub learn how to open the door by herself?"

"You must not have closed it all the way," Jules said, scooping up Bathtub, who mewed in protest.

Denise shrugged. "Well, lock it."

Jules nodded, and before I could react, they'd gone back inside, cat in tow, and shut the door. I heard the click of the latch. I was outside.

I blinked at the door. Everything had gone so wrong so quickly.

Denise turned out of sight at the end of the street. I tried the front door pointlessly, then squeezed myself down the narrow, weed-choked gap along the side of the house. This led not to a yard but to a concrete no-man's-land beneath a rickety wooden second-story porch. I climbed the stairs to the porch, tried the back door, but it was locked, too.

My mother and I rarely needed to break into forbidden places. We could just walk in, so long as someone else opened the door.

Still, my mother is a decent picklock. It comes in handy now and then. She taught me, of course, but all the tools were in her backpack, which had vanished along with her.

I circled around to the front again. Denise's bedroom

window was slightly ajar, its yellow curtains billowing in the breeze.

I'm no climber. My legs are strong, since I'm used to walking many miles a day, but my arms are not.

So it was pretty stupid when I wrapped one hand around the drainpipe at the corner of the house, wedged my sneakers (limited-edition bright red high-tops, though when I had them on, they were as pale and translucent as the rest of me) against the brick wall, and heaved. Through sheer adrenaline, I got about five feet up before my hand slipped. The drainpipe clanged against the side of the house, and I fell into the bushes and rolled onto the thin strip of lawn.

Bruised, sore, winded, I lay on my side. Focused on a blade of grass a few inches from my nose. Watched it shiver in the wind.

And then I started to cry.

I cried (silently, of course) until my face and my throat hurt. The wind dried the tears on my cheeks.

Mom would come back.

She had to.

I needed to move, needed to do something. I stood, started walking. I was still hungry, so I'd find food. We had a couple of granola bars, but those were in Mom's pack also.

Don't think about that, I told myself. *Walk. Don't think.*

Was my mother dead? Could she be gone? Really gone, forever? I'd thought it before, on the train. I refused to consider it now. I shoved all thoughts of her from my mind. My face felt puffy and slack from crying.

I walked fast, feet hitting the pavement too hard, so I

knew my shins would ache later. I tried to make the world whip past me like I was on a train, tried to let my mind settle into that rocking rhythm.

A young man with headphones bumped into me. He grunted in surprise, spun once, looked around to see if anyone had witnessed his behavior. There was no one else. He put his head down and kept walking.

That was how little I affected the world. If I was hit by a car, no one would see my body. If I died, no one would know.

I headed vaguely south. The streets changed as I went, became tree-lined, the houses moving farther apart, sprouting up into grand Victorians.

A busy intersection drew me up short. There are so many things that normal people take for granted. Like not being hit by cars. Sure, they can't wander freely into traffic, but if normal people cross a street and a car's coming, the driver will see them.

A driver wouldn't see us. Wouldn't stop. Every time we cross a street, we have to be so careful. Sometimes we have to wait five, ten minutes until the street is totally clear.

For busy streets, the best thing to do is wait until someone crosses and become their shadow.

The crosswalk signal lit up. A woman loaded down with blue grocery bags, three in each hand, was walking toward me, and I realized that I knew this street. I knew where I was.

I ran across the intersection, terrified despite the walk signal, and down the sidewalk, past a man sitting on the pavement, hunched over and head bowed, wrapped in a blanket and gripping a plastic cup. Half a block later, I whooshed through the automatic doors of the Giant Eagle Market District.

With a bare hand, I reached for a glistening pink Fuji apple. As soon as I touched it, the whole mountain of apples flickered away. A nearby woman gasped, dropped the orange she'd been holding.

That wasn't supposed to happen. Maybe it was the panic and sorrow I was trying not to think about, trying very hard to shove down deep inside me and not look at. Maybe I was broken for good now. Whatever. I couldn't make myself care. I yanked my apple away, and the display popped back.

I bit into the apple. The sweetness seemed wrong, cruel. I dropped it, let it roll away. Anyone looking would have seen it pop into existence midair. I didn't care.

I didn't care about anything.

In the deli area, a bored young woman wearing an apron and a hairnet was leaning against one of the enormous cheese slicers. I slipped around the display case, saw that she was holding her phone carefully out of view behind a pound of salami, flicking her thumb left, left, right. I grabbed a to-go container and filled it with pasta salad. I ate the salad with my fingers, watching the deli girl.

I hated her in that moment, her carelessness, her ease. So I reached out and touched the counter. On purpose this time. It flickered away. She looked up, sucked in a breath. I let go and the counter popped back. Solid, beyond reproach.

I moved on, grabbed two containers of prepackaged sushi. Two boxes of crackers. Two blocks of sharp cheddar.

Outside, I dropped a bag with one of each item I'd collected in front of the homeless man I'd seen earlier. He startled at the sound of the bag falling. Looked at it, looked around. There was no one else nearby. He looked up at the sky, over toward the grocery store.

"Shit," he said. "Oh, shit." He didn't look happy. He looked scared. Frantically, he gathered up his belongings and the food and hurried away.

I felt ashamed then.

I didn't know this man's life, and I hadn't helped him, not really. What I'd done was for me, to soothe my conscience. I should have brought him money instead, anyway.

I sank down on a nearby bus shelter bench, depleted. A middle-aged woman with a wrist brace scratched lottery tickets beside me. The *ratch, ratch* of the coin she was using on the tickets felt like it was scraping my spine. All the thoughts I'd been keeping at bay—all the guilt, the terror—came flooding in all at once, and I was lost to it.

Orlando, FL

My mother lost me once, at Disney World, when I was seven.

The park was different for me than for other kids. On the one hand, roller coasters were too risky, and obviously I couldn't have my picture taken with the Little Mermaid. On the other hand, I could go anywhere. Dance with the blue-skinned ballroom ghosts in the Haunted Mansion. Hang with animatronic pirates. See behind the smoke and mirrors.

When I got separated from my mother in a crowd, I followed the first familiar person—thing?—I saw: Mickey Mouse. A normal kid might have asked for help, but I just followed.

I ended up in a massive network of underground tunnels beneath the park—the utilidors, I would later find out they are called. Chilly, concrete-floored, lit by dangling overheard fluorescent lights, big enough for golf carts full of employees. There was a dining hall down there, bathrooms. At one point, looking for a way out, I stumbled across a whole room full of heads. All oversized, plastic and faux fur, with gaping necks and hidden mesh eyeholes. I was terrified.

By the time I found my way back aboveground, I had no idea where I was. I sat, huddled at the foot of a building, crying. The sun sank. The park closed for the night, lights snapping off in the distance. A cat with long dirty fur and the tip of one ear missing slinked past. I followed it out into an empty courtyard, and my mother finally found me.

She was furious. I expected her to yell, or to hit me, even. But she hugged me instead. Picked me up and wrapped her arms around me.

Which was unusual. My mother never hugged me. She held my hand when crossing streets, but that was a practical consideration, not a show of affection. Now that I'm older, I think I understand why my mother was like that, but when I was young, it just made me sad.

I was happy when she hugged me. As scared as I had been, as lonely and desperate for most of the day, still I thought: *It is good to get lost.*

I tried it again, on purpose, a few days later, in a Miami mansion. Hid in a closet while she called for me. I got impatient and popped out eventually. There was no hug. Only coldness.

In Georgia, a week later, I made a better show of it. Wandered away from the house where we were staying, installed myself in the home goods aisle of a store down the block.

I sat there until the store closed, and then half the night as well. I fell asleep for a while, woke with a start.

I wandered back in the wee hours. I could see my mother through a window, reading a book, as if nothing were wrong. I burst into tears on the sidewalk.

She looked up and saw me, then returned, very deliberately, to her book.

She did not hug me when I ran in and clung to her leg. She gave it a little shake, as if trying to detach me. I think, looking back, that she understood what I was doing, and she knew she couldn't reward it.

I'm sorry, I wailed.

Be quiet, she told me.

My mother was all I had in this world. She was the only other person like me. The only one who could see me. The only one I could talk to. Without her I'd be truly lost.

8

I'd known that the grocery store would be on this corner, because I had been here before.

I knew that if I crossed the railroad tracks and walked half a mile or so, I'd eventually come to a steep hill lined with private drives, the stately houses beyond them shielded from the view of passing commoners by tall trees.

My mother and I had stayed in one of those houses once.

I couldn't tell you the street names, couldn't trace the route on a map. Didn't remember it exactly, not consciously, but I let my feet carry me, snacking on cheese and crackers as I went, until I reached that house.

I'd always thought of it as the castle.

The castle of my heart.

What an idiot I was. What a stupid way to think of it.

But I was stupid. I'd been stupid two years ago and I was still stupid now.

It was a stone house, built in a Tudor style, with a sprawling lawn, an honest-to-god tennis court.

I stopped by the playhouse first. Set at the back of the property, it was a re-creation of the main house in miniature, just large enough for a kid to stand up inside. Like a dollhouse, but the doll is you. It had real glass windows. A tiny porch.

I opened the door and crawled inside. The floor was littered with outdoor cushions and dead leaves. Tess used to come out here to smoke. From the scent of sour smoke that clung to the cushions, she still did.

I pulled out the loose stone in the faux fireplace, peered into the dark cavity behind it.

There was nothing there.

Why would there be, after two years? Tess hadn't spent those years thinking of me the way I'd spent them thinking of her.

I crawled back out and made my way along the stone walkways that ringed the property. When we stayed there, my mother and I broke a window latch so we could go in and out of the house when there was no one to follow without picking locks. We chose a window in the corner of the basement, far from the family's endless racks of wine.

My heart tripped as I pushed against the dirty pane and found that it still swung open freely. No one had fixed it in the two years since it was broken.

The basement was dank and cool. The wine bottles hunkered down in their hidey-holes.

I followed Tess down here once. Watched her carefully consider the bottles, running her fingers along their dusty necks, before snatching one. She hid it in the playhouse, drank it in secret.

Up the dark stairs, through a door, and I was in her kitchen again.

Most of the houses in my life have blurred together in memory, become one endless many-roomed monstrosity. I couldn't tell you which house had the double refrigerator or the two-story stained-glass window or the tub that a spigot in the ceiling filled like a miniature waterfall.

But this house remained crisp. I could have closed my eyes and walked it in memory. And here it was, exactly as I remembered. The marble-topped island, gleaming copper pots hanging from the ceiling. The midnight-blue Aga stove, with ornate bas-relief tiles behind it depicting a sheep, a flounder, a bunch of radishes. As if those organic things had any place here. The kitchen was cold, pristine, untouched. Not so much as a dirty dish. A vase of flowers sat in the center of the marble island. It looked like a display, pretty as a magazine, waiting for someone to see.

My pulse flickered. Around any corner I might find her. I might see her.

What would I do then?

It was hurting me, I knew it was, loving someone who could never love me back, who could never even know I existed. I understood why my mother had tried to warn me off love. For all the good that had done.

I circled the first floor, saw no sign of life, proceeded up the narrow back staircase. In the old days, it would have been reserved for the servants. They don't call them servants anymore, but this family did have cleaning people who came in every day. When they hosted parties, they got caterers.

They were not the richest family we'd stayed with, not by far. They had no live-in help. No indoor pool. But they certainly did well enough. Better, it was clear, than Denise's family. There were six bedrooms in this house. Five and a half bathrooms.

I found my way to the gabled third floor, to a room I remembered well. Tess's room, with vaulted ceiling, exposed wood beams, decorative fireplace.

It was messier than the rest of the house. A pile of clothes lay heaped on the floor by the foot of the bed, a lime-green polka-dotted bra hung from one bedpost.

I pulled my backpack off and lay down on the bed, thought about sleeping here, the place where she slept every night. My stomach twisted.

It was wrong, I knew, for me to be here. Creepy.

But that's all I was. A creep. That's why in the past people had paid good money to rid their homes of my mother and me, believing us to be ghosts, demons, an infestation of raccoons. Something unwanted, unsavory, maybe even sinister.

I had known Tess the way a spy can know someone. The way a fly on the wall can know someone. I had watched her sleep. I had read her journal. I had looked over her shoulder as she wrote in that journal, following her pen as it traced the curve of each letter.

Look, I'm not proud of it.

There were things I did not do. I turned away when she was naked. I made myself do that. I closed my eyes. Afraid, disgusted at myself, at my desires.

I did catch sight of her, a few times, in almost nothing. In a bra and underwear, which is maybe no better. Maybe I was fooling myself that I wasn't disgusting.

No, I wasn't fooling anybody.

I was disgusting. I hated myself for it.

I don't know if it matters, but it was never about how she looked. I found her beautiful, but I didn't love her because of that. I think it was the other way around. She was beautiful to me because I loved her.

In her empty room, I looked beneath the mattress. Reached a hand under it, feeling for the place where she had kept her journal. It wasn't there.

I checked the drawers of her bedside table. Checked her desk. Leafed through a three-ring binder, but it was only math notes, with the occasional doodle of a stick figure hanging itself from a fraction bar.

I was reaching behind the desk, in case the journal was wedged against the wall, hidden, when I heard a door slam downstairs.

Only one person in this house slammed doors like that.

I was up and moving before I had time to think, grabbing my backpack from the bed, whipping around the corner into the hallway, bouncing down the narrow back staircase, bursting out onto the first floor, skidding to a halt at the kitchen threshold.

And there she was.

Frick Park

Here is what I loved most about Tess: she was so angry.

Her anger radiated off her like heat, localized solar flares. She threw a raw egg at a guy in the middle of Giant Eagle because he said something fucked-up to her. She scowled, walked as though she were punishing the earth with each step, threw middle fingers with abandon.

I saw her expressing everything I felt but couldn't let out. That's probably what made me like her to begin with: that brash and visible part of her.

But that was only the surface of her anger. That was what everyone could see.

There was more to it, a secret side, that only I knew about.

It started like this: I followed her, one evening just before sunset, when she left the house quietly, easing the back door shut softly behind her. I thought she must be sneaking off to a party or a show. Thought I could watch teens be teens, watch all the things I was supposed to be doing. All the things I never would do.

I followed her through the neighborhood of Squirrel Hill to Frick Park. I followed her deep into the park, off the paved walkways, away from the picturesque couples, the small dogs. Followed her down a dirt path, into a culvert, past shipping crates tucked against a hill, past a mountain of gravel, past a place where only a low divider kept us from tumbling down a steep slope beyond which the western part of the city was spread out, a mess of little twinkling lights, far below.

I followed her down a trail that was more a suggestion, a mere parting of branches, than a true path. I followed her, as the sky grew darker, deep into the woods, where maybe it was dangerous for a teenage girl to go alone.

But she wasn't alone. Not anymore. I was there, and already, that first time, I was pretty sure I would do anything for her.

When she was far enough into that large wooded park that there were no visible signs of civilization, no people, not even voices carrying, just Tess and the trees and me—that first time and many other times after—then she would stop and she would break shit.

Stuffed in her pockets would be china teacups she'd brought from home. Wineglasses. Little crystalline statuettes. Her mother's bracelets. Tiny, precious, expensive things.

Tess would take whatever she had brought and throw it, hard, against the nearest tree. The delicate wineglasses would explode. Some of the other trinkets would survive, so she'd throw them again and again until they shattered. Then she would gather the shards of glass or china or crystal or twisted metal into a pile, stomp them over and over or smash them with a stone until they were obliterated, as broken as she could make them.

When they were ground into fragments, into dust, into the dirt, returned to the earth, she would cast about, frantic, not yet satisfied. She would grab dry fallen branches, crack them over her knee, tear them apart with her bare hands until her palms were scraped and bleeding.

By then she'd be sweating, breathing hard, wrung out.

She'd wipe her hands on her jeans, wipe her brow with the hem of her shirt, pale strip of stomach exposed to the night for a moment. Then she'd turn around and walk out of the park.

Silent, I'd trail after her.

9

Now she stood only ten or twelve feet from me. Tess.

Her appearance hadn't changed much in two years. Her hair was shorter. She still wore dark clothes. She was still wiry. And I don't just mean thin. She had this quivering tension, like a taut guitar string. Like she might snap at any moment. It had been that, as much as the jacket, I think, that had made me jump off the bus when I did. That girl from the other house, Neely—she had a little of that, too.

I heard Tess's mother shouting her name from upstairs. I hadn't realized that anyone else was home. Good thing I'd been moving quietly out of habit.

Tess dropped her backpack on the floor, crossed to the fridge. She pulled out a carton of chocolate milk, reached for a glass from the open shelves.

I took a step toward her, hardly daring to breathe. I was close enough to see the texture of her skin, her chapped lips, that little divot of a scar on her cheek under her left eye. The spray of freckles, fainter now than when I knew her in the summer.

This was a moment I'd dreamed about for two years. I had

rehearsed a thousand variations in my mind. Where we'd be. How she'd look. What I'd say. Imagined soliloquies, grand declarations.

She poured the milk into the glass.

I breathed in.

Hello, Tess, I wanted to say. Something simple, to start.

I opened my mouth to speak.

She gulped some chocolate milk.

I breathed out.

There was a wall between us. A window, closed. Glass. I could see through it, but that was it. I couldn't break through.

There had been too many years of silence, of training myself to be quiet. How could I do it? How could I possibly speak to her?

This was stupid, reckless. My palms were sweating. My heart was thudding.

If my mother hadn't been sick, if she hadn't been . . . gone, I'd had a plan. Not a good one. I'd worked it out only a few days ago. We'd get to Pittsburgh. Go to the Mattress Factory museum. Get lunch, maybe. Then I'd say I wanted to go see a movie. I'd picked out the perfect one. A recent release. It even had explosions. My mother, I knew, would tell me to go on my own. The theater would be too crowded for her, too loud.

And off I'd go, but to Tess's house instead. I'd find her. See her.

Here, the neat plan fractured into a hundred shards of possibility, each one sharper than the next, more terrifying, more thrilling. I'd need to break through that glass wall some-how, smash it.

"Tess," I managed. Just a whisper. Barely audible.

She went still, rigid. I remembered Christy and the Lego house all those years ago, the way she'd screamed, and I wanted to run away.

But I had to be brave. Had to be a person.

"Tess," I choked out once again, my voice raspy, strained, but slightly louder.

She dropped her glass. It clattered to the floor but didn't break. Just thunked, rolled, spraying chocolate milk in a muddy arc.

She walked very fast out of the kitchen.

"Mom!" she shouted. "Hey, Mom!" A nervous note in her voice. A moment later, I heard her feet pounding up the stairs.

Not quite as bad as Christy, maybe. But not great.

I was so stupid. I shouldn't be here. I should never have come. My mother was sick. My mother might be dead.

Tess's backpack was on the floor where she'd left it. I un-zipped it, looking for her journal, pulled out a textbook, a school planner covered in stickers. When I opened the plan-ner, a folded half sheet of paper fell onto the floor.

I picked it up, unfolded it. It was a photocopy of a hand-drawn flyer with a sketchy drawing of a bat at the top. Block letters beneath the bat read: HALLOWEEN PARTY. DON'T TELL ANYONE. LIVE MUSIC BY SQUIRREL KILL. Below that a time, an address.

Recognition bloomed. The street name, the house number. It was the house I'd followed Neely to this morning. The house where my mother had disappeared. I remembered the flyers I'd seen Denise pull from the drawer.

The party was tonight. Tess had an invitation.

So maybe this was fate.

Then again, I'd followed Neely because she looked like Tess. So it wasn't entirely surprising that they ran in the same circles. I carefully replaced the flyer, then hurried down the stairs to the basement, out the window, across the broad lawn.

As I headed toward Denise's house, I told myself that my mother would be there when I returned. Maybe she'd be angry at me for leaving. I'd welcome her anger.

Guilt began to gnaw at me. I should have stayed closer to the house. What if she needed help? I made a wrong turn at one point and ended up at an enormous fenced graveyard. I followed the fence for several blocks, past a tall metal gate, before I found the right street. When I finally reached Denise's house, the door was still locked, so I sat on the front stoop to wait, to think about how I was the worst daughter who ever lived.

Each time a person or a car passed down the street, I leapt to my feet, then sagged back down.

The sun was starting to set by the time Denise appeared. I spotted her blue-purple curls at the end of the block, and relief washed over me. She carried an oddly shaped package, wrapped in a trash bag, and several grocery bags, which, as she got closer, I could see were mostly full of soda. She made her way up the walkway to the house, and I whooshed through the door after her like a gust of wind.

I ran past her, up the stairs to the second floor. Denise's room was as I left it, the futon overturned, the sheets and blankets tossed in the corner. Cindy stared blankly at the window.

"Mom?" I called softly. No answer.

I circled the room. I needed my mother to be here, to be okay.

That desperate feeling was building inside me again, that silent scream. While I'd been gone, I could imagine that when I got back everything would be fine. But now here I was, and nothing was fine.

I searched the house. Went downstairs. To the living room, where Jules was arranging the bleached skulls from the bathroom on the mantel above a bricked-over fireplace. To the kitchen, where Denise was unpacking the grocery bags. No sign of Mom.

Back upstairs, I checked the bathroom, then eased open the doors I hadn't been through yet. One led to a room the same size as Denise's but with a large bed instead of a futon. The walls were covered floor to ceiling with drawings and photographs. I recognized Jules and Denise in some of them. This seemed like the room of an adult, a parent.

The final door on the second floor led to another narrow staircase. I padded up it and found myself transported into a jungle.

Terra-cotta pots and orange industrial buckets lined the

floor, each overflowing with green. More plants hung from the ceiling, long spidery leaves reaching down to brush my hair. Vines snaked along the wall, following a path of nails plotted out for them. The last rays of the setting sun came in through the dormer windows.

It reminded me of a place in Albuquerque where we once stayed. I wanted to tell my mother that. I wanted to show her this room and say, *See, just like that woman in the desert who couldn't get enough green.*

"Mom?" I said. No answer, of course.

The floor creaked wildly as soon as I stepped forward. I cringed. The floorboards up here were blue, with the paint stripping off in places like bark, the bare dark wood showing through.

Farther into the room, a twin mattress sat atop two wooden pallets. Next to it, a freestanding metal rack was draped with colorful clothes. There was a dresser, too, the top crowded with potted succulents. Golden bangles and beaded necklaces hung from branches of a skinny cactus.

Several canvases were leaning against the dresser. I pulled one out to look at it—an explosion of colorful blobs, signed JULES in the corner—when something on one of the nearby plants caught my eye. A strange flower. Silver, shiny. I moved closer to check it out, but as I bent down, I realized it wasn't a flower at all. I picked it out from the tangle of leaves.

It was a granola bar wrapper.

In her backpack, at the time she disappeared, my mother had ten of these same granola bars.

It had to mean something. Right? It couldn't mean

nothing. I crinkled the wrapper in my hands, smoothed it again, crinkled, smoothed. Nothing, something.

It had to mean that she was alive. Eating granola bars. Littering. My mother wasn't dead. She was here, somewhere.

Invisible. Even to me.

Albuquerque, NM

In the Southwest, everything is shorter, the buildings and the trees. Or maybe it just seems that way in the shadow of the mountains. People have rocks for lawns. It's too hot and dry for grass. The rain, when it comes, dumps down in sudden torrents. The ground, surprised, doesn't know what to do with all that water. It floods the streets for ten minutes and then is gone, the air no cooler, the scent of creosote lingering as strong as smoke after a fire.

The sides of the highways in Albuquerque are painted with turquoise stripes. The windows of houses, covered in turquoise bars to keep out the tweakers. Or us.

My mother and I stayed for two months downtown in a 1970s bungalow with a terrarium for a front room. Walking into that house was like walking up the stairs into Jules's attic room: it was like entering another world. The contrast between the outside, hot and dry, sun blazing, and the inside, green and cool, wet from the swamp cooler, was near miraculous.

The woman who lived there had all kinds of plants. Every morning she'd come in and tend to them lovingly, as carefully as though they were her children. She'd pluck the dead leaves. Water or spritz or give a trickle of plant food. She would sing to her plants, stroke their leaves.

I would sit in my favorite place, tucked behind a banana leaf palm and a fiddle-leaf fig, and imagine that the woman was singing to me, too, talking to me. I imagined that I was a plant being coaxed to grow. I imagined being loved.

10

I had carved out a hiding spot in the corner of Jules's attic room, like the one in Albuquerque, wedged myself between the wall and a huge potted plant with leaves like elephant's ears. A screen of green between me and the world. It was night now, and the attic was dark. I finished off the cheese and crackers from my backpack and waited for another sign.

After maybe an hour, Jules came upstairs. They changed into a different outfit (I closed my eyes), then sat for a long time in front of the vanity mirror, painting their face.

And I do mean painting. They weren't using makeup but tubes of watercolors, squeezed out onto a Tupperware lid and applied, in swoops and swaths of bright color, with a long-handled brush. A thick book lay open on the vanity, and Jules referred to it periodically.

When they finished and went downstairs, I crept over and saw that it was an art book, open to a page showing a portrait by Matisse. *Woman with a Hat,* 1905. Jules had been copying it, re-creating the colors and shapes. A pale lilac line down the cheek. A spot of yellow on the nose. I sat where they had been sitting, took a good look at myself.

I am vainer than you might think, for an invisible girl.

I'm no vampire. Mirrors reflect a bit of infrared, so I can see myself in them, though other people can't.

The way I look changes depending on what is behind me. I appear, to myself, transparent. A girl of glass. A girl who is a window. If I stand in front of floral wallpaper, I am full of roses.

I have experimented to find the most flattering combinations. I have tried on other people's faces. Taped magazine pages to the wall behind me. If I angle my face right, I can line my eyes up with the eyes of models, celebrities. See their noses slot into mine. Angle my mouth to fit their expression.

A costume, a mask.

What is the point of it? No one can see.

I don't really know what I'd look like, opaque. My mother and I are faint and nearly colorless. We are not brown, tan, beige, or pink. Our hair is not black, red, blond, or brunette. We are the color of soap bubbles but without the rainbow iridescence. Dull dishwater.

I've always thought that I was ugly. From what I can see of my features, they are plain, unappealing, my nose sort of lopsided, one of my eyes a little bigger than the other, smudges obscuring a pleasant view out a windowpane.

So it should have been a blessing—right?—that no one could see me.

Downstairs, the front door opened and closed several times. I pressed my ear to the floorboards. Many voices reached me. More people were here than Neely, Denise, and Jules. Distant music started up.

"Mom," I said to the room, "if you don't come back right now, I am going to this goddamn party."

Someone laughed downstairs, muffled. But up here: only silence, darkness, the sound of plants growing.

I made myself wait, returned to my hiding spot. I tried to judge from the muffled din how many people were downstairs. Doors banged opened and shut. Voices rose and fell. If the party was big enough, I could melt into the crowd. I had a costume ready, though I'd meant to wear it in New York, not here.

When my watch told me it was ten, I decided I could wait no longer.

As I crept down to the second floor, I told myself it wasn't just Tess, wasn't just selfish restlessness. The party noise became steadily louder. I stopped by Denise's room, circled it, calling my mother's name softly, keeping an eye out for another wrapper. All I saw was Denise's purse, sitting on the floor by her desk. I knelt, dug around until I found her house key. Now I wouldn't have to worry about getting locked out again.

I went into the bathroom, shut the door, bolted the latch.

I shrugged off my backpack and pulled out the carefully folded dress. It cost five thousand dollars.

Or it would have if I'd actually bought it. It cost me nothing, of course. I'd just taken it from a bridal boutique in downtown Chicago.

I'd imagined people admiring it at some enormous, glamorous Halloween party in Manhattan.

The dress was floor-length and long-sleeved (important).

Rows of pearlescent beads and tiny crystals followed intricate patterns along the bodice and sleeves. I'd picked the dress for exactly that reason: with all that crystal, it was heavy. Hard. I needed all the armor I could get.

No matter how much I look forward to going out in costume, it also terrifies me.

I changed out of the jeans and long-sleeved tee I was wearing and into my underdress. It was long-sleeved, too, and tight, with a high neck, though the skirt ended above the knee. It was meant for showing off your curves, but on me it was a layer no one would see.

I pulled on two pairs of tights. The top pair, since it didn't touch my skin, was visible. Next: two pairs of gloves. My normal pair, the lilac silk, tucked carefully into my sleeves. And over those, a second pair I'd taken from the bridal boutique: looser, white, visible.

The dress took some wiggling to pull on. It rustled and crinkled. I had to contort myself to reach the back zipper. No doubt that was usually the bridesmaid's job or something. Maybe my mother would have helped if she'd been here.

I thought of the mural I'd seen earlier, of the bride on the steps. She'd been alone, too.

Someone knocked on the door. Instinct made me freeze and go silent. It took me a few tries to find my voice.

"Someone's in here," I tried to say, but it came out a strained whisper.

There was more knocking. I tried again. Louder this time. "Someone's in here."

A queasy thrill ran through me.

Someone. Me.

I remained frozen for a few moments, faint with fear, but there was no answer. I returned to the zipper.

Once the dress was on, I checked it carefully in the mirror. None of it was touching my bare skin, so it was solid, visible. I moved around, making sure it never flickered into transparency. I had planned this carefully, as I did every year, making sure the bottom layers would cover my skin completely.

Finally, I pulled on my sneakers and tucked a black ski mask into the neck of my dress. Over that, a skull mask, bones picked out in white plastic. To top it all off, a cascading death-white wig, which I pinned to the ski mask as quickly as I could.

There was knocking at the door again. Heavier, more insistent.

"Just a minute," I called, the words coming easier this time. I turned my head side to side to see through the eyeholes in the mask, which narrowed my vision to a tunnel.

I was visible. Or my clothes were, anyway: wedding dress, gloves, a plastic skull mask, a wig. Not me, exactly, but a face, a body. A role I could play.

I shoved my backpack into the tub, where the skulls had been before, hidden behind the shower curtain. I kept the house key I'd taken from Denise's room, though, tucked it into a sneaker (the wedding dress did not, unfortunately, come with pockets).

My hands were shaking terribly as I reached for the doorknob. *This is merely a play,* I told myself. *A performance you've been rehearsing for.*

You are not feeling fear, I told myself. *You are feeling excitement. You are about to step onto the stage. The curtains are about to part.*

Of all the idiotic things about me, this might be the stupidest: when I was a kid, my greatest dream in life was to become an actor.

A job all about being seen. Impossible.

I opened the door, swept past whoever was standing there without looking at them, which was easy enough, since the mask cut off all peripheral vision. I didn't want to give them a chance to say anything like *Where the hell did you come from?* or *Who the hell are you?*

My skirt dragged on the stairs, the beads and crystals clinking against each other. It was stifling hot, but I needed all the layers. I kept one hand on the wall, trying not to trip. Turned at the bottom of the staircase, stepped into the living room.

And heads turned. Eyes focused. Looking. Right. At. Me.

Somewhere in Maine, I think

The first time I wore a costume was in a small New England town I've since forgotten the name of. It's silly but I got the idea from a cartoon. My memory of it has collapsed down to one moment.

Me: perched silently on the back of the couch while some visible children watched TV.

Onscreen: a floating white sheet-ghost with blank eye-holes, drifting down hallways, creeping people out. *Don't be scared,* declared one of the characters. *It's obviously just a person wearing a sheet.* Smug, triumphant, so certain of his interpretation of reality, the character reached out and yanked away the sheet.

But underneath: nothing.

Just empty air.

It struck me like a revelation. *That's me,* I thought. *That show is about me.* I tumbled off the back of the couch and ran to find my mother.

I explained to her about the ghost, the sheet. She didn't get it, didn't understand the earth-shattering existential significance. I had to spell it out for her. If I wore a costume, people would think there was someone normal underneath it. They would assume.

So why couldn't I do that? Why not, for Halloween this year, join the other kids?

It took weeks of convincing, of wheedling. *If you want candy,* my mother said, *I can get you as much as you want.* But of course, it wasn't about the candy.

When trick-or-treat night finally rolled around, when the children of the house we were staying in headed out in their pink Power Ranger/tiger/witch costumes, I hid in the hedges and then followed, wearing a sheet with holes cut out for the eyes (and a ski mask beneath that and double tights and a double shirt and double gloves).

I didn't speak a single word that first night, not to another child, not to any of the adults dispensing candy.

But I can still remember the shock, the little spark that shot through me every single time I knocked on a door or walked up to a porch and someone looked at me, looked right at me. *Hey there, little ghost,* they'd say. I'd hold out my pillowcase, small gloved hands trembling. They'd smile at me, drop in a bite-sized Butterfinger. Maybe make a joke about my silence, my commitment to character, or ask me, with a hint of concern, if I was out here by myself (my mother was always nearby, hovering unseen on the sidewalk).

My mother hated it, but I begged every year, and she relented.

I'd spend months planning my costumes, gathering or crafting the components. Always costumes with a full-face mask, of course, full body coverage. The second year, I managed to occasionally mumble *Trick or treat* quietly and *Thank you* when my costume got compliments. By the third year, I spoke, haltingly, to other children. *Hello. Nice costume. Trade candy?* Things that probably came naturally to them, but for me each interaction was a mountain. To speak a single word was to rappel up a sheer cliff face, seeking footholds, gathering courage, and then to fling myself down the other side in free-falling terror. I'm sure the kids thought there was something wrong with me. I mean, there was, I guess.

Some kids were kind. Others laughed at me or ignored me. I lived off those small interactions for the rest of the year, the bad and the good, played them over and over in my head. Weighing them, evaluating them, imagining how they could have gone differently, planning how to do better the next time.

It was enough.

It was not enough.

But it was all I could allow myself to have.

11

The party was less packed than I'd expected, though I heard music coming from somewhere else in the house. I turned my head side to side, scanning awkwardly. A jellyfish and a girl with cat ears sat on the couch. Harley Quinn and a few people in costumes I couldn't identify stood by the fireplace.

I stuck out. Tess was the same age as me, and Neely had teased Denise about being a high school dropout, so this must be a high school party. My dress was way too fancy. I touched my mask with a gloved hand to reassure myself it was still there. I just needed to play my part, act like a normal high school girl at a party.

Whatever the hell that meant.

A drink. That's what my character, Normie McNormal-Girl, would want. I rustled my way through the living room, feeling dizzy, drunk already on the glances people were giving me. No one had actually challenged my presence, at least.

Six white pillar candles in glass holders were arranged on the mantel, burning glossy and flickering. The skulls I had seen in the bathtub earlier were arranged between the candles. I nodded at them, skeleton to skeleton, and slipped into the kitchen.

The counter was crowded with drinks. Soda. Six packs of Pabst Blue Ribbon. Bottom-shelf vodka. Red plastic cups. I poured myself a vodka and 7UP, hands shaking, before realizing that there was no possible way to drink it through my mask. It would probably be nasty anyway.

My mother let me have my first drink when I was fourteen. A single glass of champagne at New Year's. *You should know that alcohol isn't magic,* she said. *It is not the forbidden fruit of the tree of knowledge. It's just a drink with some nice side effects followed by some unpleasant ones.*

I passed the test, I guess. Had my one glass of champagne, didn't ask for more. After that, we'd occasionally share drinks lifted out from under the noses of distracted patrons in upscale but dimly lit cocktail bars or taken from the private wine cellars of the filthy rich.

Maybe it wasn't normal, but nothing about us is.

I suppose it turned me into a snob. I like a sloe gin fizz, a Sazerac, a sidecar. I like a mint julep on a wraparound porch in Mississippi. A Vieux Carré on a rooftop in the French Quarter of New Orleans.

Everyone at this party would probably think I was a pretentious asshole. I know most kids my age, if they drink at all, drink to get drunk, drink whatever they can get.

I don't really know what it means to be seventeen. I always feel older or younger. A wizened old man sipping top-shelf whiskey or a naïve infant who doesn't know how to drive a car or check out at a grocery store or talk to another human being.

I heard footsteps behind me, whipped around, the beads on my dress clacking. Jules stopped in the doorway, brow furrowed. I must have looked absurd, standing there, frozen, clutching my Solo cup. Jules wore a silky floral top, a long skirt, and a big blue sunhat. Their face, streaked in blocks of bright color, was a spot-on re-creation of the Matisse painting.

Silence stretched a moment, two, three. Long enough that it was awkward. Long enough that I felt sure, as they opened their mouth to speak, that the words that came out would be some variation on *Who the hell are you, and what are you doing in my kitchen?*

"Matisse," I spat out, all blind panic.

Jules's look of concern dissolved instantly into a grin. "Is that you, Shawna?" They peered more closely at the mask. Involuntarily, I took a step back.

Jules was still smiling at me. I realized I was supposed to respond. Of course I was. That's how a conversation worked.

I shook my mask no. This was so simple and I was so, so stupid. So unprepared.

"Oh." Jules cocked their head. "Who are you, then?"

I had to say something. "Sam."

It was one of the names Neely had mentioned to Denise that morning. From a show, she'd said. It was a risk. Sam might be a boy. Maybe that didn't matter. This seemed like a queer crowd, which was cool. But Sam might already be here.

"Who invited you?" Jules asked.

Nobody.

"Neely," I said instead. I was speaking too quietly, I knew, my voice muffled further by the mask. Jules was leaning in to hear. My heart pounded.

"Well, I'm Jules, Denise's cousin." Jules popped a PBR can free from its plastic ring. "Do you know Denise, too?"

I nodded slowly, uncertainly. I'd backed up more without even realizing it. The edge of the counter pressed into the small of my back. The inside of my mask was damp with condensation. I wished I could take it off. But the mask was, for all intents and purposes, my face.

"Do you go to CAPA?" Jules asked.

This conversation was going way too fast for me.

Should I say yes? No? I didn't know what CAPA was. I was exhausted already.

Buying time, I raised my cup to my mask, tried to take a sip. A few drops made it into my mouth, but most of it dribbled down the front of the mask, dripped onto the dress.

"Shit," I said. At least vodka and 7UP were both clear.

Jules laughed. "You need a straw!"

They turned and rummaged in a cupboard, turned back a moment later.

"Voilà!" They held out a paper-wrapped straw.

My hand shook as I reached to take it. I was careful not

to let my glove brush against Jules's hand. Not that anything would happen if it did. But still.

I fumbled to unwrap the straw. What an idiot I was being. I should say thanks. I should say more than one word at a time. I was sweating. I was so bad at this.

As soon as I could, I shoved one end of the straw through the hole in the mask and took a long inelegant slurp of my drink. It was awful. A thin veneer of viciously sweet over a solid base of rubbing alcohol. I took another slurp anyway, let it burn at the back of my throat.

"Is Neely here?" I asked. My longest sentence so far.

"She's in the basement." Jules pointed to a door in the corner that I hadn't even noticed. "Her band is playing."

I hurried over to it. Realized, a little too late, that I probably should have said thanks again, or bye, or something. I was too relieved to be free of the conversation to care.

Which is so stupid. Everything about me is so stupid.

All year I dream about talking to people, but as soon as I get the chance, I choke. As soon as I get the chance, I run away like a coward.

It wasn't Neely I wanted to find, really, but I hadn't dared ask about Tess. I couldn't possibly explain how I knew her.

The basement door was ajar. Music pounded up from below. I pushed the door open, and the sound hit me. I took one step onto the rickety wooden stairs, another.

The basement was dim and cramped. Christmas lights looped along the low ceiling beams. Each strand of lights was different—one white, one blue, one multicolored, one blinking.

In the far corner, a band played, their instruments set up on a threadbare carpet. A guy dressed as Guy Fieri played guitar, Neely played keyboard, still in her leather jacket, and between them, wearing glittery red devil horns and wailing into a microphone, was none other than Tess.

The Castle

I'd had a lot of crushes before. I collected them. It was something to do. They were always fleeting. Some lasting no longer than a train ride, a bus ride. A pretty boy or a girl with interesting hair. Passing in and out of my life the way my mother and I pass in and out of houses.

Why did it turn, with Tess, into something more? Was it just brain chemicals, coincidence? I said I loved her because she was angry, but it was more than that, too. I had some sense that if only circumstances were different, if I wasn't who I was, we could have gotten along. Could have understood each other. I don't know.

We lived in her house for several months. So the crush had time to grow. To change. To go wrong.

It became painful. To be so close to her and yet so far away. I wished sometimes that I'd never seen her, that I'd never had these feelings.

I could never talk to her, never reach her. There was a glass wall. Between me and everyone. Unbreakable.

And yet I had stood there and watched her break so many things. Her bloody knuckles.

So I broke through, too, just a little bit.

I started taking things to give to her. Expensive things from fancy stores. The kind of things her mother would buy. Porcelain dolls, porcelain teacups. I'd tuck them into likely places around the house. The china cupboard. The attic.

As far as she knew, her mother was simply ordering these things during her late-night online-shopping sprees. It was plausible. I had once watched the mother click "buy" on an eight-hundred-dollar painting at two in the morning like it was nothing.

It was enough, for a while, to see Tess touch the things I had brought her. To see her smash them. Every one of them my heart.

What a sentimental idiot I was. One night I got an idea. A romantic idea. A stupid idea. It seemed like the kind of thing people did in movies and TV when they were as hopelessly in love as I was. So I did it.

I sent her a note.

12

Everything about Denise's basement was anathema to me. It was hot, it was loud, it was crowded. This is why there hadn't been many people upstairs. They were all down here. There was no room to move, no space to breathe. Nowhere to hide. People were jostling each other. Not quite dancing. More like violent group swaying, with a single person occasionally breaking free of the group to pinball to and fro.

It reminded me of ants or bees. Cells. All these individuals moving together, becoming one large organism. Part of something larger.

I was never part of anything.

Nonetheless, I descended. Hugging the wall. Walking slowly so as not to trip on the trailing hem of my heavy beaded dress.

The sight of Tess up there on the makeshift stage was like something out of a dream.

In my dreams, I'd always be doing something else, fighting a demon train conductor or trying to climb a mountain while carrying five kittens, and then suddenly she'd be there.

Sitting on the side of the mountain. Standing at the other end of a train car.

Oh, how my stomach would twist. How my heart would soar.

My stomach twisted now, all right.

But in my dreams, she'd look at me. She'd smile. In dreams, her eyes met mine. In dreams, my eyes were more than slight black pinpricks disturbing the air like motes of dust.

Would I be brave enough, this time, to talk to her? I had a mask now. I had a drink.

What I really needed was practice.

Half the people down here didn't seem to be in costume as anything other than themselves. Punk kids. Some wore face paint or glitter. I caught a glimpse of a shaggy-haired boy with fake blood smeared across his face. Or was it real blood?

I spotted Denise against the far wall, watching the band intently. It didn't look like she was in costume, either.

I picked my way toward her, sliding past people as best I could. The band was finishing up with a buzzing crescendo as I reached her. She turned and I saw that I had been wrong about her costume. Her clothes were normal only to the left shoulder. There, her gray sweater devolved into a gradient of gray-black feathers. Her arm was completely encased by an enormous wing, outstretched. The tip brushed against the wall.

Here in the dark of the basement, the effect was breathtaking. This was not some store-bought wing. No cheapo Victoria's Secret Angel–wannabe fluff on wire. It looked real. Each feather meticulously placed in an interlocking pattern.

I stared. She stared. The band struck up another screeching song just as she opened her mouth and spoke.

"What?" I said.

"Creepy," she repeated, louder this time, gesturing with the great wing toward my face. The feathers fluttered.

"Do I know you?" shouted Denise. She was smiling. "I can't tell. You could be anybody under there."

I am the ghost in your house, I thought. *We have already met, in a way.*

"Sam," I said instead, more prepared this time. "Neely invited me."

"Oh yeah. Neely invited almost everybody. She's the popular one."

Denise turned back to watch the band. Tess was leaning into the microphone, bending it forward, full of an intensity that made my stomach turn over. She was shouting, a staccato refrain that I couldn't quite parse into words. Or a tune, really.

"Cool costume," said Denise. I realized, with a start, that she was looking at me again.

I couldn't get over that. I didn't think I would ever get over that. Being looked at.

"Thanks," I made myself say. I told myself that the fuzzy distorted howl of the guitar was like the sound of a train. That this was no different from talking to my mother.

"Where did you get that dress?" Denise asked.

I didn't want to say I'd stolen it. I wasn't sure what to say. Why would a high schooler have a wedding dress? Family heirloom? It wasn't vintage, though.

Conversations were so complicated.

"Where did you get that?" I asked instead, pointing to the wing.

"I made it." Denise flexed the wing. It reminded me of a fairy tale I'd read once about these seven brothers whose stepmother cursed them to be swans for some reason, I don't really remember, and their sister had to knit seven sweaters out of nettles to save them, but she didn't finish the arm on the final sweater and so all her brothers were turned back into normal boys except the last one, who was stuck with a single swan wing for life.

"The seventh brother!" I blurted out, and then faltered. Denise looked startled. Jules had seemed pleased when I identified their outfit, but I'd known I was right that time. I'd cheated. Maybe this was also a painting. Or a Greek myth? Or maybe it was a recent pop culture reference. Something from a new TV show I hadn't seen. Or a music video. "That story," I muttered, looking down at the ground. "The fairy tale. Your costume."

I must have sounded like an idiot. My face felt hot. Was I blushing? Maybe. It didn't matter. No one could see.

"Oh my god!" Denise said. "You are the only person so far who has gotten that."

I glanced up. Denise was grinning.

"Jules and I had a bet," she said. "They thought nobody would. But you've just won me five whole dollars!"

I smiled, but she couldn't see that, either. When you don't have friends and you spend a lot of time on trains, you read books. Lots and lots of books. They are the only way I've really lived.

"Shit, are you a literary reference, too?" Denise scrutinized me.

I felt ashamed, suddenly, of my costume. Of myself. I was a little kid playing dress-up. A fraud. A liar. An idiot and a loser. If she knew who I really was. If anyone ever knew—

I shook my head.

"Just a bride who died?" Denise asked.

I nodded. Inside, screaming at myself: *Say something, you idiot.*

"Fatal case of cold feet?" Denise prompted, still smiling despite my stupidity, my silence. She was being so nice, trying to make this easy. If I couldn't talk to her, no way would I be able to talk to Tess.

"I was left at the altar," I said. I still wasn't talking loudly enough. Denise was leaning very close to hear me. She smelled like coconut oil. "And I died immediately of pure rage."

The song ended abruptly with a jangled fuzz of electric guitar static and then silence.

Speaking quickly, before I lost my nerve, I continued: "Since then, I've roamed the earth, seeking revenge on the one who stood me up."

"Any luck?" Denise asked.

"Not yet. But that's why I'm at this party."

Denise laughed and I felt a pang of something—happiness, maybe. Like a sliver, a tiny glimpse, a fraction of a fraction of a fraction, of what it felt like to have a friend.

"Oh," she said, then, turning away, "they're taking a break."

The band had set down or unplugged their instruments. Tess was talking to the guitarist. Neely scanned the crowd, spotted Denise, started over toward us. With horror, I remembered I'd said I knew Neely. I needed to get out of there.

I turned, but the crowd was surging as one toward the stairs and my way was blocked by bodies.

"Hey, Neely," I heard Denise say behind me. "Sam guessed my costume."

I spun back around. Neely's hair was sticking up in all directions, and she'd sprayed it black with, it looked like, some cheap Halloween-store dye. Her eyes were lined with thick geometric blocks of black.

"Yeah?" said Neely. She looked me over but didn't ask who I was. Maybe she thought I was someone else named Sam. Maybe she was just bad at names. Maybe she didn't care. "Well, do you know who I am?"

Neely, I almost said, until I realized she meant her costume. I was an idiot. I stared at her. The makeup was distinctive, certainly.

"Uh, punk Cleopatra?" I offered.

She rolled her eyes. "Siouxsie from Siouxsie and the Banshees."

I didn't know who that was. I'd failed the coolness test. I mean, I knew what a banshee was, but I doubted that would help.

Neely sighed. "I need a cigarette," she said. "Tess!"

Over on the makeshift stage, Tess turned toward us.

Neely was waving her over. This was a dream. Oh god. I was dreaming.

Tess. Her pale face approaching through the crowd like the moon crashing toward earth, coming closer and closer, blotting out everything else. Oh. I was an insufficient astronomer.

"Hey," said Tess.

"Hey," said Denise

Hell, said my heart. *Goddamn.*

"Come on," said Neely. "Let's go outside."

And with that, she and Tess swept away. Denise trailed after.

I stood, frozen, watching them go. When Denise reached the bottom of the stairs, she turned back, head swiveling, until her eyes rested, finally, on me. She waved at me, and it took me quite a few moments longer than it should have to realize that she meant for me to come with her, meant for me to follow.

The Playhouse

I'd been having imaginary conversations with Tess in my head for weeks by the time I wrote the note. Still, I didn't know what to say.

Tess, I love you, I wrote on a piece of fancy stationery I'd lifted from a boutique in Shadyside. I read it over and laughed aloud. Idiot. I added a letter and a word.

Tess, I love your style.

I left the note in the playhouse. She often hid cigarettes behind the loose rock in the fake fireplace, so I put the note there.

Later, I followed Tess outside. Watched her find it. She frowned at it, turned it over, scrawled a reply.

What? Is this some joke? Who the hell is this? Do I know you?

Sorry, I wrote back, after she'd smoked and left. *I didn't mean to freak you out. I go to your school.*

That wasn't a lie. I did go there sometimes. I'd followed Tess on the bus twice. I'd told my mother I just wanted to see the high school, sit in on a few classes.

Tess checked the playhouse again the next day.

Talk to me at school, then, she wrote. *Why are you trespassing on my property? If my parents find out, they'll call the cops.*

I'm afraid to, I wrote back. *Sorry. I'm very shy. I live nearby.*

Nearer than she realized.

Her reply came a day later: *You probably think this is romantic or something. Well, sorry, buddy, I'm gay.*

I'd suspected this about her, I can't say why, just a feeling, but I hadn't been sure. I had no hope anyway, of course. Still, it made my heart flutter to have her confirm what I'd guessed.

I kept my reply simple: *So am I.*

She looked at this note for a long time. Turned it over, looked at the back. Traced the letters with her finger. When she did that, it felt like she was touching my skin.

Okay, she wrote back. *Well, tell me about yourself. Are you punk? What bands do you like?*

That was the beginning of the good part.

13

I followed Denise up the stairs, through the kitchen, and out onto the back porch. There was a roll of plasticky green AstroTurf laid out along the planks. A fake yard floating above the concrete. I gravitated, instinctively, to the farthest corner, wedged myself beside a small rusting grill. Tess leaned against the porch railing and pulled a crumpled pack of cigarettes from her boot. She took one, lit it, held the pack out for Neely.

"So do your parents know you're throwing this party?" she asked Denise.

"Oh," said Denise, "this is my aunt and uncle's place, actually."

"I thought you lived here."

"I do." She looked uncomfortable. "Can I get anybody a drink?"

"Yeah," said Tess. "Vodka cranberry. Make it strong."

"I'll take a PBR," said Neely.

"Sure," said Denise. "Sam?"

It took me a moment to remember that this was me. I shook my head no. Denise squeezed back through the door to the kitchen, her wing going last. I was oddly sorry to see her go. Technically, Tess was the only one here who wasn't a total stranger, but in my brief conversation with Denise, she'd been easier to talk to than . . . well pretty much anyone I'd ever spoken to in my life.

Except my mother, of course.

Thinking of her gave me a stab of guilt. I'd barely thought of her at all since the party began. This was wrong. I had no business trying to enjoy myself.

"How many drinks have you had?" Neely was asking Tess. "You should take it easy."

"Jesus. Lay off me, Officer."

"Come on. If it weren't for me, there wouldn't even be alcohol at this party."

"Nobody would have come if there wasn't." Tess flicked ash off the edge of the porch. I watched her hands.

"Harry would have. He's straightedge."

"Lame." Tess made a face. "If this was my party, it would be a rule that everybody had to drink. No straightedges allowed."

Neely rolled her eyes. "How about no straights allowed."

They talked so easily, so effortlessly, both smoking their cigarettes. I could never talk like that. They so clearly belonged, both in their black jackets and boots.

I didn't belong here. And yet here I was, trapped in the corner of the porch. Visible. Stuck. Starting to feel light-headed. It was hard to get a full breath in the plastic skull mask.

Denise came back with the drinks. She was accompanied

by Jules and the Guy Fieri guitarist. Jules's face was melting, the colorful paint dripping down their cheeks like tears, the colors mixing, pretty in some places, going muddy in others.

"It's too damn hot in there," Jules said.

I agreed, though I didn't say so out loud. I was sweating buckets in my double layers, even out here on the porch.

The light-headedness was turning into full-blown dizziness. What was I doing? This was dangerous and bad and wrong, and my mother wasn't here and she might be dead.

"Slots only takes good photos because he's rich," Denise was saying to the others. I'd missed some of the conversation.

"Being rich isn't everything," said Tess. She sounded a touch defensive, the anger I knew so well simmering just under the surface.

I should try to talk to her. That's what I was here for.

"Yeah," said Denise, "but he can buy anything he wants. All the fancy lenses and shit. I have to rent a camera from school."

I pushed away from the railing. Took a shaky step forward. Toward Tess. My heart was racing.

Hello, I practiced in my head. *Hey. Hi.*

Tess's eyes flicked over to me for a moment. I was breathing too fast, too shallow. I felt like I might faint.

There was a crash from inside. Everyone turned at once to look at the back door.

"Shit," Denise said as she hurried inside.

"That better not have been our instruments," Neely said. She and Tess stubbed out their cigarettes and headed after Denise. With a jolt and a shiver that went from my scalp to my spine, I realized that someone was standing right beside me. I turned. It was Guy Fieri.

"What was your name again?" he asked.

Head spinning, I pulled up my heavy beaded skirt and fled inside.

In the kitchen, I braced myself against the counter, my back to the room, trying to catch my breath. I squeezed my empty cup in my hand so hard it cracked. Someone brushed past behind me, stepped on the trailing hem of my dress, said, *Oh, sorry.* I didn't turn to look.

The parties that we were planning to go to in New York, the kind I'd been to the year before, were huge, hosted in fancy nightclubs. There was anonymity in that. The rooms were large and dimly lit, with so many corners to fade into.

Last year, dressed as a seventeenth-century plague doctor, with dark robes and a long-beaked mask, I had floated from room to room, my mother tagging along, unseen, behind me. Mostly, I had merely observed, as I always did, though I reveled in the occasional glance sent my way. I'd spoken briefly to four people: a bartender, when I ordered cocktails (they'd checked IDs at the door, but I'd been invisible then), two people who had complimented my costume, and one woman at the sink in the ladies' room. None of these exchanges had lasted longer than a minute or two.

I hadn't realized how much worse a small party would be.

"Sam?"

I spun around. It was Jules.

"You okay?" they asked.

Absolutely not. Not even a little bit.

I nodded.

"Oh." Jules glanced down at the floor by my feet. The straw from my cup had fallen there. "Here." They opened a drawer again, extracted another wrapped straw, held it out to me.

"Thanks," I forced myself to say as I took it with a shaking hand.

Tears pricked my eyes. This was stupid.

I'd held real diamonds in my hand before, and yet here I was, getting choked up over the gift of a disposable straw.

I grabbed a new cup and the nearest bottle of booze and poured half a cupful. My first slurp through the straw almost made me choke. I topped off the cup with soda, took another sip.

Jules poured themselves a glass of water. We were the only ones in the kitchen now. There were shouts and laughs coming from the living room.

Jules seemed nice. Quiet in comparison to the others. Their face paint had dripped onto the collar of their shirt. They adjusted the big blue hat perched atop their black curls.

"Do you know Tess?" I asked.

"Tess? Yeah, of course. I mean, we're not good friends or anything." Jules shrugged. "I'm not really friends with most of the people here. They're all from the grade above me. Honestly, I feel a bit out of place."

"Oh." I felt a surge of warmth. Connection. "Yeah, me too."

"Why do you ask?"

"I"—I took a deep breath—"I just wanted to tell her I like her singing."

"Well, come on," said Jules with a grin.

They beckoned me into the living room. It was crowded now. People sat on the floor, the coffee table, on the back of the couch, perched on the arms. They leaned against the walls. Denise was kneeling in the corner, restacking piles of books that had been knocked over. I scanned the room but didn't see Tess.

She appeared a moment later at the opposite doorway, holding a bottle of whiskey and a stack of little paper mouthwash cups.

"Shots!" she shouted, before marching over to the mantel. She lined up cups next to the skulls and candles, dispensing a splash of whiskey into each.

She turned as Jules and I approached, held out a paper cup.

"Did you take these from our bathroom?" asked Jules, frowning.

Before she could answer, Neely appeared and snatched the cup out of Tess's hand. She crumpled it. The whiskey ran down her fist.

"What are you doing?" Neely demanded. "We have to play the second half of the set still."

"So?" Tess arched a brow.

"So you can't get hammered."

"That was for Jules," said Tess, pointing to the crumpled mouthwash cup. "You should apologize."

"It's fine," Jules mumbled.

Neely scowled. "Just take it easy, okay?"

Without breaking eye contact, Tess reached out, grabbed one of the cups on the mantel, and downed the shot.

Neely made a noise of disgust and stalked away.

Jules cleared their throat. "Uh, hey, Tess, have you met Sam?" Tess turned to look at me. Her eyes were slightly glassy, like maybe she was not taking it easy at all. She had been fond of sneaking drinks from her parents' supply even two years ago.

I felt frozen. Deer in headlights. *Come on,* I told myself. *This is what you've been waiting for. This is it. If you don't say anything, you will regret it. You will obsess over this moment for months.*

"I . . ." My voice sounded small, childish. Pleading. "I liked your singing."

Tess grinned. "Oh, cool, thanks. Shot?"

I blinked at her. I wanted to capture this moment, save it forever. Her smile. Her gaze, fixed on my face. Well, on my mask, actually, but close enough.

The boy with fake-or-maybe-real blood on his face had come up beside me. "Can I have one?" he asked.

Tess turned to him. "Yeah, here." She busied herself dispensing more shots.

The moment was over. Still, my head was buzzing. I'd spoken to her. She'd spoken back.

The Auditorium

Our notes got longer. Turned into letters. I'd catch Tess staring out the window for twenty minutes at a time, eyes fixed on the playhouse. There was only one window in the house you could see it from, in the attic. She'd sit up there with her headphones on, blasting her music so loud I could hear it as I sat a few feet away, watching her while she watched for me.

I brought her packs of cigarettes. New tapes of bands I thought she'd like from the record store in Squirrel Hill.

In her notes, sometimes she'd still ask who I was. She'd make guesses. *I've figured it out. You're that chick Taylor from the grade above me, aren't you?*

At school the next day, I'd try to figure out which one was Taylor. I'd see who Tess was eyeing. I'd started going with her to high school most days. Staying late in the auditorium to watch the school play practices (she was part of the crew).

Look, it wasn't a proper romance, I know that. But it was the most exciting thing that had ever happened to me. She took over my thoughts, my every waking hour. All my life became a letter to her.

Tess, I would think, I see you across the auditorium. You

are crouched at the back of the stage, working on the scenery. You are painting a wooden backdrop some hideous shade of green, and the actors are in front of you, they are singing, they are posing, they are waving their arms and dancing. But you are all I see. You are all I ever see.

I left a china teacup with the next note. It was stupid.

She had said something in one of her notes, something about smashing everything, had complained about her mother's fancy belongings. So I guess I'd thought that was enough to make it plausible. But really, I was just forgetting, blurring the line between myself and the character I was playing, the note-giver. Because we weren't really the same. We couldn't be.

Nobody knew that Tess broke shit in the woods. At least nobody was supposed to know.

When she found the teacup (I was watching through the playhouse window), she picked it up and stared at it for a long time. She looked around. Her face bore a strange, haunted expression. She wrote back right away, in the margins of the note I'd left.

WHO ARE YOU? she wrote. *Tell me now or I won't talk to you anymore.*

That was the beginning of the end.

14

As Tess was swallowed up by a crowd of partygoers drawn by the promise of shots, I backed away, toward a less packed corner of the room. I found myself standing next to Denise, who had finally finished righting the stacks of books.

"Hey there, Ghost Bride," she said.

I jumped a little, which was stupid. I hadn't expected anyone to talk to me. No one ever did, normally. But here they could see me. This was wrong and dangerous.

And exciting. Wonderful.

"Found the bastard who stood you up yet?" Denise asked me.

It took me another second to remember what she was referring to. The story I'd made up for myself. About a jilted bride wandering the earth, forever seeking vengeance. I smiled behind my mask. Shook my head no.

"Ugh, who invited him?" said Denise, eyes going to something behind me.

A tall boy had walked through the door. Dirty blond hair, pink complexion. He was dressed as Jesus Christ, wrapped in a sheet, wearing a plastic crown of thorns.

"I think you did," said Jules, who had wandered over. "Didn't you invite everyone in your class?"

Say something, I told myself.

"That's him," I said. "The man on whom I have sworn revenge."

I sounded so stupid. I knew it. Was that even the correct usage of whom?

"Slots?" Denise arched an eyebrow at me. "Why the hell would you ever want to marry Slots?"

"Um," I said.

Really A-plus conversation there. Sparkling, some might say.

I tried closing my eyes. I'd simply pretend I was talking to no one. Or talking to my mom.

"Well," I started, "maybe it's not him. Maybe it's been so long I've forgotten exactly what my betrothed looked like. So maybe I just go around killing any man who kind of resembles him."

"So just basic-ass white dudes?" said Jules. "There's plenty of them."

Denise laughed her big wonderful laugh. "That's perfect. Kill Slots because he's so generic. The most fitting death for him."

Her laugh made me feel better about everything, somehow. I opened my eyes, blinked at Denise. Then turned back toward the mantel. I caught a glimpse of Tess amid the crowd, a glimpse of the twinkling candle flames on the mantel, the bleached skulls. The Jesus guy, Slots, was over there now, taking a slug from the whiskey bottle itself, talking to Tess.

Maybe I should go back, try to talk to her again. Say more this time.

I was having a proper conversation with Denise, wasn't I?

"Do you actually know Slots?" Denise asked, sounding slightly worried.

"No," I said quickly.

I took a step toward the mantel, toward Tess.

"Show starts again in five!" Neely shouted from the doorway of the kitchen. People moved toward the basement, Tess leading the way.

"You want to come watch the band?" Denise asked, stepping up beside me.

I'd missed my chance. Should I go back down into the crush of the basement? It was so strange that Denise was even asking me. So . . . nice. Almost like we were friends.

My choice was delayed by Slots, who appeared, suddenly, to block our path. He stared intently at Denise's blue and purple curls.

"Whoa," he said, his voice slow and thick-sounding. "What happened to your hair? Did you dye it?" He reached for it, but she flinched away. He swayed a little.

"How are you this drunk already?" Denise asked.

"I pregamed," he said. I craned to see past him. Tess had already vanished.

"Did you make your sister buy you alcohol?" Denise asked.

Slots shrugged, reached for her hair again. She slapped his hand away. I stood, frozen, wishing for invisibility, safety.

"Don't be a dick," he said. "It looks good. How'd you get it so bright?"

"It's extensions." Her tone was flat, guarded. Her expression matched.

"Oh, weird, so it's not even your hair."

Denise's face twisted in disgust for a moment before returning to neutral.

"It's mine. Now move out of the way."

She tried to step around him. But he wasn't done.

"Tess said you were talking shit about me," he said, moving to block her. I remembered Denise complaining about this guy out on the porch. I don't understand why Tess would tell him about that. I wouldn't have. It couldn't achieve anything but trouble, hurt feelings.

But what did I know?

"So what if I was?" Denise asked.

"Well, say it to my face." He took a step toward her, menacing all of a sudden, like a flipped switch.

"Leave her alone," I said.

He wheeled to face me, looking confused.

I felt equally baffled. What was I doing? I must be almost as drunk as he was.

"Who the hell are you?" asked Slots.

Good question.

I was getting carried away, losing myself in the role. I had lied my way in here, pretended to be one of these people, to be normal. Denise wasn't my friend, not really. But for a moment there, it had felt like she was.

I was drunk on that feeling, I think, as much as on the alcohol.

"She told you to move," I said to him.

He reached out and pushed me. I mean, he actually put his hand on me. On my shoulder. Pressed.

The shock of that was electric. And not in a good way. I felt like I'd been shot.

"Sam," said Denise. I couldn't tell, in the moment, if it was admonishment or concern.

I pushed him back with both hands. Hard. So hard he lost his footing.

He pinwheeled, reaching out desperately for something to hold on to. His left hand latched onto my long white wig, grasped a fistful of hair.

He fell anyway, his momentum carrying him back. But he didn't let go. My head jerked forward, and before I could react, my wig was being yanked off, and the plastic skull mask, to which it had been so carefully pinned, went right along with it.

I stood still for a moment, too shocked to do anything.

Someone screamed.

Without the mask limiting my view, I could take in the whole room, and it was like a dream. A nightmare. All those people. Staring at me, their eyes wide, mouths open. All those eyes on me, pinning me, pulling me apart.

I still had the ski mask on, but it didn't matter. That was touching my skin. It was as invisible as I was.

All anyone would see was a long beaded wedding dress with a high collar. And above that collar: nothing.

"What the fuck?" someone shouted.

Shocked back into motion, I snatched the skull mask from where it had fallen to the ground, tripped over my own dress, banged my shoulder against the mantel. The nearest candle toppled, knocking a skull into the next candle. They all fell, one after another, blazing dominoes. The final one plummeted to the floor. A lick of flame leapt up from the edge of the rug.

But I was already scrambling away, running for the door, frantically pulling the skull mask back on.

People were shouting. I heard someone calling my fake name, but I didn't turn around. The mask was on crooked. I could see only through one eyehole, barely. I banged out the front door, ran down the path. Tripped again on the long hem of my dress, and fell forward.

There was the sound of ripping fabric. Gravel stabbing my palms. More screams from the house. A hand grabbing at my arm.

I shoved the hand away, stumbled to my feet, hauled up my skirt, and ran like hell. I paid no attention to which direction I was going. Just away away away.

The Cathedral

The notes stopped.

I started to consider it—telling Tess who I was. I knew I shouldn't do it, I couldn't, but those notes had become everything to me. They felt necessary for life. Her words were water, and I was on fire.

I thought that maybe I could talk to her. Maybe if I explained, she would understand.

Maybe she would love me back.

I started following her from dawn to dusk. Waiting for the right moment, trying to gather enough courage to break through.

And that's how I found out about Taylor.

I saw Tess pass this girl, Taylor, a folded note in the hallway of the high school. I saw her hand brush against Taylor's hand, just for a moment. I saw them talking together, laughing together. But I didn't want to see that, didn't want to believe it.

"So you swear it wasn't you?" I heard Tess asking her one day.

"I swear," she said. She was sporty. Wore her hair in a

tight ponytail, played on the school varsity basketball team. She was nothing like Tess. I didn't get it. "It sounds like you had a stalker, honestly. It's kind of creepy."

"Yeah. I guess you're right."

"Let me know if they send you any more stuff."

One day, they left school together instead of taking their separate buses home. I followed them down to Oakland, across the lawns of the Pitt campus. They both wore their school uniforms, knee-length navy skirts, jackets. Looking almost alike. Looking like they belonged to something. Belonged together.

I saw them slam through the doors of the Cathedral of Learning. When I got in there, I spun around, looking for them. The place was like a castle, all stonework and arches, winding staircases, parapets. They could have gone anywhere. Down one of the narrow corridors or up in the elevator to the top floors.

But then I spotted them again, up on a stone balcony. They were both laughing, red-faced, out of breath from running. Taylor said something I couldn't hear from down below. She reached for Tess's hand. And then Tess leaned forward and kissed her.

It shouldn't have been a surprise, shouldn't have been a shock. But it was.

I was one of her teacups. Stomped on, shattered.

I turned, ran, slumped to the floor in one of the outer corridors. Slammed my fist against the wall. A moment later: shouts.

The wall was gone, the whole wall, the broad green lawn

beyond clearly visible. The students who'd been lounging out there were all jumping to their feet. Many had phones out.

I yanked my hand away, of course, but it was too late.

It wasn't until later that I'd realize the full extent of what I'd done.

I felt guilty, looking back. How terrifying it must have been, up on the fortieth floor, to turn around, expecting wall, and see only sky.

But right then, in that moment, I wasn't sorry at all. Right then, I wanted the world to match my heart. I wanted to break shit.

15

Weighed down by the wedding dress, I was out of breath in a few blocks. The inside of my mask was wet with sweat and tears and snot. The key I'd taken from Denise's room had slipped around from the side of my sneaker to the bottom, and it stabbed my heel with every step.

I dragged myself down a narrow gap between two houses, stumbled to the paved backyard, which was dark, unfenced. Crouched behind a trash can, threw off my mask, contorted myself to reach the dress zipper. I was breathing so hard I thought I would pass out. I coughed, gagged. The zipper broke when I yanked on it.

I had to squirm out of the dress. A butterfly in reverse, emerging from my gilded chrysalis a boring old caterpillar once more.

Only once I had stripped down to a single layer—one pair of gloves, the spandex dress, one pair of tights, which I ripped open at the toes so my skin would be in contact with my shoes—only then could I pause. I was invisible again. Safe. Erased.

My hands shook. I let my head fall against them as I kneeled on the concrete.

I was alone. Really truly alone in a way I'd never been before. I had no idea what to do, where to go. Had no idea where my mother was. How to get her to come back.

In the eyes of the world, I didn't even exist. Had no ID, no birth certificate. I couldn't go to the police, couldn't go to anyone.

I had no one.

As soon as I thought that, I realized it wasn't completely true. There was exactly one other person in the world besides my mother who knew that I existed. I hated to ask for help, but I couldn't see any other choice. I bunched up the dress and shoved it, plus mask and wig, into the trash can.

I picked myself up, brushed myself off, double-checked that no part of me was visible, and walked away.

It took me several blocks to find what I was looking for. A neon sign on the side of a brick building: NICO'S RECOVERY ROOM. A bar. Inside, it was dark and loud. Good.

I approached a group of girls laughing together, all of them with their phones out on the table. I didn't need to pick a pocket. I didn't even need to wait for them to look away. I grabbed a phone with a rhinestone case and slipped back out the way I'd come.

There were no alleys here, only streets and smaller streets, and everywhere felt too exposed. Several blocks away, I ran into the giant graveyard again. The gate was closed and locked, but I found a low tree growing near the fence and managed to climb up and lower myself down.

The phone had a pattern code, but it was easy to guess from the smudges on the screen. Sitting at the base of a stone mausoleum, I dialed the one and only number I knew by heart: my father's.

The phone rang. Rang again.

It was late. Nearly midnight. He might not pick up.

"Hello?" came a voice from the phone.

My voice got stuck on the way out, became nothing more than a sad croak.

He was my father, not a stranger, and I'd talked to so many strangers tonight, yes, but it was still hard. I didn't know what to say. How to start the conversation.

I hadn't spoken to him in nearly a year. Hadn't seen him in ten.

"Annette?" he asked into the silence. My mother's name.

"No," I said.

"Pietà!" He sounded delighted but also casual, as if this was no big deal. As if it weren't the middle of the night. As if I were the kind of daughter who just called sometimes. "It's so good to hear from you. Where are you?"

I took a deep breath, let it out audibly.

"Mom's sick," I said.

"Oh." His tone was hard to read. Flat, cursory. Was he shocked? Annoyed? Disappointed? My father never let on what he was truly feeling.

"Really sick," I said. "I need help."

"Where are you?"

"Pittsburgh."

He laughed, which seemed like entirely the wrong response. "Was that you? A while back. The Cathedral of Learning?"

For a moment I was surprised. How did he know about that? But of course. The local news covered it. And he alone would have the information needed to guess what had actually happened.

"Yes," I admitted.

"I thought so. I went there when I heard about it. Tried to find you."

That made me feel oddly warm. Happy, almost. That he wanted to find me. Wanted to see me.

"We left right after," I told him.

"I was afraid of that."

"Are you still here?" I asked. That would be good. I could go to wherever he was living. I could . . . stay with my father?

It was a bizarre thought. I hadn't even met him in person until I was seven. Hadn't seen him again since then.

"Nah, I'm up in Michigan. But look, I'll make some time for you. I can drive down there first thing tomorrow."

"Okay," I said, relieved. "Thanks."

He was far from perfect, but he was an adult. He could help. I didn't have to handle this all on my own.

"Probably take me about five hours. So if I leave early. . . ." He muttered a bit, not quite audible, counting. "How about we meet up around one? At the Carnegie. The art side. You know where that is? In Oakland?"

"Yeah," I said, though I wasn't thinking about the

museum. How many hours between now and one? What would I do until then?

"It'll be great to see you," Dad said. He sounded so upbeat, as if he'd forgotten what I'd told him about the reason for my call. "Does your mom know?"

"What?"

"That you called me?"

"Oh." I didn't want to explain over the phone. Didn't want to say it out loud and make it real. Maybe by tomorrow she'd be back and I wouldn't have to tell him she wasn't just sick but gone. "No."

"Well, that's all right. I'm glad you did. See you tomorrow, sweetie. Hang in there. We'll get everything figured out."

His tone was so cheery it verged into customer service. I wanted to believe him, wanted to believe everything would be fine.

"Okay, thanks," I said. I hung up, stared at the phone in my hands, angled it back and forth so the rhinestones caught the distant haze of the streetlights and glimmered faintly. I didn't believe that everything would be fine. I felt uneasy, uncertain whether I'd done the right thing by calling him.

My father was a thief, a con man. My mother said he rarely showed anyone his true face. Even us.

I didn't mind that he stole for a living. Technically, my mother and I did, too, though I didn't really think of us as thieves. I mean, I guess we were. But we had no choice. No other way to live.

The problem with my father was that he lied as easily as

breathing. I could never tell what he really thought, what he really felt. I barely knew him.

My father was perfectly visible. And yet, in his own way, he was as insubstantial as we were. He, too, could be seen only wearing a mask.

Austin, TX

I met my father only because my mother thought I might die.

My mother had never hidden my father's identity. Quite the contrary. She told me about him all the time. Mostly about what a bastard he was, how foolish and reckless they'd both been in their art-heist days.

Still, there was a hint of fondness in those stories.

Usually when I'd been sick, my mother had treated me herself. She'd sat in on a half semester of medical school when she was pregnant and become well acquainted with how to sneak medicine from hospitals and doctor's offices. She'd splinted my wrist when I sprained it, stolen and administered the necessary vaccines throughout my childhood.

But this time, I had a fever that wouldn't break. She was scared. She called my father.

He came to the town we were in, booked us a motel room. I was seven. Delirious with high fever, dehydration. Before that, I'd known him only as an occasional voice on long-distance phone calls.

They fought. I can remember listening to them shouting as I drifted in and out of consciousness.

"Where is she right now?" I remember him saying, because of course he couldn't see me.

"You aren't even really her father," I heard her say.

"What?" He sounded confused suddenly instead of angry.

"Well, biologically you are. But that's it. It doesn't mean much."

Still, he helped us. Brought us things we needed while my mother stayed at my side. Even after my fever broke, after I started being able to keep down liquids, we stayed. I thought maybe we would live with him then. We moved to the next town over, got another motel room. Went out to eat. He ordered food for all three of us.

And we took things for him. Little things at first. Then bigger. *Hey, kiddo,* he'd whisper into the air. *Go grab me some cash.*

He never touched me. Never even shook my hand.

"A hug?" he asked at one point, looking in the general direction of my mother but pointing down toward a spot to her left where he believed me to be standing.

"No," she said, in a tone like the sheer face of a glacier. To her right, I sagged with disappointment. I would have liked a hug. My father just shrugged and gave a sad smile.

"You cannot trust him," my mother told me. We left suddenly one morning, without saying goodbye, for no reason as far as I could tell. "You cannot trust anybody," she added.

I knew she was right. She was always right.

16

My feet were sore from running, and the cold crept in through my ripped tights. My mother and I wear sandals most of the year, but with boots or sneakers, we either have to cut holes in our socks or go without, to make sure our skin touches the shoes.

There are a lot of little things like that. Things I barely even think about half the time, until suddenly I'm watching someone get dressed and I'm hit with how easy things are for everyone else.

How do people do it? They all make it look so effortless. To be seen. To talk to each other. To touch each other. How does it not drive them insane?

I'm not naïve. I've read plenty of books, seen plenty of movies. I have watched people touch each other in all kinds of ways.

Sometimes I think there must be an extra sense, like touch or taste, that everyone else has but I don't. Like how I can see a little bit of infrared that visible people can't. There's some extra dimension of the world that is totally blocked off to me.

The sense that lets you connect.

Tess could never ever, ever like me back. No one could. I might as well be a ghost. Might as well be dead.

I waited a long time in the graveyard, just sitting there in the dark, thinking, *This is where you belong.*

Finally, I made myself get up, shake a little warmth and feeling back into my limbs. It was nearly two. The stolen phone had begun to ring incessantly—the drunk girl I lifted it from must have noticed it was missing—so I ditched it by the graveyard gate.

I walked down the dark streets, glancing into the occasional lit windows, into worlds I was not and would never be a part of.

After a few wrong turns, I made it back to Denise's house.

To my relief, the windows of the house were unlit. No music or voices drifted out to the street. The party must have been over.

I pulled off one glove, fished the stolen house key from my shoe, unlocked the door, eased it open. I slipped in, eyes on my feet in case the cat tried to make another escape. The house was dark.

"Hello?"

I jumped at the voice, turned.

Denise was bent over in the living room, illuminated faintly by the streetlights. Even in the gloom, I could see that the room was trashed. Denise held a partially crushed beer can in one hand, a trash bag in the other. She had paused mid-motion, staring at the door.

"Neely, is that you?" Her voice was high, a little shaky.

I was frozen. Silent.

Denise shoved the beer can in the bag and moved sideways, reaching for the lamp, never taking her eyes off the door. I noticed her enormous swan wing propped gently against the stairwell. Now she just wore her black jeans and a black tank top.

"Neely," she said, voice rising even higher, "if you're messing with me, it's not funny."

Maybe I should have gone somewhere else. But where? I needed to be here in case my mother came back. And I'd left my backpack in the tub. There was nothing irreplaceable in there—we moved around too much to get attached to belongings—but it felt like the only thing I had in the world right now.

I felt myself tearing up again. Stupid. All I could do today was cry.

"Jules?" Denise pulled the lamp cord.

The light blazed on, illuminating: nothing.

She dropped the bag of cans with a crash. Cast about around her, grabbed an empty forty bottle. Held it up like a bat.

I saw that the edges of the rug in the middle of the living room were scorched, the wall and the mantel smoke-blackened. In my panic, I'd completely forgotten about knocking over the candles when I fell. I felt guilty. At least I hadn't burned their whole house down.

"Fuck," Denise said under her breath. She was scared. The hand that held the bottle was shaking. Her eyes looked puffy, red. Had she been crying, too?

I don't know what possessed me.

"It's okay," I said. Out loud. "I'm not going to hurt you."

Her eyes went wide. She took another step back, not reassured at all. This wasn't the party. I had no mask on. She couldn't see me.

"Who is that?" she asked. "Who's talking?"

It wasn't too late. I could have kept my mouth shut, pretended that I'd never spoken. She'd be forced to conclude that she'd imagined my voice. That she was too tired. Too drunk.

"It's me," I said instead.

The Glass Wall

Walking down a street at night, I pass dark houses with bright windows. Behind the panes are warm little worlds, lit up like fish tanks. I can walk right up, press my palm to the glass, watch as bright strangers flit from room to room.

People I can never touch, never talk to. People who will never see me, never know I was even there.

Even if they happen to glance out, even if they look right at me. Even if I leave the window and walk through their front door.

Even if I were to stand in front of these people, close enough to count the tiny veins in the whites of their eyes, the glass pane would still be there between us.

I carry those windows with me everywhere I go. They are always closed.

17

It's me.

What an idiotic thing to say.

"I can't see you," said Denise. Her voice shook as much as her hands.

"Yeah," I said, because I didn't know what else to say. "Sorry."

"Why can't I see you? Where are you?"

"I'm right here," I said. What the hell did I have left to lose at this point? This was rock bottom. "I'm invisible."

"Oh shit, oh Jesus. It's happening, isn't it?" She dropped the bottle, which clinked off the edge of the coffee table and rolled away. She clamped her hands over her ears.

I didn't know what she meant, but I thought of Christy, my first not-friend, who taught me how monstrous I was, how no one would ever be happy to know about me. I would have to leave now. Grab my backpack and go. I couldn't stay.

I sighed, walked into the room. Slumped onto the couch. Denise saw the movement and jumped back.

"What the ever-loving fuck?" she said.

"You swear a lot," I said. I put my head down in my hands

and lost it. Couldn't hold back any longer. I sobbed. Silently of course, but with uncontrollable spasms that wracked my chest, twisted my muscles.

I gasped for air, opened my mouth in a soundless scream. This is how I always cried: silently, painfully.

I didn't care what happened to me anymore. Didn't care if she started screaming or if she called the cops or if she bashed me in the head with a glass bottle.

Whatever happened, I probably deserved it. I was done. I was giving up.

"Sam?" Denise's voice had changed slightly. There was a note in it that hadn't been there before. Hope, maybe. Relief?

I jerked my head up, blinked at her through blurry tears. She was staring at me. Well, not quite at me but at the couch, at the divot I was making on it. Close enough. It was disarming.

"Your voice," she said haltingly. "I recognize it."

"Yeah," I said, my voice barely above a whisper.

"Your face fell off," she said.

I laughed, then choked on the sound and let out one small audible sob before subsiding.

"So this is just a prank," she said, "right? I'm not going insane?"

"You're not insane." This wasn't going the way things had gone with Christy. Denise wasn't screaming, wasn't running. She wasn't calling me a demon, either, or trying to exorcise me from the house. Not yet, anyway. "Who even are you?" she asked, tone returned to wary. "Neely said she didn't know who you were. I asked her, after you ran off all headless and stuff."

Why was she talking to me? She should be running away by now. Should be freaking out.

"Sorry," I said, shrugging though she couldn't see it. "I crashed your party."

Denise stood up and moved toward me, hand outstretched in front of her. I jumped up from the couch and backed away rapidly. Denise stopped, dropped her hand.

"*Am* I crazy?" she asked. "Am I hallucinating this?"

"I don't know." I had once known a man who experienced frequent hallucinations. I used to pretend he was talking to me when he spoke to the air, but he'd never actually known I was there.

Denise swung her head around to face the direction my voice had come from, though she ended up looking a foot or two to the left of where I stood.

"Was that whole bride story true? Are you actually a ghost? Are you here to haunt me or some shit?"

"No."

Maybe she was mentally ill. After all, she *was* still talking to me. We were having a conversation. Like we had at the party. But no mask. Only me.

"Am I just really, really high?" Denise asked.

"Are you?" I asked.

She laughed, short and sharp, rubbed her eyes. "Why are you here?"

If I'd been able to think of a plausible lie, I'd have told it.

But I couldn't, so I told the truth. "I just don't have anywhere else to go."

"I don't get it. How did you do the trick at the party? How are you doing this?"

I wish I knew. "I'm not doing anything. This is just how I am."

She shook her head. Blinked once, long and slow. Turned on her heel and strode out of the room.

So that was that. It could have gone worse, I guess. Did I dare stay?

No. This was the stupidest thing I'd ever done. Idiotic.

I would try to find another house nearby. Maybe I should leave a sign for my mother. A note hidden in that same plant where I'd found the wrapper. Could I sneak up there without Denise noticing?

I should just leave. I was feeling nauseous, exhausted, the drinks from earlier sitting uneasily in my stomach.

I moved to the front door. Tried turning the knob one millimeter at a time. So slowly. I would ease it open, slip out, ease it shut. Glide away into the night, unseen once more.

The floorboards creaked behind me. I'd only twisted the doorknob partway, hadn't even cracked the door yet. I turned.

Denise was back, carrying two glasses. She set one on the table and took a seat on the armchair.

She looked over at the smoke-stained mantel, where I had been standing before.

"I can't sleep anyway," she said. "So go ahead, spill your shit."

Portland, OR

My mother's silences came in waves.

I could see them coming, sometimes, from a long way off. But I could no more stop them than a person standing on the beach can stop the tide.

As isolated as our lifestyle was, for my mother, sometimes it wasn't enough. When the wave broke on the shore, she'd withdraw. Stop talking to me, except for a begrudging word or two. She'd lead us as far from people as we could get, walking for hours through the woods, the desert. Sometimes there would be a house out there, a seasonal rental sitting empty or a rich person's remote vacation home.

More often, though, we'd shed our borrowed luxury and rough it. That's how it was when I was sixteen, in Portland, when my mother took us deep into Forest Park. She'd grabbed a tent, set up camp in a remote area, far from any trails. You weren't supposed to camp there, but of course no one could see us or the tent so long as one of us stayed with it. The woods there felt prehistoric. Full of ferns. Damp, too.

My mother allowed me to trek the mile and a half out of the park each day, alone, to bring back supplies.

There was a small tent city by the side of a highway ramp that I'd pass on my way in and out. I started lingering, desperate for the sound of voices, for the proximity of other human beings, unwilling to return to the woods, to silence. That's where I met Javier.

He talked to people who weren't there. The fact that there *was* someone there—me—well, that was merely a coincidence.

Javier was not very old, early twenties at most. But he was gaunt, his skin rough and cratered, weathered as an older man's. He used drugs. A lot of the people in the camp didn't. Whole families lived there. Mothers, young children. Some were like Javier, struggling with addiction or mental illness or both. Others, I knew from listening to them talk, had just run out of money. Lost a job or an apartment and fell into a gap.

It seemed wrong that my mother and I were living in a tent by choice while they were doing it because they had no other choice. Technically, we were homeless, too, but I knew it wasn't the same. I took things from the ritzy boutiques I walked by in town. Snatched wallets from people standing in line for trendy brunch spots. Brought money and trinkets back to the tent city. None of it was what any of them really needed.

I spent the most time with Javier, sitting near him as he conversed with the voices no one else could hear. Sometimes his unseen companions seemed to be on his side as he told them his troubles. Other times, it was clear he was angry with them, or afraid. Sometimes he would cover his ears and moan or shout at them to shut up.

I'm ashamed of this, but I was almost jealous. *At least,* I thought, *he's never alone.*

He needed real help, needed a safe place to live and a safe way to calm his terrors, his racing thoughts. Many times, I thought about speaking to him. I thought it wouldn't even be risky. He'd assume I was another voice. I could be a kind one. Whisper encouraging things to him.

I never did, though.

18

I hadn't said anything. Hadn't moved, one hand still on the partially turned doorknob. I'd been too stunned, too uncertain. Denise was leaning forward, hands on her knees, waiting. Silence ticked on. The ice in one of the glasses she brought cracked. Denise's forehead creased.

"Are you still there?" she asked.

I could undo it, right? I could stay quiet.

"Fuck," she said softly and put her face in her hands. I thought she was going to cry.

And so again, without thinking, I moved away from the door, toward her.

"I'm really sorry about the fire," I said.

Her head snapped up, expression flashing quickly from sorrow to relief.

"Oh," she said. "No. That wasn't your fault."

I sat back down on the couch opposite her. "It was."

She straightened up. "Well, Ed stomped it out before it spread. Thank god all punks wear thick-soled boots."

She was smiling, genuinely smiling at me. Or nearly at me. In my general direction.

I couldn't understand it.

My stomach churned. Stupid, stupid, stupid. I should have left more quickly. Should have gotten out while I could.

I thought for sure I was going to puke. Had I caught whatever my mother had?

"Still," I said. "Sorry."

She shrugged. "It was foolish of us to throw a party like this. My aunt said it was fine if we had a few friends over, but she obviously didn't mean, like, a hundred friends. And if she ever found out there was booze . . ." Denise groaned. "Ugh. She's really cool, you know? I mean, I guess you don't know. She and my uncle offered to let me live here when my mother went to the hospital the first time, and then they let me stay because it's closer to my school. But, like, I know money's been tight and all."

Had she forgotten who she was talking to? It was bizarre. Denise just talked and talked. It was kind of wonderful. Like Javier, except she knew I was there.

"Fuck," Denise said. Spat it, really. I jumped. She put her hands to her temples, rubbed. "This party was so stupid. I should have been working on my project. And I'd like to say Neely talked me into it, but it's not like I really needed that much convincing."

I was grinning despite myself. This was surreal. Was it just because she was drunk? I reached forward for the drink she'd set on the table and then hesitated. Talking was one thing. But if I touched the glass, it would either disappear or, if I put my glove back on, float around in midair like a thing possessed. Surely that would be enough to convince Denise she should be freaked out.

"Wait," Denise said, looking up sharply, "this is stupid. I'm talking about my problems to a goddamn invisible girl. You're supposed to tell me what your deal is."

"Oh . . ."

I had imagined this so many times. I'd told my story on the couch of TV talk shows, told it to the vague outline of a future love interest (it was hard to make this person seem real, but I tried). And of course, I had played out this conversation so many times, in my mind, with Tess. Sometimes she would react well, sometimes terribly. Sometimes she would embrace me, sometimes run screaming, depending on how willing I was to suspend my disbelief.

I should have been prepared, with so much practice.

I was not.

"Why are you talking to me?" I asked.

Denise blinked.

"Why wouldn't I?"

"Because . . ." What should I even say? How was it not obvious to her? There were so many reasons. I was an abomination. I shouldn't exist. I had broken into her house.

"I'm a stranger," I said.

"Not really. We met at the party."

"But I wasn't supposed to be there."

She seemed about to say something. Stopped. Her face changed. "Look, honestly, I'm not even really sure you're here now. I'm still not sure it hasn't happened."

I didn't know what she meant by "it," but this whole

thing felt barely real to me, too. She picked up one of the two glasses, swirled it around, watching the ice hit the sides.

"You haven't told me to murder anyone yet, so maybe it's okay." She looked up, eyes narrowed. "Do you want me to murder anyone?"

I thought she might be joking, but I did my best to sound serious, nonthreatening. "No."

"Cool, good. I mean, that's a stereotype anyway. That's not how it is for my mom."

I thought of my own mother then, of course. How furious she'd be if she could see me now, breaking every single rule.

"Your mom?" I asked.

"We have a history," she said, "in my family. My grandma had a break—a psychotic break, that's what doctors call it—and my mom did, too." She gave a half smile, one corner of her mouth quirking up slightly and then dropping again. "Anyway, I've always been half waiting for my turn. I guess here it is."

She gestured broadly in my direction.

"Well," I said carefully, "I am really here. I promise."

"Can you stop being invisible?" She sounded curious rather than angry or afraid.

"No. Sorry."

"Why are you like that?"

"I don't know. I was born this way."

"Like the song?" She laughed, a hoarse barking laugh. "Oh, wait a second. Were you here before the party? Are you the reason the door opened on its own earlier today?"

I nodded sheepishly before remembering that I was not talking to my mother. Denise was visible. It kept hitting me: What was I doing?

"Yeah," I said.

"What was that all about?"

"I'm sorry, we just—"

"*We?*" She jumped on the word. "There's more of you?"

Before I could protest, she had stood up, bristling, on guard, eyes darting to all corners of the room.

"No," I said. I was so bad at this. "I mean yes, but only one."

"This is it," she said, pacing. "Paranoia, right? Delusions of being watched?" She nearly tripped over the trash bag of beer cans on the floor.

"Are insane people this self-aware?" I asked.

"Sometimes." She frowned in my direction. "My mom— she's like anybody, really. She's not stupid. Or even crazy, at least not the way people mean when they use that word. She just has episodes sometimes."

Mine, too, I almost said.

"I'm sorry," I said instead. "I came here with one other person. My mother. And she's not here now."

"Okay." Denise stopped pacing, though she still glanced around the room nervously. "Are you sure?"

Well, no, I wasn't. God, this was a mess. How had I let it get this far? Was it too late to get out of this?

Did I want to?

"I'm sorry about coming into your house uninvited," I said. "My mother—she was sick, she needed to lie down. We just picked your house randomly. That's how we live. We stay in other people's houses."

Denise blinked at me. "Is the world absolutely full of invisible people? Am I bumping into them all the time without realizing it?"

"No," I said. "My mother and I have never met another one in all our lives."

"Oh." She tilted her head and frowned. "That's sad."

I looked away, rubbed at the surface of the sofa with my thumb. It was a mustard color, the fabric wearing thin at the corners of the cushions. A tuft of stuffing poked up from a small hole.

"So where is your mom?" Denise asked.

"I lost her."

"She died?" Denise's eyes had gone wide with horror.

"No," I said quickly. "I just don't know where she is."

Denise laughed. "Oh, I get it. Because she's invisible, right? So you can't see her!"

I didn't say anything. Thinking too much about my mother felt dangerous. Like standing at the edge of a bottomless pit of guilt and fear. One push and I'd keep falling forever.

Denise stopped laughing. "Shit, no, I'm sorry. This is so weird. I can't see your face, so it's hard to tell when you're being serious. You're serious, aren't you?"

"Yes," I said. I took a deep breath, poked the errant tuft of stuffing back into the couch cushion. "My mom and I can see each other, even though other people can't."

"Weird," said Denise. "So how old are you? I guess you

could be, like, fifty or something, and I'd have no way to know. I mean, you don't really seem fifty."

"I'm seventeen."

"Oh." She brightened. "I'm eighteen. Well, if you are real, consider this an official invitation."

She held out her hand. I stared at it.

Denise waited.

Surely this was too far, right? This was beyond all reason.

Denise blinked, eyes drifting restlessly through the empty space in front of her. I held my breath, reached out.

A Complete List of the People I've Touched

My mother, mostly when I was little and she would hold my hand firmly as we hurried down a train platform or wove our way through a store or ran across a street. Sometimes she'd grip my small hand so tightly that my fingers would go numb, but I never minded. It made me feel safe.

Christy, just for a second. Her arm.

Slots, when I pushed him.

A few people by accident on a subway or a train because they tried to sit on me, not realizing I was there. This would result in a panicked collision of limbs as I tried desperately to escape, heart racing. For them, the experience seemed to be one of mild annoyance and confusion. But my skin never touched their skin, of course. Never. And I never touched any of them on purpose.

Myself, obviously. More than I'd like to admit.

That's it.

19

My right hand, gloved in lilac silk. Seams along each finger. Three pearl buttons at my wrist.

Her left hand, bare. Skin warm brown in the light of the lamp. The palm lighter, crossed with dark lines. The pink crescents of her nails.

She waited, expectant.

Our hands were inches away. It felt like an uncrossable distance.

But I did it. I moved my hand a little farther. It was shaking. I let my gloved fingers graze hers. She let out a small involuntary gasp. I yanked my hand away.

The moment was strange for both of us, but in different ways.

My pulse was racing now, my brain telling me to run, though nothing was happening. There was no danger. I tried to tell myself that. It was only a hand.

It was nothing, really. A normal person would barely have noticed.

Denise smiled.

"You're welcome to sleep here on the couch," she said.

"Really?" My fingers tingled from the brief contact. Our skin hadn't even touched. I wondered what the texture of her skin would have felt like. Soft? Rough?

"Of course. People crash here all the time. This is a punk house." She said it proudly. "Or sort of. Not like Ed's place. But Aunt Larissa does let us host shows in the basement sometimes. And if people need a place to sleep, they've got one. Larissa is on board with that. She lets Neely stay any time she wants."

"Thanks," I said, overcome. I couldn't take in most of what she was telling me. But I understood the wildest, most unthinkable, most unprecedented part: she was letting me stay.

She wanted me to stay.

"There's a lot of posturing and stuff sometimes," Denise went on, "with the punk kids around here, and everybody thinks it's about hating shit and being angry, and don't get me wrong, society sucks. But part of why it sucks, if you ask me, is that people shut themselves off from each other. Real punks are fucking kind." She shrugged. "Or, I don't know, that's what I think, anyway."

She jumped up and darted out of the room again, ran up the stairs, but I'd learned now that this meant nothing. I sat alone in the dark, blinking hard. The room felt like it was spinning. I was exhausted. Physically, emotionally.

Denise returned a minute or so later with a sheet, blanket, and pillow, which she dumped on the couch.

"You still there?" she asked.

"Yeah," I said. "By the way, I left my backpack in your bathtub."

"You did?"

Before I had time to say anything else, she was gone again, running up the stairs. I stared at the pillow, the blanket. Was this real?

Denise came thudding down the steps, holding my backpack. She set it down next to the couch. Its familiarity was a relief. Sure, I've left behind other backpacks countless times, but right now I was happy for any tether to normalcy, to my mother, however small.

"Here you go," said Denise, eyes fruitlessly scanning the sofa.

"Thanks."

"Where are you?"

"Here." I bounced a little on the seat so she could see the sofa cushion move.

She plopped down on the opposite end of the couch. I stiffened, but she didn't try to reach toward me or anything. "Luckily your backpack wasn't invisible," she said.

I gave a small uncomfortable laugh. "Um, yeah."

"Wait," she said, eyes going wide.

My heart sank. Had she changed her mind? Was she going to kick me out?

"Are you naked?" she said.

"What?"

"At the party you were wearing clothes and stuff and I

could see them, but then your mask fell off and you were invisible. So does that mean you can't wear clothes?"

"Oh," I said. I'd never had to explain this to anyone before. I pulled my left glove off, tossed it onto the coffee table so Denise could see. The moment it ceased making contact with my skin, it popped into visibility. "I wear clothes. It's kind of complicated, but basically, at the party I was just wearing layers."

Denise laughed, eyes on the visible glove. "Sorry, that was probably incredibly rude."

"It's okay. Thanks for letting me stay."

"No problem. I know it looks kind of scummy, but it's honestly really comfortable." She patted the sofa affectionately. "We got it for free. I spotted it on the curb and told Larissa and she came to check it out right away. We drove home with it sticking out of the trunk."

I get everything I own for free, I thought. My voice felt raw from use. I'd talked so much this evening, to so many people. And now, finally, this. The most insane and magical conversation of my entire life.

"There is a stain here in the shape of Texas." Denise pointed to a dark patch on the cushion between us.

"Is that from the party?" I croaked out.

"No, that's always been there. Probably why it got thrown out. Well, that and the leg was missing." She pointed out a leg in the back that, unlike the other three, was not ornately carved dark wood but an unvarnished hunk of two-by-four. "We fixed it. Tried to get the stain out, but it wouldn't budge.

Jules thinks it's blood, but I think it's definitely red wine. Someday I'll visit this stain."

"What?"

"Texas, I mean."

"Oh." It was amazing the way she just talked to me, as if everything was normal. As if I was normal. It almost made me feel like I was. "You should go see the swimming holes outside Austin. They're really gorgeous."

"You've been there?"

"We lived there for a while."

"Damn. I bet you've just had the most exciting life ever. Will you tell me about it? Tomorrow?"

I didn't think my life was exciting at all. I'd spent most of it so far looking out of windows. But I said, "Okay."

"Oh!" Denise said. She jumped up, went into the kitchen. Returned a moment later with a scrap of paper, a roll of tape, and a Sharpie.

DO NOT SIT HERE, she wrote on the paper. She taped it to the back of the couch.

I was pretty sure it was the sweetest thing anyone had ever done for me.

"Good night," she said.

It wasn't until after she'd left and the warm glow of those words had washed through me and faded away that I remembered I should have said it back.

An Incomplete List of the Places I've Slept

The perfect houses are the ones so large, so excessive and wasteful, that the beds outnumber the people. Houses with rooms exclusively for excess stuff. Forgotten rooms no one goes into. Rooms for us.

But we don't always get those houses. It takes time to find them. Rich people rarely live right next to the train station.

Sometimes we've had to leave somewhere in a hurry or arrived in a new city at a strange hour. We have slept in mattress stores and department stores—walked in before closing, stayed after everyone locked up. They are cold, full of mechanical hums. We've slept in closed libraries. Coffee shops. A clothing store, on a pile of coats.

Sometimes we sleep on couches. Or sneak the winter comforters out of storage and make ourselves a nest in the attic or some out-of-the-way corner.

And we have slept outdoors. When Mother is having her silences. When even an attic is too close to people, even the sound of their voices drifting up through the floorboards too loud.

We have gone into the woods. Gone into the desert. Gone into the mountains. Slept in sleeping bags. Slept on the bare ground.

I've slept on trains, of course. Slept all over this country.

Rarely have I slept somewhere I was invited. Once, in a motel room my father booked with money my mother brought him.

And then again, on this sofa with a stain in the shape of Texas.

20

"Sam, are you awake?" Denise asked. Her voice was kind of husky, like she had a cold.

It was morning. I had slipped into consciousness only about ten minutes earlier. Had remained on the couch, wrapped in a fragment of a dream, unwilling to wake fully and face my situation.

I was used to waking in strange places. Normally, I would get up quickly, clear away any sign of my presence. Normally, my mother would have woken me.

"Sam?" said Denise. She stood in the doorway, staring at the couch.

This was not normal. I lay, frozen, muscles tight, absolutely and terribly awake.

I was terrified of her.

She took a step into the living room, frowning at the sofa.

"Are you there?" she asked, voice quavering slightly.

She knew about me. We had talked. This was different from everything. Different from watching people, getting to know them slowly by their habits, by the way they eat their breakfast when they are alone.

That is safe. That is normal for me. That is how I love. Like a museum. Distant, untouching, silent.

"Sam?" she said. She sounded sad now.

I couldn't answer. Not answering was the best choice, wasn't it? It would be so easy to pretend I was not there. Natural. Normal. That was what I always did. I could slip away, never speak another word, let her think she had succumbed to her family history of mental illness. Let her think she was alone. That we were both alone.

I felt the word bubbling up inside me, felt it strain at the back of my throat.

The night before had been foolish. We'd both been drinking. It was different now, in the cold light of day.

I couldn't speak. I shouldn't. There was no way she'd be as calm and accepting now as she had been then.

Was there?

"Yes," I whispered. Quiet, so quiet, I thought there was no way she could have heard me. But she froze, head swiveling side to side, like she was listening.

"Hello?" she said, taking another step toward the sofa. She was whispering too, now.

I licked my lips. Took a deep, shaky breath. Sat up. My head swam.

"Hello," I said, only barely louder than I'd spoken before. But she definitely heard this time.

"Holy shit," she said, her eyes going wide, but not with fear. More like . . . *delight*?

Could that be? Or did I just want it to be true?

"Where are you?" she asked, eyes flicking back and forth

from one end of the sofa to the other. She still sounded kind of hoarse. Maybe from all the drinking. "I don't know where to look."

"Uh." I felt a bit dizzy. "The couch. The left side? Near Texas?"

"Well, shit," she said, hoarse but definitely happy-sounding now. She moved forward and I flinched, but she simply plopped down on the easy chair across from the sofa. "I was worried that I imagined the whole thing. I woke up this morning and thought it must have been a dream, but then I saw the sign." She gestured at the note taped to the back of the couch. "So then I thought I was right and I'd had a psychotic break after all."

My breathing was getting fast, sucking short and shallow, in and out through my nose, like I couldn't get enough air. I tried to slow it. Tried to ignore the signals my body was giving me to run like hell. This wasn't safe. Couldn't be safe.

My mouth was dry. My head pounded. I was hungover, probably. Dehydrated.

"Do you eat and drink and stuff?" Denise asked.

I breathed in, out. Slumped down into the couch and squeezed my eyes shut.

"No, sorry, that was a stupid question," said Denise. "Of course you do, right? You were drinking at the party. You want some coffee?"

I opened my eyes. Denise was smiling at a point slightly above my head. She was still being nice to me, still talking to me like I was a person.

"Uh, sure," I managed to say.

I couldn't understand it. Last night might be written off as drunkenness. And yet here she was this morning, still chatting away. As if this were normal. Almost as if we were friends.

She darted off to the kitchen.

The stairs creaked. I straightened up.

Jules appeared at the bottom of the staircase, in the same flowered robe as the day before. They stepped into the living room, frowning at the burned carpet. Their eyes drifted over to the couch. I held very still, barely breathing.

Jules moved closer to me, leaned forward, squinting at the note Denise had taped to the couch the night before.

"Hey," they called into the kitchen. "Did someone puke on the sofa?"

Denise came running back into the room, eyes darting between Jules and the couch. "Uh, no."

My pulse spiked, instinct torn between freezing and running.

"Why shouldn't I sit there?" Jules pointed at the note.

"It's . . . well, it's up to the couch if it wants to tell you what happened to it."

Jules gave Denise a skeptical look.

Bathtub the cat chose that moment to weave her way into the room, meowing at the top of her small lungs. We all turned to look at her.

The cat made her way to the couch and jumped up beside me. I remained motionless, uncertain what to do. I liked cats, though I rarely had a chance to interact with them. Bathtub sniffed cautiously in my direction, startled back, moved forward again, little nose working furiously. She extended a paw, prodded the air, startled again when her paw collided with my thigh.

"The hell?" said Jules. "Is the couch haunted?"

Denise laughed.

Bathtub, apparently deciding I was not a threat, walked directly forward and onto my lap. I held very still. Bathtub circled once, then curled up in a ball, paws tucked into her body, nose touching tail.

Jules was blinking rapidly. "Is the damn cat haunted?"

To them, of course, it appeared that the cat was levitating about a half foot off the surface of the sofa. I was being stupid. I should have jumped up and run away the moment I woke up. I should never have let this happen.

I pushed Bathtub off my lap and stood. The cat settled back on the couch in the warm spot I had left, perfectly content.

Denise tried to give me a significant look, but I'd already sidled quietly away. I was standing closer to her now.

"Can I tell Jules?" she asked the couch. "They're trustworthy, I promise."

My mother always told me never to trust anyone. Never to tell anyone about myself. Never to reveal my presence. I eyed the door, wondering if I should make a break for it.

Last night I'd broken all the rules. I'd spoken to Denise. I'd told her everything.

And yet Denise had been kind. Nothing terrible had happened.

"Okay," I said.

Denise jumped, not expecting my voice to come from right beside her.

"Sorry," I said, already doubting whether I'd made the right choice.

Jules was frowning, forehead creased with confusion.

"Jules," said Denise, gesturing vaguely in the direction she now believed me to be standing. "This is Sam. Sam, Jules."

I hesitated, but then I remembered the straw. It had been such a simple thing, Jules offering me a straw so I could drink through my mask, but it had almost made me cry.

"We met," I said, "last night."

"What?" said Jules. "What is happening right now? Ventriloquism?"

"No," said Denise. "Weirder than that."

And she did the explaining for me.

The Train Yard

I found a kitten in a train yard once when I was younger: a bedraggled, barely living ball of fur curled beside a stack of rotten wooden railroad ties. It squeaked feebly when I picked it up.

My mother told me to put it back. Said it was none of our concern. But I slipped the kitten into my shirt when she wasn't looking, cradled it gently against my waist with one arm. Touching my skin, it became invisible. I smuggled it onto the train with us.

Mom got wise to my trick once the train got moving, but I told her I would scream if she tried to take the kitten away from me. It wriggled at my waist, pressed minuscule paws against my skin. It was warm, soft, needy. I fed it bits of cheese and ham, rolled into tiny balls, from a café car snack tray. It never made a peep the whole train ride. A handful of fleas jumped ship from its dirty fur, peppered my midsection with itchy red bites.

When we got off at Little Rock, my mother found us a proper mansion, with six full baths. She filled one of the oversized tubs with lukewarm water and dish soap, dunked the kitten in, and then me, to get rid of the fleas. I dried the kitten off with a towel. Fed it tiny scraps of trout with saffron sauce pilfered from the kitchen.

I fell asleep in a spare bedroom, in a spare bed, with the kitten curled up in my armpit. Its tiny frantic heartbeat ticked against my bare skin, the buzz of its purring. I loved it more than I had known it was possible to love something.

When I woke in the morning, it was gone. I sprang from the bed, mad with fear. My mother said it must have wandered off. I skidded from room to room of that huge, half-empty house, sick to my stomach with worry. Finally, I stopped in the downstairs sunroom, where the mother of the house and one of the three children were crouched over something on the ground.

It was the kitten. When I got closer, I saw that it was perfectly fine, unharmed. Its fur was all fluffy from yesterday's bath. It wobbled charmingly around on blunted legs, sniffed at the pattern on the Oriental rug.

"Well, I just don't know where it could have come from," the woman was saying, "but I suppose we can keep it, so long as it doesn't have any kind of disease."

My heart sank. I took a step forward, but my mother was there at my arm, pulling me back.

"We can't keep it invisible," she signed to me. "It wouldn't be fair. A kitten needs to roam and play. It will be much happier if we let it go live a normal life."

I nodded sadly. She was right. I knew it.

A strange sad expression came over my mother's face. She looked at me, and then back at the kitten.

"It should have a normal life," she repeated.

21

It was weird how, well, not *normal,* exactly, but how *un-catastrophic* it felt, fifteen minutes later. The three of us sitting in the living room. Drinking coffee. Eating stale bagels with peanut butter (their fridge was woefully bare).

Jules had, after hearing Denise's explanation and, with permission, gently touching my arm, come to accept that I existed.

"Why are you invisible?" Jules asked me.

I had asked the same question many times over the years. My mother gave me various answers. *Don't question a blessing,* she said once. Or, *Maybe it's just because I grew you inside my body, because we touched continuously for nine months.*

Epigenetics, she had once said proudly, after the semester we lived next to a college campus so she could sit in on classes.

The real answer was: she didn't know, either.

"It's just how I am," I told Jules.

Jules had more questions, about what happened last night, how my "power" worked, how I'd come to be in their house. I answered as best I could. And then, to my surprise, the conversation moved on, moved past me.

I learned that Larissa and Terrance—Denise's aunt and uncle, Jules's mother and father—were away for a weekend anniversary trip and would be back Sunday. Tomorrow.

"What the hell are we going to do about all this?" Jules asked, gesturing to the burned rug, the smoke-darkened wall above the mantel.

Denise sighed. "Let's hope it comes off, or we're screwed."

She fetched a bucket of soapy water and some rags from the kitchen, and the three of us set to scrubbing. I left my gloves on. Jules was delighted by the sight of the soapy rag seeming to wash the wall on its own.

"That's some straight-up *Fantasia* shit," they said, pausing to cue up the soundtrack on their phone.

As we worked, the ghostly gray stain left by the smoke came away, as did a decent amount of the paint.

"Our landlord is cheap as hell," said Denise.

We opened the windows to air out the room. Took down the curtains to wash. Mopped the floor with lemon cleaner. Scraped the pooled wax from the mantel. There were several burn marks in the white wood that no amount of scrubbing could undo, so Jules ran up and got a tube of white paint.

In the end, the only thing we couldn't do anything about was the rug. The fibers were fused and blackened around the ragged edges of a fist-sized hole, and the whole rug smelled strongly of smoke.

The three of us rolled it up and dragged it down to the basement. Denise shoved it in a corner, behind the stack of pallets. The basement seemed so much smaller now. I could hardly fathom how so many people had crowded in here last night.

"We'll have to figure out what to do with this later," Jules said.

"Yeah," said Denise. "Thanks for helping, Sam."

I contemplated telling her that Sam wasn't my real name, but it seemed much too late for that. I didn't even like my real name. This way I could be someone new. Someone better.

"It was my fault," I said, but I couldn't make myself feel truly sorry. I was glad my face had fallen off. Glad I'd spoken to Denise.

Glad—no, I wasn't glad about my mother. I couldn't be.

I shouldn't let myself be happy.

"We should help you," Denise said.

"You let me stay here," I pointed out.

"Sure, but you need to find your mother, right?"

"Oh." I was startled, as if she'd read my mind. But of course, I had told her about my mother last night. "Yeah."

Then we had to fill Jules in. Explain how my mother had vanished. Vanished more than was normal for an invisible person, that is.

"But you think she's still here?" Jules asked. "In the house? But, like, hiding or something?"

"Well, I found this on the third floor after she disappeared." I pulled the granola bar wrapper out of my backpack and held it out in a gloved hand so they could see it.

"It's not mine," said Jules.

"I think my mother left it."

Jules frowned. Perhaps they were freaked out that I had been in their room. Maybe now they'd realize that they shouldn't trust me. I waited, tense, for anger. For admonishment.

"It's a clue," said Denise. She was smiling. "This is like a proper mystery."

She nudged her cousin.

Jules nodded. They looked serious but not angry. "Maybe there's more," they said. "Let's search the house."

An Incomplete List of
the Best Meals I've Ever Eaten

A slice of white truffle pizza with poached duck egg and shaved Parmesan, taken off a table in Chicago.

A selection of sushi rolls from omakase meals, snatched one at a time off black platters in Manhattan.

Bites of turnips with miso ghee, fire-roasted Indian street corn, *pani puri,* and cardamom-roasted beef shank in Miami.

Sicilian cassata cake with champagne sabayon and pomegranate foam at a wedding we crashed in Tucson.

A whole bowl of Wagyu beef ramen with matsutake mushrooms from a food truck in LA.

Steamed king crab legs with shaved bottarga, salt-roasted Japanese sweet potato with macadamia milk–espresso dressing, and caramelized creamed sunchokes with beeswax and honey from a pop-up in Brooklyn.

Soufflé potatoes with béarnaise sauce, oysters Ohan with eggplant and andouille, and café brûlot made by a private chef in New Orleans.

That stale bagel I ate with Denise and Jules in their living room.

Yes, I mean that last one. I honestly do.

22

We all went up to the third floor first, since that was where I'd found the wrapper. Jules rifled through their stacks of art supplies, while Denise and I peered between the leaves of plants.

"Your room is a mess," Denise said.

"Look who's talking," Jules shot back.

We didn't find anything. I hadn't held out much hope that we would, but the fact that the two of them were looking at all, that they were helping me, gave me a warm feeling.

We moved down to the second floor. Jules checked their parents' room, while Denise and I searched her room. She opened the drawers of her desk. I moved aside the yellow curtain to check behind it.

"Oh," said Denise, "I can see your hand."

"What?" I was so startled I dropped the curtain, took a step back, bumped into the window.

"I mean the outline of it, a little bit. Go on, hold the curtain again."

Cautiously, I did.

I saw, now, what she had meant. The gauzy fabric draped

over my arm, dipped between some of my gloved fingers, taking on the rough shape of my hand.

"That's so cool," Denise said. "Can I take a picture?"

I knew I should say no. Evidence of our existence was dangerous. My mother had taught me to avoid it at all costs. But I'd already told Denise so much. This was hardly worse, right?

"Sure."

She picked up the bulky camera from her desk, snapped a few shots. I noticed a serial number written on the camera body in silver Sharpie, remembered what she'd said at the party about renting a camera from school since she couldn't afford one of her own.

"You're a photographer?" I asked.

She laughed. "I'm trying to be. I've got a big project due on Monday, so I should have been working on that instead of planning a stupid party."

She snapped another photo, held out the camera so I could see it on the viewscreen. My hand and arm—safely covered by glove and sleeve—didn't show up in the picture. Just the curtain taking their shape.

"That does look pretty cool," I said. "Here, how about this?"

I experimented with moving the yellow curtains, tried to hold them up like they were wafting in on a breeze, pushing both my hands against them so it looked like a ghost was straining through, while Denise snapped shot after shot. It was fun. More fun than it should have been. More fun than I had any right to be having.

Denise pulled a curtain down then, had me drape it over my head. At first, of course, it blinked away as soon as I did, but after I explained the rules, she found me a knit cap and a scarf to tie around my face so the curtain would stay visible, and the outline of my body beneath it, too. Like my first Halloween costume: sheet ghost.

"What's your project?" I asked her.

"It's supposed to be a ten-image series with a theme," she told me. "Here, I can show you."

She pulled up images on her laptop, clicked through them.

There were pictures of Denise and the wing she'd worn at the party, though these shots had been taken outside, in front of a river.

"I did those with a timer," she explained. "The series has to have a theme, so I picked transformation. But like partial transformation. Being halfway between one thing and another. And like maybe stuck, or maybe just in this state of possibility."

There was a shot of the mannequin Cindy, but with a real human arm reaching out from her socket.

"That's Neely's arm. It took forever to get the angle right. I wanted to do all the effects in-camera."

She clicked through to the next one. It was her again, in the bathtub this time. I recognized the tiles. The tub was half full, and Denise was slumped over the edge, facedown, arms hanging limp onto the tiles, her hair wet and streaming and teal. Her back bare, skin glistening.

"I'm a little nervous about showing this one," she said.

Her bottom half, the half in the water, was a fish. Blue

green, scaled, tapering to a semi-translucent fin. The distortion of the water made it look real.

"I mean, you can't see anything," Denise rambled on. I liked how she did that. Just talked, didn't need me to carry my half of the conversation. "But I didn't have a top on, you know. And my arms look fat here." She prodded the photo. "I wish I didn't care about that. You probably don't have to think about that kind of thing, do you?"

"Um." I didn't know what to say. I'm not thin. Somewhere in the middle, I guess. My mother caught me once when I was eight or nine pinching a roll on my stomach, as I'd just seen the woman we were staying with do in the mirror, and she slapped my hand. *Don't buy into any of that bullshit,* she told me. *It wouldn't matter how you looked, even if people could see you.*

Denise sighed. "I used to think I wanted to be a fashion photographer. I'd spend hours looking at editorials in, like, *Vogue* and stuff. But all the models looked like her." She pointed at Cindy. "None of them looked like me. It kind of messed with my head."

"It's a beautiful picture," I said. It was. And Denise was beautiful, too. The long brown curve of her back in the photo. The curve of her cheek, catching the light as she stood beside me.

She laughed, uncomfortable. "Thanks. It's okay. I don't know. They never turn out quite how I imagine them in my head. I spent way too long on the fish scales and the wing. That's why I'm behind on this series. Ugh, Slots will probably just take pictures of his buddies doing skateboard tricks. That's what he does for every assignment. The worst part is, he actually gets some pretty great shots." She stared forlornly at the screen. "I should scrap my project idea and do a whole ghost series instead."

"Isn't being a ghost a partial transformation?" I offered. "Stuck halfway between alive and dead?"

"You're right." She grinned. "Hey, Bathtub, what you got there, girl?"

The cat had wandered in and was batting at something stuck in the floorboard.

Denise crouched next to the cat and pulled a tiny, folded slip of paper out.

"Oh," she said after unfolding it, "I think this might be for you."

Since I still had the curtain draped over me, she could look right at me. She held the paper out, and I took it with a gloved hand. Denise stared, eyes wide. To me it was just my hand, my normal hand, holding a scrap of paper. But she saw the paper floating on its own. Magic.

Letters were scrawled across the paper, loose and shaky, in a hand I recognized immediately.

My mother's.

I'm okay, the note said. *I am here but I can't reach you. I hope this note does. I'm sorry.*

I felt a surge of relief—*I'm okay*—and then confusion—*I am here but I can't reach you*—and then anger.

I read it again and again, eyes racing frantically down the

slopes of the words, searching each time for something more. Some extra meaning in this insufficient collection of pen strokes.

"Is it from her?" Denise asked, leaning forward. "Your mom?"

"Yes," I said dully, still scanning the note over and over.

Each time I read it, I felt an echo of the emotions I'd experienced the first time, with the anger gradually growing to overtake everything else. This was all I got? She'd vanished. And this was the best she could do? This was worse than all her silences put together.

And that last line.

I'm sorry.

What did that mean? What was she sorry for? What had she done?

"Hey, Jules," Denise shouted, "we found something."

A moment later, Jules appeared at the doorway.

"What is it?" they asked, eyes snapping to my curtained outline. Mutely, I held the note out so they could read it, too.

Why couldn't she have said more? Told me what was happening, told me how to help her?

"She's here?" Jules asked. They darted their eyes around the room.

"Don't be stupid," said Denise. "We obviously can't see her. Sam can't even see her."

"So she went, like, *double* invisible," said Jules.

That was an odd way of looking at it. "Maybe," I said. "I don't really understand this."

"Well, how do we find someone none of us can see?" Denise asked.

"Bathtub could sniff her out," Jules suggested.

The warm glow I'd felt earlier, the gratefulness that they were willing to help me, had dissipated. This was just a fun puzzle for them. They didn't really care about helping, did they?

They couldn't possibly care. They didn't even know me. No one did. I was alone.

Hopelessness threatened to swallow me. My mother was gone. My mother had left me behind, had left me nothing but a cryptic note.

"Oh, I have an idea," Denise announced. She ran downstairs. Jules and I trailed after, caught up with her in the kitchen, where she was banging open cupboards.

"Aha!" she exclaimed, emerging from one with a bag of white flour.

"You going to bake a bread so delicious that all the ghosts come out of the walls to smell it?" asked Jules, mocking.

"No. And they aren't ghosts. Right, Sam?"

"Uh, right," I said, though it certainly felt like my mother was haunting me.

Denise yanked opened the bag and spilled it.

"Hey," shouted Jules. "Watch out."

Plumes of white dust puffed into the air and then settled into a fine coating on the floor.

"Sam," said Denise. "Walk across there."

I understood, then, what she was doing. I wasn't sure I

liked the idea, but I went along with it. I walked through the flour. My shoes left prints, scuffs in the white dust.

"See!" exclaimed Denise, pointing, clearly delighted.

She moved into the living room, scattering flour across the floor as she went, leaving just a thin path around the edge of the room. I just watched, too despondent to care much.

"We can do the other rooms as well," she declared, "before we go to bed tonight."

"We'll have to clean it up tomorrow morning," Jules pointed out. "Mom and Dad are supposed to be back in the afternoon."

"Fine," said Denise, "but now we can see if anyone walks through the room other than the three of us. What do you think, Sam?"

They both turned to look at me, which was disarming. I shrugged. They could actually see me do it, too, since the curtain was still draped across my head and shoulders.

"You should leave that on," said Jules. "Then we can see where you are."

The curtain cast everything I saw in vivid yellow, buttered the world. A constant sun. I wasn't wearing a mask, nor was I invisible. I was halfway between one thing and another. Maybe stuck, or maybe in a state of possibility.

The front door opened.

I whipped around, hoping against hope that it was my mother. Though she didn't have a key, as far as I knew.

It was not my mother.

Instead, it was a tall woman with long hair in small neat

braids, her skin a few shades darker brown than Denise's, her perfectly shaped brows arched in consternation at the flour scattered across the room. We all froze.

"What," she said, "in the name of sweet baby Jesus have you kids done to my floor?"

Mobile, AL

I was in the attic of a Queen Anne Victorian mansion, sitting on the floor, the room dark but for the flickering light of a small television, muted, with closed captioning on. I kept one finger on the power button as I watched.

From far below, the sound of the doorbell. A vague and distant susurration of voices.

A few moments later, the stairs creaked. Reluctantly, I switched off the television.

But it was only my mother. The instant I saw her turn the corner, I flipped the TV back on. I'd only missed a minute or two.

"You should see what's happening downstairs," she said, speaking low.

"I'm in the middle of a movie."

"We need to leave."

So I strapped on my backpack, followed my mother downstairs. In the dining room, the family of the house was gathered. With them, a man in black. They stood, clustered at one end of the room, watching two teenage girls who wore cream-colored sweaters over collared shirts and long denim skirts. Each girl held a silver cross.

"We drive you from us," called the younger of the two girls, her face bright and shining, cheeks dewy. "Whoever you may be, unclean spirits, all satanic powers, all infernal invaders, all wicked legions."

"Does she mean us?" I signed to my mother.

"Yes," my mother signed back. "The family spoke about strange noises in the house."

"In the name and by the power of Our Lord Jesus Christ!" cried the other girl. Her eyes were squeezed shut. She brandished the cross in front of her, hands gripping it so tight her knuckles turned white. "We drive you from this place. We cleanse this house of your wicked presence."

The man in black was nodding solemnly, smugly, watching the two girls. His daughters, I thought.

"God the Father commands you," said the younger, "and God the Son commands you and God the Holy Ghost commands you."

The other girl dropped to her knees, cross thrust above her head like an umbrella. Several of the watching family members gasped. The girl began to shake. When she opened her eyes, cast upward, they were full of tears.

"The glorious mother of God, the Virgin Mary, commands you," she shouted, her voice raw with emotion. I was riveted. This was a performance, a pretty good one, too, and I, in a strange way, was part of it.

"The faith of the holy apostles Peter and Paul and of the

other apostles commands you. The blood of the martyrs and the pious intercession of all the saints command you."

The girl collapsed to the ground, writhed, speaking now in unintelligible tongues.

My mother tugged on my arm. "Come on," she whispered, "let's go."

She headed for the foyer, the front door. I started to follow but then took a detour around the side of the room, brushing very near the smug man in black.

Before I left, I reached carefully, ever so carefully, into his pocket. Pulled out the cash I had been sure I would find there.

Cash that the people who lived here had paid him to get rid of us.

23

Wild-eyed, Denise shot a glance at me, a ghost draped in a curtain. She stuck a hand out quickly and plucked the curtain off my head.

The woman in the doorway—who must have been Larissa, home early—blinked at the empty space where I stood. She shook her head. "This better not be cocaine," she said, gesturing to the flour all over the floor, "or I will lose my damn mind."

"It's not cocaine, Ma," said Jules. "Just flour. Denise was doing a photo."

A man came in the door behind Larissa, herding two suitcases. "Uh-oh," he said, taking in the mess. This was too much for me. I slid along the wall, inching toward the door.

"Vacuum this nonsense up," said Larissa.

"Yes, ma'am," said Denise.

"Where's the rug?" asked the man, who must have been Terrance, Jules's dad. Jules and Denise exchanged panicked looks. I slid farther.

"Uh, I spilled my pop on it," said Denise. "I moved it to clean it."

"And what is this?" Larissa went over to the mantel,

where the paint we'd used to cover up the burn marks still glistened wet.

Larissa fixed her gaze on Denise.

"Well? Cat got your tongue? Do I got to call your mama?"

"No." Denise's voice was small. She hung her head.

"We didn't think you'd be back until tomorrow," said Jules.

This felt like as good a time as any to go. I dashed the last few feet to the front door, as quietly as I could.

"Sam?" I heard Denise say as I eased the door open just wide enough to slip through.

"What?" I heard Larissa say.

And then I eased the door shut.

A few blocks later, I passed a bank and saw that there was still an hour until one, when I was supposed to meet my father. I walked leisurely toward Oakland, using only the least-crowded sidewalks, waiting for a long time before crossing each road.

Less than an hour later, I was outside the Carnegie Museum of Art, staring at a big hunk of rusty sheet metal. It was in front of a museum, so I guess it was art.

I found a seat near the front doors by the fountain. Though it was less a fountain than a strip of concrete intermittently spitting upward. No doubt that was also art. A kid played chicken with the water, darting in and out.

My father showed up maybe twenty minutes later, wearing a rumpled gray suit, carrying a large duffel bag. He was thinner than the last time I'd seen him.

The only other time I'd ever seen him in my life.

He didn't see me, obviously. He took a seat at one of the tables. Leaned back. Lit a cigarette. All casual ease.

I walked up behind him, my footsteps inaudible over the hiss of the fountain and the noise of passing traffic.

When I got close, I could see that there was a small spot, at the whorls of his part in the back, where the hair had thinned almost to bald. A tender little spot. I leaned in close, peered at it. Wondered if he knew it was back there. I felt a surge of fondness for the spot. It seemed like maybe the only honest part of my father.

I had no idea how old he was. My mother was forty-one. My father might have been much older, for all I knew. If I asked him, I felt certain he would lie. My father was vain. During the month we stayed with him, I'd watched him check himself in every mirrored surface he passed.

I reached out with one gloved finger and poked the bald spot. I wanted to startle him. To catch him off guard. I was hoping for a yelp. A genuine reaction, something he couldn't act.

He straightened but didn't turn. Smooth and casual, he pulled a cell phone out of his jacket pocket, held it to his ear. His old strategy for talking to us in public without looking weird.

"Hello!" he exclaimed, sounding upbeat, delighted. "So good to hear from you."

I was glad I was behind him so I couldn't see his face, the cheesy grin I felt sure was plastered there. A con man's smile. I wasn't sure if he could turn that off even if he wanted to.

"Thanks for coming," I said cautiously.

"It's cold out here," he said. "I'm headed inside. Let me call you back."

He jumped up and started walking toward the door, slipping the phone back into his pocket. It wasn't that cold, and no one had been close enough to hear us. The fountain provided plenty of cover noise. We could have talked outside.

But I had no real choice. I couldn't shout for him to come back.

He'd left his duffel bag sitting on the ground by his chair. An accident? Or had he meant for me to take it? A gift, perhaps. I pulled off my left glove, snagged the handles of the bag, and hurried after my father.

He pushed through the first pair of heavy glass doors, held them open several moments longer than strictly necessary. I slipped in behind him, prodded him in the back. He continued, held the second set of doors for me, too.

I hovered outside the small gift shop while he bought a ticket and hung the little paper tag from a suit button. I was relieved he hadn't asked me to steal him one of those tags so he could weasel out of the admission fee. That was the kind of thing he always did when we stayed with him.

He asked the ticket counter lady, a little louder than he had to, where "one might find the Classical art," and she pointed up the stairs. He strode off, leaving me, once again, no choice but to follow.

I caught up to him on the stairs, which seemed like they must be some interactive art exhibit of their own, since they were exactly the wrong pitch for human legs. You were forced into a bizarre rhythm of uncomfortably long strides or tiny, shuffling half steps. The art of the awkward. Fitting for the moment.

"Dad," I said. There was no one else on the stairs, but I still spoke quietly, wary of echoes in the wide modernist space. "We need to talk."

"Mmm," he said, gazing out the glass wall to our left at a sculpture garden. He wasn't making this easy. He hadn't asked me anything about what was wrong. Hadn't asked about Mom at all. He was almost ignoring me. Should I just shout it all at him? Force him to pay attention?

He pushed through another door at the top, held it open. A guard glanced at him, then returned to her rounds. I didn't dare talk in front of her, even after all the insanity of the last day and a half.

Dad strode off down the gallery. This was his kind of art. Towering oil paintings in enormous gilt frames. Over-wrought and gaudy. He pulled his phone back out.

"Hello?" he said, as if answering a call.

"Dad," I said, hovering by his shoulder. "You left your bag outside."

"I'd like to talk about acquisitions," he said. He paused in front of a small portrait. "It's definitely time that we grew our portfolio."

He was enjoying this, I was sure, this faux–business speak. Probably thought himself terribly clever. He leaned in to in-spect the portrait. It was probably the smallest painting in the room. It showed a pale, blank-faced girl with golden ringlets and a lumpy hat. She looked a bit bored, I thought.

"Yes," my father said, "I want that one." He turned away. "Make it happen."

He continued down the gallery.

I stood, rooted to the spot, staring after him.

I should have realized what it meant when he suggested we meet here, of all places. But I'd been naïve. Believed that he'd be happy just to see me. Happy to help. I was wrong.

He wanted me to take the painting.

The Other Side of the Ocean

My mother used to go to museums to touch the art, she told me. To run her fingers along forbidden brushstrokes, feel the cracks in the ancient layers of oil. To kiss all the statues right on the mouth.

Just because she could.

She was wilder in her younger days. It's hard for me to imagine that now. It's hard for me to imagine, too, that she could ever have revealed her existence to another person. But she did.

She met my father at a museum. After weeks of watching him, following him from gallery to gallery—because he visited the museum every day—she spoke to him.

My father was a sculptor. Or at least that's what he was studying in college. He never finished his degree. He never sold any of his work.

He tried to make a sculpture of my mother once, she told me, re-creating her face from touch. She found the half-finished piece unnerving. One night she snuck it outside and tossed it in the river. *That* I can imagine.

She stole for him. Small things at first. A bit of cash. Art supplies for school. And then actual art. Jewels, valuables. They took a boat across the ocean. Spent blissful months roaming Europe, going where they pleased, stopping into museums, churches. My father would point out the pieces that caught his eye, and my mother would wait until he'd left and then take them. They were untouchable, stealing by whim, never by force. The things they took were usually small. Sometimes it was days before anyone noticed that anything was missing. My mother told me she'd find the MOVED FOR CLEANING signs in the back rooms of museums and hang those out in place of the things she took.

They kept moving, never staying anywhere for long. They dined lavishly. My father would order too much food and share it with my mother. She took bottles of wine for them. Took French silk and Italian leather.

It was foolish, of course, my mother told me. *I regret it.*

Sometimes, when she'd talk about that time—and I would often beg her to, because I loved to hear about it—I'd catch the hint of a smile tugging at the corner of her lips.

Still, I know it ended badly.

24

"Are you still there?" I heard my father ask from somewhere in the next gallery over.

"No," I said, but too quietly for him, for anyone, to hear.

I'd done it before, of course. Taken things for him. From stores, wallets, restaurants. And my mother and I take things all the time.

I'd never taken anything from a museum. That did feel like kind of a big deal. There was no way to justify it as necessary for survival.

My mother had been an art thief, though, and I had to admit that her stories always made it sound kind of glamorous.

I wouldn't have minded if my father had just talked to me first. If he'd acted a little more like he actually cared about me and my mother. This was why he'd been willing to drive to Pittsburgh right away. Not to help, not really.

He just wanted stuff.

I walked leadenly to the next gallery, letting the duffel bag drag on the floor behind me.

My father was waiting patiently in front of an enormous painting of Jesus, who glowed in the middle of a gaggle of adoring acolytes, all of them staring at him like they were in love. Jesus was probably supposed to look beatific, but to me he looked smug.

"Dad," I said. He turned toward my voice. "I need help. Mom, she's . . . I'm really worried about her."

A flicker of something—genuine emotion?—passed across his face. It was there and gone before I could get a good look.

"Pie," he said. He was looking in the right direction, but his eyes were focused on a painting behind me. "I had a job lined up back in Michigan. Now obviously family is more important." His tone softened, going treacly with sincerity. "So, of course, I dropped everything and came right down here. No-brainer. But I've got to recoup my losses somehow."

It was a lie, I was almost certain of it—he'd delivered it too well. There hadn't been a job. Had there?

"You two left me in a bit of a lurch last time," he went on. He spoke lightly, smiling all the while. "I've got to make a living, you know? I'm no help to anyone if I can't keep a roof over my head."

On the phone once, I'd asked him what happened to all the art they took in Europe. He'd told me himself that stolen art is almost impossible to fence. The art they took had remained in his "personal collection."

So he probably wasn't even going to sell these. The story was a lie.

One thing he'd said was true, though. Last time. Ten years ago. My mother and I had simply up and left without warning. We hadn't even left a note.

He'd had no way to reach us until the next time we called, months later.

The few times he'd brought this up on the phone over the years (*I thought I wouldn't hear from you again*), he'd spoken the same way he was speaking now, his tone so light and breezy he might have merely been discussing the weather. It was hard to tell how he genuinely felt about the whole thing. Angry? Hurt?

One thing I had learned about my father, in the short time we'd lived with him, was that the more casual he sounded, the more he was probably hiding.

So I guess this was a test. I didn't trust him, and he didn't trust me, either. He'd help me, but only if I helped him first.

"Okay," I said quietly.

"Great," he said, switching back into his faux-businessman act, "fantastic, always a pleasure doing business with you. There are two other properties I'd like you to look into when you get a chance."

I followed him, resigned. He indicated, via close gazing at the title placards and a muttered *Interesting,* two other paintings he wanted.

"I'll meet you at the dinosaur when the deal is finalized," he said and strode out of the gallery.

I was not meant to follow.

I returned to the first painting he had indicated. *Portrait of a Young Woman.* I stuck my tongue out at her. She remained, as ever, slightly bored. I pulled off my other glove.

The frame was attached to the wall with a sturdy hook,

but I could lift it right off. I went slowly, lifting gently, but there was no resistance. No alarms, either.

The duffel bag was full of bubble wrap and rags, into which I gently nestled the bored young woman. My father cared a lot about art. Cared about it more than me, probably.

Next up was a diminutive beach scene, with women in broad skirts holding colorful parasols. The painting was dwarfed by its ornate gold frame, but it was still easy to lift from the wall and place in the bag.

My father's final choice, *Flowers in Green Vase,* was a whimsical still life of, you guessed it, flowers in a green vase, the artist having apparently run out of creativity by the time he got to the title.

I pulled it from the wall, shoved it in the bag, yanked one glove back on.

Backtracking through the maze of small galleries, I passed a child staring at the empty spot on the wall where the beach scene had once been. I walked faster.

In the final gallery before the stairs, a security guard spoke urgently into his walkie-talkie, eyes alert, scanning the area.

My pulse sped up. They must have been alerted to the theft. Pushing through the heavy double doors would draw unwanted attention. But what if they locked them? I shifted from foot to foot, indecisive.

I was saved when the security guard from the landing rushed in. Before the doors swung shut behind her, I slipped through.

I ran down the awkward stairs, silently cursing my father,

duffel bag bumping against my legs, frame corners jabbing me. There'd be bruises for sure.

Two security guards had stationed themselves at the front door. I squeezed in behind a young woman as they checked her purse. When they waved her through, I shuffled after her, so close that I bumped the back of her knee with the duffel bag. She spun around but saw nothing.

The bright sun outside felt like a blessing on my skin. Safety.

I clutched the duffel bag to my chest and walked fast to the big fiberglass diplodocus in front of the natural history half of the museum.

My father was leaning against one of the gargantuan legs, as casual as can be, smoking a cigarette. I shuffled the dead leaves loudly on purpose as I approached.

He stubbed out his cigarette, lifted his phone to his ear. "Well, how did it go?"

In answer, I shoved the duffel bag against his chest, so that frames poked him in the ribs. He startled, recovered.

"You're an absolute gem," he said.

"Take it," I whispered.

"Not here," he said. "You had lunch yet?"

He didn't give me a chance to answer before striding off. What could I do but follow? I shadowed him down the block, across the street, into a noodle place.

"Just me," my father told the waitress, "and could I sit by the window?" He indicated a table over in the far corner, where there were fewer people. "Please," he added, voice suddenly low, earnest, cracking slightly. "I get nervous if I can't have my back to the wall. War will do that to you." He put a hand to his chest. I rolled my eyes. He'd never been anywhere near the army.

"Of course, sir," said the waitress.

I stood awkwardly beside the table while the waitress took my father's drink order. Once she departed, he pulled out his phone. "So," he said, "do you need a place to stay? Medicine?"

"No," I whispered. He leaned forward a little to hear me. "It's more complicated than that."

"What is it? Cancer? We could probably find a doctor who'd stay quiet for enough money."

Carefully, with my gloved hand, I pulled a chair out just far enough to slump into it and shove the duffel bag under the table. I explained, haltingly, keeping my voice low, how Mom had vomited, flickered, vanished. I told him about the note she'd left that hadn't explained anything.

My father listened, unruffled. When I was done, he leaned back in his chair, silent for a minute, considering.

"Well," he said, "it's obvious to me what happened."

"It is?" I felt a flicker of hope.

My father grinned. "She finally did it to you, too. Ran off and left you."

"What? No." My hope snuffed out as quick as a candle. "It wasn't like that."

Was it?

"Seems to me that it was," he said, shrugging. "Don't take it so hard, kiddo. That's just what she does."

I wanted to argue, to tell him he was wrong, but my mind kept running the words of the note over and over. The note hadn't said, *Come find me.* The note hadn't said she needed help. The note hadn't been any help at all.

I'm sorry.

What if he was right?

"You can come stay with me," my dad said. "What do you say? The two of us, we'd be a great team."

"No," I told him. He couldn't be right. She wouldn't have left me on purpose. Right? "I want to find her."

"So did I," he said. He spread his hands, palms up, a gesture of defeat. "Seventeen years ago. God knows I tried. I've been trying ever since."

Las Vegas, NV

My mother left my father before I was born. She left him in Las Vegas, in a hotel lobby.

She walked in the door with him, into the optical-illusion-carpeted, gilt-mirror-walled lobby. He was paying for their room with money she'd stolen. He strode to the elevators, got in one, pressed the OPEN DOOR button to give her time to follow him.

She didn't.

She stood in front of the elevator and watched the doors close. Then she turned and walked out of the hotel. Walked the mile and a half to the train station. Got on a train and left.

He hadn't done anything wrong. They hadn't gotten into a fight. Nothing had changed except that, the day before, she'd taken a pregnancy test and it had confirmed what she'd suspected for a while.

Me.

This was, according to my mother, about a month after they returned from Europe. She'd smuggled most of their illicit haul back across the ocean and hid it in the attic of my father's childhood home.

She called that house two and a half years later. Made up some lie about being an old college friend, got my father's current number from his mother.

His phone rang, out of the blue, and he found out for the first time that I existed. I don't remember it, but my mother says when she put me on the line, at my father's request, I was too shy to speak. He hung up half convinced she'd made me up.

We kept calling. Not often. Once or twice a year. I overcame my training and spoke. Our conversations tended to be brief, perfunctory. *Happy birthday, kiddo,* my father would say, or *Merry Christmas, kiddo. Get any cool presents?*

No, I would say, because I never got presents. If I wanted something, I just took it.

25

The waitress returned, and my father ordered too much food for one person.

"There's someone I know," he said when she'd gone, "a contact, who might be able to help."

"Someone you know?" Honestly, I wasn't sure my father had friends any more than I did. Only marks.

"Two years ago," he said, "after the Cathedral of Learning thing, this guy helped me look for you two."

"What?" My voice rose, accompanied by a queasy rush of panic. "You didn't tell him about us, did you?"

A woman a few tables over glanced at us, having heard my voice. My father fumbled showily with his phone, made it appear he was turning down the volume.

He gave me a disapproving look. "You could have just stayed with me, you know. You both could have stayed. It's okay to trust people sometimes."

"You're a con man," I shot back. What the hell did he know about trust?

He'd told someone about us. He'd probably told lots of

people. Of course, he had. Why would he bother to be careful, to follow my mother's rules, when he had nothing to lose?

"Look," my father said, "he can help, I bet. I think he'd be willing to talk to you."

To me? Did he realize what he was saying?

"This was a mistake," I said. "I shouldn't have called you." I stood up. My chair moved slightly as I did so, and a panicked look flitted across my father's face for an instant.

"Wait," he said. "Trust me. Just listen."

I didn't trust him, but I wanted his help, so I waited.

"You'll want to see him," my father said. "I promise you will. And he'll want to see you."

"He can't see me," I pointed out. Was he just being difficult on purpose?

"Oh, but that's the thing." My father grinned like he was telling the best joke. "He can."

"What?"

My father grinned wider. I don't know what that man had done to his teeth, but they were several shades brighter than teeth had any right to be. Maybe he ate Crest Whitestrips for breakfast.

My own teeth were clear, of course. The sun shone right through them. So I guess in a way I could grin as brightly as my father. As insubstantially.

"He's invisible," my father said. "Like you."

"That's not true," I said. No one else was like me.

He gave me a pitying look. "Don't tell me you thought you were the only ones out there. Didn't she tell you?"

It couldn't be true.

I had always believed we were the only ones in the whole world. It was part of the loneliness that lived inside me, that inhabited my bones, curled up inside instead of marrow.

Once, many years ago, in Central Park, I thought I saw a man in the distance with skin like a soap bubble, but he was swallowed by the midday crowds before I got a good look. Still, I ran across the park trying to find him again. My mother chased after me. We were both exhausted by the time she caught up and convinced me I must have imagined it.

"He won't talk to me, unfortunately," my father said, shrugging. "We had an, uh, *difference of opinion* a while back. But I still have his address. I doubt he's moved since then."

Difference of opinion?

If my father was lying, if he was making someone up— why make up this part of it? Why pretend the guy hated him? Was he self-aware enough to know that this detail, more than anything, would make me want to believe him?

I felt dizzy.

The waitress came with the food. When she was gone, my father slid one of the noodle bowls over to my side of the table. I sat, pulled off my gloves, lifted the bowl.

We ate in silence. I slurped about a third of my noodles before discomfort overtook hunger.

As soon as I pulled my hand away from the bowl and it popped back into existence, my father snapped to attention.

"Pie," he said, and it wasn't a question. There was a hint

of warning in his tone. He wasn't going to let me slip away the way my mother always had.

I could have just walked off. What was he going to do about it? He couldn't follow me.

"Okay," I said instead. "I want to meet him."

26

My father's van was parked a few blocks away. Dark curtains blocked the back windows, and the tan-beige paint flaked off heavily in places. This van looked like it had been through some shit. Possibly attacked by a pack of feral hogs.

He held open the front passenger-side door for me. I climbed in. Another curtain hung behind the front seats. A strong odor of stir-fry filled the small space.

My father slid the duffel bag under the curtain, into the back of the van, and then started the engine. I dug my fingers into the faux-leather seat.

"Can you go slower?" I asked, after he'd pulled away from the curb and accelerated.

"You aren't used to cars," he said. "I forgot."

Cars are probably the number one thing normal people take for granted. People get in them every day like it's nothing. Like they aren't death incarnate, these hulking tons of freewheeling metal that turn the world into a paved wasteland of highways and parking lots. Like they aren't completely terrifying. Too fast. Too unpredictable.

If I were in charge, I'd get rid of every car. Make it so

that trains ran through every state, like arteries, and buses branched off from each station, capillaries that could carry you anywhere.

Trains make sense. They stick to their tracks. They go where they're supposed to.

And anyone can ride a train. If you're very old or very young. If you use a wheelchair. If you can't see. Or if you can't be seen. Doesn't matter.

When we jerked to a stop at a red light, I gasped audibly. I was gripping the edges of my seat so hard my hands were cramping.

My father frowned over at the passenger seat. "You can get in the back," he said.

"Thanks," I gasped. He held the curtain aside while I climbed awkwardly over the gearshift, squeezed between the seats.

I tumbled into the back. It was not what I expected. Not that I had been inside many vans, but I didn't think most of them had hardwood floors or fleur-de-lis wallpaper. More importantly, I have to assume very few of them were lined with gold-framed paintings, some of them almost as tall as the van itself. The paintings, I was sure—every one of them— were stolen. I knelt in front of a large Baroque still life: an explosion of flowers and fruit against an inky darkness studded with moths. Had my mother taken this one?

Nestled among the art, I spotted a tangle of blankets, a rusty hotpot. My father was living out of his van, it seemed. A rope strung up in one corner had several damp socks hanging from it, a sharp contrast to the opulence of gilded frames.

When the van was once more safely parked, I squeezed back up to the front seat. We were on a steeply inclined street lined with houses.

"He lives there." My father pointed to an unassuming two-story with a small porch.

"Are you going to introduce us?" I couldn't tell if my pulse was racing from the lingering anxiety of being in a vehicle or from nervous excitement.

"Better if I don't."

"Are you going to just drive off as soon as I get out of the car?" I demanded. I had a sinking feeling. Was this all a lie?

"What?" He gave me a wounded look. "I would never."

"Give me your car keys."

"Why?"

"Collateral."

My father was a con man. He conned people. He came up with something they wanted, and he pretended he was going to give it to them. Then he took their money.

Well, maybe he'd only pretended to know another invisible person. That was something I wanted, right? To be less alone in this world.

"It's not a lie," he insisted. "Go see for yourself. He'll talk to you, probably. He knows me as John Darnsen."

That wasn't my father's real name. But who was I to judge? Denise still thought I was named Sam.

I reached over and grabbed the keys out of the ignition with my bare hand, making them vanish.

"Hey!" my father shouted. "Give those back." He grasped

at the air, but I pressed myself far into the corner, and he couldn't see where to grab. I fumbled the door open, hopped out.

"I'll give them back," I said, "when I'm done." I slammed the car door shut and strode up to the house my father had pointed to.

The blinds were drawn on the front windows. The door was heavy wood, no glass.

I knocked. No answer. I knocked again.

An intercom I had mistaken for a fancy lock crackled on.

"Please leave the package outside, thank you," said a man's voice, staccato, matter-of-fact.

"I don't have a package," I said.

There was no answer.

I knocked again.

"I do not want to change my cable or gas company I do not want to buy any fundraising items I do not want to hear the word of the Lord have a lovely day goodbye." This was recited like a poem, without pause, and then the system buzzed off.

"Wait," I said quickly, "my father knows you."

Silence. I searched in vain for a speak button on the intercom, but it was a featureless plastic grill. Anonymous, unyielding.

I kept knocking. I even jiggled the doorknob just in case, but the door was firmly locked. What now? Should I just stand here?

"Vacate my property immediately," said the intercom.

The voice sounded different this time. Same man but, I suddenly realized, those other two statements had been prerecorded, perhaps preprogrammed.

"Sir," I said, the words tumbling out as breathless and unpausing as his previous messages, "my father is John Darnsen and he said he used to know you and that you are like me and maybe you could help me I need to talk to you please."

"Is this a prank?" the voice said.

"No. I'm very serious."

"Where are you? Stand in front of the door so the cameras can see you."

"I am standing in front of the door," I said.

"You're not. I can't—" He stopped abruptly midsentence.

"Hello?" I said.

The intercom crackled off.

Well, I would wait. Or I would go and get my father and make him come here, since this was his stupid contact.

But a few moments later, I heard the rasp of a lock turning. And then another. And then a bolt sliding free, and a chain jangling.

The door swung open. Just inside stood a man.

He wasn't very tall. He was balding. He wore glasses. His hair was long and put back in a neat ponytail. Overall, an average-looking nerdy guy, I guess. Older than me, but younger than either of my parents.

None of that was interesting. None of that is what I noticed first.

Because the man who stood in front of me seemed like a miracle.

A man made of water. A man made of glass. A man I could see right through, the light not stopping but bending and refracting through him. A man like a double exposure in a photograph. A man like me.

"Holy shit," I said.

"Yes," he said, eyes sweeping up from my feet, pausing at my eyes, *seeing* me. "Nice to meet you, too. Your father is an asshole."

Encino, CA

The entirety of Southern California has a temporary feeling, like an overgrown resort. Identical apartment complexes ring enormous turquoise pools. Everything is terribly new. The oldest houses are from the fifties or sixties. Sprawling shopping malls take the place of downtowns. Instead of history, there is artifice. Architecture in a pastiche of Mediterranean styles, terra-cotta roofs, arched courtyards. Non-native palm trees that don't even thrive in that climate.

Rich people are different depending on where you go in the state. In SoCal, they flaunt their wealth. Live in giant houses with glass walls overlooking the ocean. Designer clothes. Fast cars. Makes them easy to spot, to follow home. In San Francisco, rich people like to pretend they are salt of the earth. They make their own peanut butter, wear Birkenstocks. You wouldn't know, necessarily, at first glance, that their company just went public.

The roads are as big as rivers in Southern California, everyone zipping around on twelve-lane freeways. It could be a frightening place for us, but walk far enough and there is majesty, too. The Mojave Desert, the mountains, the beaches and coves. We went there often in the winter, for the mild weather.

One evening, my mother and I stood on the limestone patio of a house outside LA, looking at the lights of the city, when the ground slid beneath our feet. First one way and then the other, the world suddenly drunk. Water sloshed over the sides of the pool. The glass in the mansion windows shimmied.

It lasted a full minute. We were far enough from the epicenter that there was no damage. Still, I will never forget what it felt like to have something that you thought was solid, something you thought was certain, suddenly shift.

27

His name was Steve. A boring name. A normal name. He hadn't been able to see me on the feed from the front-door security camera, since the camera couldn't pick me up. But he could see me now.

I sat on an armchair in his living room, which was spare and neat. He sat across from me. I could see, through his face, the poster of the periodic table hanging on the wall behind him. His right eye was nickel, his left manganese.

We sat in silence for what felt like a long time. I suppose he was waiting for me to explain myself. He didn't look right at me. Out of politeness, perhaps. Or annoyance. I couldn't tell.

"I never knew there were other people like me," I said finally.

His gaze flicked to my face and then away. "Well," he said slowly, "we are hard to spot."

Was that a joke? I couldn't tell. He wasn't smiling. His face was impassive, but I didn't get the sense that he was hiding anything like my father did. Why would this guy need to put up a façade? Nobody was ever looking at him.

I wondered if I, too, made fewer facial expressions than

visible people. Perhaps not, since I'd always had my mother around.

"Did you know?" I asked.

"Not at first," he said. "But, yes, I've met others."

I was struck with a vision of silent, unseen hordes. In every corner, one of us. Crouched under tables, pressed into nooks and crannies, lurking just out of sight. It's what Denise had worried about, that first night we talked.

"How many others?" I asked.

Surely if there were many of us, my mother and I would have noticed one or two, wouldn't we? It's a big country, yes, but we've been all over it. I thought of the man I might have seen in Central Park.

"In person," Steve said, "only one."

"Oh."

"Two now, counting you. And I maintain an online correspondence with a woman in Montreal who claims to share our condition."

I was disappointed. I hadn't realized it was there until it burst, the little bubble of hope that had swelled inside me when he said he'd met others. I wanted a whole secret community. A network. A family.

"Did you know about me?" I asked.

"In part. Your father was always cryptic when he spoke about you—I often thought he was lying. He said only that he knew two others like me."

He still wasn't looking right at me. Every now and then, his gaze would flicker across my face and then return to a point above my left shoulder.

"My father," I started uncertainly. "He said maybe you could help me."

"No," Steve said, so abruptly I jumped in my chair. "I no longer engage in any of the type of activities your father finds helpful."

"That's not—I mean, I just wanted some information."

Steve's tone, level and emotionless to begin with, had gone icily flat. "You mean like credit card information?" He stood.

"Of course not," I said, and stood up also. "Look, I'm not my father. I'm nothing like him."

"So," he said, "you mean to tell me you are not a liar and a thief?"

I flinched a little as his eyes met mine for a moment before he looked away again. I wasn't used to people looking me in the eyes. Perhaps he wasn't used to it, either.

"I—" There wasn't any good way to answer his question without lying, which would kind of defeat the point. He was right, of course. I'd been lying a lot lately, to my mother, to Denise. And I was absolutely a thief. Sure, maybe I stole to survive, but you could argue that my father did, too. And let's ignore the fact that I had just robbed a museum. "Aren't you?"

"Not anymore."

"Well, then, whose house is this?" It couldn't be his. Maybe he lived with a visible accomplice who bought things for him. That would be the only way to live without stealing, though I didn't think it gave him any right to judge me.

"Mine," he said.

"Okay, who else lives here?"

"No one."

"And this stuff? How'd you get it?" I gestured at the room's few furnishings—the armchairs we'd been sitting in, a side table with a stack of books. He must have taken these from somewhere.

"I bought it."

"How?"

He tilted his head at me. "Is it really so inconceivable? Here, I'll show you."

Without further explanation, he walked out of the room. I hesitated, unsure if I was meant to wait or follow. After a moment, I heard him call "Come along" from another room, and I hurried after him.

He stood in a room at the back of the house, the one window covered by a dark curtain. A curved desk wrapped around three walls, with a futuristic-looking ergonomic chair in the middle. Almost all available desk space, and some of the wall space, was crowded with monitors, several displaying a feed from cameras mounted on the outside of the house. Others were open to browser tabs, something that looked like lines of code, a paused computer game.

"I order anything I want," Steve said. "It arrives on my doorstep. I speak to no one or, if I must, to a delivery person via the intercom."

"But the money—"

And even as I said it, I realized that the answer must be the same. There are plenty of ways to make money on the internet. Online poker. Cryptocurrency.

"I am gainfully employed as a programmer. I work remotely."

"I guess I never thought of that."

"There," he said. "I have given you valuable information. Now you can leave."

He sat at the desk, turned his attention to one of the monitors, started typing.

"No," I said, my frustration building. "Wait. Aren't you interested at all? Don't you care that I'm like you?"

To me, meeting this man was a miracle, a revelation. And yet he acted like it was nothing. I couldn't understand him.

"You are not like me," he said without turning.

"I am," I insisted. Maybe our personalities were nothing alike, but he just had to look at me to see what we had in common. When he didn't respond, I reached out and nudged his shoulder.

He flinched so violently that he nearly fell out of his chair. I jumped back, startled by his reaction.

"Shit," I said. "I'm so sorry."

"Your father and I had an agreement," he said, staring down at his hands. "He would leave me alone forever, and in exchange I would not submit any evidence of his crimes, which I possess, to the authorities. Evidence which I believe is sufficient to convict him. If you do not leave immediately, I will consider the agreement breached by proxy, and I will make good on my threat."

I took that all in. "Fine by me," I said.

Why should I protect my father? Not that I really wanted

him to get arrested, but I couldn't say I was feeling particularly loyal after how he'd acted at the museum.

Steve was silent for a while. Long enough that it was uncomfortable.

"What is it that you want?" he asked, finally, glancing up at me. In that silence, it seemed, an agreement had been reached.

"My mother," I said. "She's like us. Invisible, I mean. But she disappeared. Just blinked out like a light right in front of me. I don't know what happened to her and I'm worried and scared and I didn't even know other invisible people existed but you do and so I hoped maybe you'd know something more than I did about why we're like this or what happened to her and what I can do."

"Ah," said Steve, tapping his finger against the side of the desk. "Your mother. It must run in families, then. Though I am not aware of any other cases in my own line."

"Can you help me?" I asked.

"Perhaps," he said. "I am not an expert. I can give you little more than hypotheses, with data drawn from an inadequate sample size."

I blinked at him. He was the most peculiar man I'd ever met. He was, in a sense, the *only* man I'd ever really met besides my father.

"What I can tell you," he said, "is that what you describe is not unprecedented. I am a firsthand witness to that fact."

"Wait," I said, trying to catch up to his formal way of speaking. "You've seen it happen?"

"Yes," he said. "Just once."

28

He agreed to tell me the story in exchange for a haircut. It was one of the few services not accessible to him in any form. No one could see his hair to cut it.

He sat rigidly in a chair in his kitchen, stiffening further if my hands ever strayed too close to his shoulders or ears—in danger of touching. He just wanted the hair shorter, he said—it didn't really matter how it looked. Which was good because, while I'd cut my mother's hair plenty of times, I'd never had much of a knack for getting it even.

While I worked the scissors, he talked. His words seemed to come easier when he didn't have to look at me. He told me his story, starting nearly from the beginning.

Like my mother, he was born visible and had been consumed by the need to get away when he was a teenager. But not for the same reasons. There was no abuse. His parents, he told me, were well-meaning, quiet and detached, like him.

Everything and everyone else, though, was a problem.

School, unbearable. Stores. Streets. All too loud. Too

chaotic. Clashing lines and colors. Music, lawnmowers, voices. Faces.

"Faces," he said, "have so much information, all of it coming at you so fast. Have you ever noticed?"

It was as though everything in the world was screaming at him all the time.

So he left. Walked away one day when he was seventeen, into the forest outside town. He camped out, made midnight runs into town. Broke into his own house, the houses of neighbors, to take food, borrow books. He felt guilty, but he couldn't stand the thought of having to face anyone.

"You were a thief, too," I said, still prickly about his accusations.

"I was," he admitted.

As time wore on, he faded. Soon he no longer needed the cover of night to sneak into town. No one could see him. He took more things, took from stores, set up a luxurious campsite in the woods, well hidden. He wasn't content with his life, exactly, but he didn't know how else to live.

Three years later, my father showed up. He tracked Steve down, drawn to town by reports of mysterious disappearing objects, daylight thefts that seemed impossible. My father caught Steve midheist. He couldn't see him, but he spoke to him, seemed to know about invisible people. Seemed to think, at first, that Steve was someone he knew.

My father must have been searching, I realized, for us. My mother and me.

Once my father realized that Steve was a stranger, he

offered him a deal. My father wouldn't tell the people of the town about Steve in exchange for some favors.

And so Steve became my father's accomplice. He stole for him, got access to private information useful for cons. My father, meanwhile, set Steve up with a nice, quiet apartment in the city. He brought him groceries, takeout.

It was through my father, indirectly, that Steve met the other invisible person. My father was tracking this person, noting patterns of strange disappearances around town. Steve helped search, and he was the one who found the guy—Felix—first. He didn't tell my father. Instead, he tried to help Felix, without coercing him into a life of crime.

Felix was only sixteen, and he was running away. Steve never pushed for details. But he knew Felix had come from a strict religious family. He had displeased them somehow. Been locked in a room to fast and pray until he could be cleansed of his sin.

"It must have been this," Steve said, "which precipitated his fade. I believe it is a defense mechanism of sorts. Camouflage."

It was the same thing my mother had said. I wished she were here, wished she could hear this.

Steve let Felix sleep on his couch, supplied him with food so he didn't have to steal. Hid him from my father and from his family.

"He was very nervous," Steve told me. "He felt certain that someone would come find him despite his invisibility. He flickered, the way you described. This went on for a few weeks, and then one day, someone knocked on my apartment door—it was your father, not his family tracking him down—and he just flickered away. Never returned."

"Do you know where he went?" I asked. I'd gone still, scissors hanging in the air. Here we were, right on the edge of an answer. Hope thrummed through me.

"I do not."

He waved impatiently for me to continue my work.

Hand shaking slightly, I went back to cutting his hair. "You didn't look for him?"

Steve shrugged, which knocked the cut I was making even farther away from straight than it had been to begin with. "I respected that he wanted to be left alone. It is what I want, as well. Are you done yet? This is taking too long."

He lifted a hand to feel the back of his head. I cringed, but he didn't recoil in horror at the uneven mess his fingers encountered.

"That's good enough," he said, and stood, sending loose hair cuttings cascading off his shoulders to the kitchen tiles.

It was not good enough. He must know more. I needed him to know more.

"What do I do now?" I set the scissors on the counter, took a deep breath, determined not to cry. "How do I get her back?"

Steve was crouching, pushing the fallen hair into a pile. "I do not know."

"Did Felix ever send you a note or anything?" I asked, feeling desperate now.

"I never heard from him again."

My heart sank. So much for hope.

What had I learned? Not much, except that this had happened to someone else. Did it happen to all invisible people, in the end? Would it happen to me someday?

The guy in the story had wanted to run, to hide. Well, so did my mother. All the time. Maybe both of them had just figured out how to get to the next level, how to leave the rest of us behind.

"Thanks for talking to me," I said to Steve, who was sweeping up the hair cuttings, which were visible now that they were no longer attached to his head. It might not have been as helpful as I'd hoped, but it was clear he'd been reluctant to speak to me at all.

"Yes," he said. "If you want, you may send me a letter sometime. I find writing preferable to talking. Now, please leave and never come back."

Too accustomed already to his brusque manner to take any offense at this, I laughed. He gave me a curious sideways glance. Playing at the corners of his mouth: the closest thing I'd seen so far to a smile.

"Okay," I said.

He walked me to the front door.

"Can I ask you one last thing?" I said as he undid the locks and chains that held the door secure.

"If you must."

"Aren't you ever lonely?"

"No."

"I'm lonely all the time," I confessed as he slid the final bolt free.

"I used to be lonely," he stated, the way you might say

that you used to be a child. A fact obvious and uninteresting. "When I had to be around other people."

"That doesn't make any sense," I said.

"I always had to pretend, back then," he said. "Trying to act the way I was supposed to, to understand what people wanted from me. Alone is not synonymous with lonely. Out in the world, everyone tells you to Just Be Yourself but then punishes you when you are." He pushed open the door, held it for me. "And yet they are right. Alone, I can be myself."

A Complete List of People
I Would Rather Be Than Myself

Pretty much anyone.

29

My father was waiting in the car, his eyes closed. I tapped on the window, and he flailed so violently he hit the horn. He'd been asleep.

"Well?" he asked me, rolling down the window. "How did it go?"

I pulled his keys out of my pocket with a gloved hand, dangled them through the window. "He said you were an asshole."

"That tracks," my father said. He snatched the floating keys.

"And he knew someone who disappeared the way Mom did."

"Really?" My father raised his eyebrows. "He never told me that. So does he know where she went?"

"No."

"She'll come back," he said. "Don't worry, kiddo. This is just what she does. She's done it to me twice now. Well, go on, hop in."

I eyed the van. "I'd rather walk."

"Where are you headed? Let me give you a ride."

I didn't know precisely where we were, but in the distance, I could see the top edge of the Cathedral of Learning peeking over a hill. It would work as a makeshift compass. The van was too small, too fast. It made me feel trapped.

"I'll walk," I said, tone firm. I moved away from the window.

"Let's meet up tomorrow," my father said. "We can do lunch again." When I didn't answer, he leaned his head out the window. "Pie? Are you still here? Look, there's something else I wanted to show you. A note from your mother."

That stopped me in my tracks.

"A note?" I asked.

"Yeah, she sent it to me a couple of weeks ago. Maybe it's got something to do with all this. Come have lunch with me tomorrow and I'll show it to you. Same time, same place. Okay?"

"I—"

"Great," he shouted, "see you there!"

He revved the van engine, and I jumped onto the sidewalk moments before he peeled away.

If there really was a note, he could have shown me at lunch today. He could have shown me just now. It was bait, or maybe insurance. A way to get me to meet up with him again, or to keep me from running off the way my mother always did.

He was supposed to offer marks something they wanted. And yes, I wanted information.

But he could have hooked me so much faster and better if he'd just been able to act, genuinely, like he cared about me.

Buses rushed past as I trudged back in what I hoped was more or less the direction of Denise's house, but I didn't dare take one, even though my legs were tired. I didn't know the routes, didn't want to end up in an unfamiliar part of the city all alone.

My father's words from earlier echoed in my head as I walked.

Don't tell me you thought you were the only ones out there. Didn't she tell you?

I knew it was true now. There were others like us. Had my mother known? Had she lied to me?

She finally did it to you, too.

And if she had, what else was she lying about? She hadn't been entirely honest with me yesterday on the train when she started feeling sick.

It made a terrible sense, what my father had suggested. Maybe he was right. Maybe my mother left me on purpose. Maybe she found a new way to run.

Don't worry, kiddo. This is just what she does.

I stopped by the Giant Eagle on my way, to pick up something better than stale bagels for Denise and Jules. I was far more careful this time, breathing slow, thinking calm thoughts, touching only one item at a time, slipping it into my backpack.

At the deli, I recognized the girl from the day before, the one who'd seen the counter disappear. I waited until her back was turned before snatching a handful of roast beef and some salami out of the glass display case. A paper-wrapped packet of freshly sliced turkey sat on the food scale—I grabbed that, too.

I was walking away when I heard the deli girl shout, "Where the hell did that turkey go? Jessie, did you take my turkey?"

I glanced back. The girl was pointing at the food scale, eyes wide.

Her coworker, Jessie presumably, ambled over. "I didn't go anywhere near your damn turkey."

"I swear I just sliced some. It's like I was telling you the other day, there is something weird going on here. Maybe that lady was right. Maybe I should call her."

Lady? I moved back toward them so I could hear better.

Jessie, an older woman in a hairnet, leaned against the counter and picked at her long fake nails. "You get all kinds of people spouting nonsense. Don't pay none of them no mind, that's my policy."

"She said she was a paranormal researcher," the girl insisted, seeming almost excited now. "She said she'd seen this kind of *phenomenon* before."

"Sounds like a load of nonsense to me."

"You didn't see what I saw. I swear, Jessie, the whole counter just vanished. Like, poof!" She demonstrated, waving her hands.

"That lady was probably playing a joke on you."

"I hadn't even told anyone yet," the girl said. "You're saying it's a coincidence that she walks right up to the counter and asks if I've seen anything disappear lately? It was like she *knew.*"

A chill went up my spine. Maybe it was only because I was standing in the extremely air-conditioned deli section. But regardless, I shivered.

Someone had been asking about me.

My first thought was my father, but the girl had said it was a woman.

"What I think," Jessie was saying, "is that you got too much imagination for your own good."

"Maybe you haven't got enough," the deli girl answered.

Jessie snorted and then turned to address a customer who'd wandered up. The other girl grabbed some more turkey to slice.

The unease stayed with me as I made my way through the rest of the store. I filled a big tub with fancy olives. Grabbed some fancy cheese, hummus, cookies, non-stale pita bread and stuffed it all into my backpack.

On the way back to Denise's house, I passed a small concrete porch with a shrine set up in the corner: a statue of the Virgin Mary surrounded by fake flowers inside a glass block. The kind some windows are made of. Light filled the rest of the empty space. It could have been in a museum.

I stopped and stared at it for some time. Thinking of the glass wall between me and the world. How it kept me safe. How it trapped me, too.

How I'd broken through.

30

When I made it back to Denise's house, I did something I have done only once or twice before in my life: I lifted my hand to the front door and knocked. It was a risk.

As I waited for someone to answer, my heart raced almost as fast as it had in the museum, post–art heist. What if Larissa came to the door? What if no one came?

The door swung open. Standing behind it: Denise. I breathed out, let the tension in my muscles ease.

She squinted at the empty stoop and then, realization dawning: "Sam?"

"Hi," I whispered.

"Well, come on in. Hurry up."

I felt like a vampire or something. Invited. I felt full to the brim.

"Is that Neely?" Larissa's voice shouted down the stairs as I followed Denise inside.

"No," Denise shouted back.

"Who was it?"

"Uh . . . Mormons!"

Denise sauntered into the living room, plopped onto the

couch. She patted the seat next to her. I hovered uncertainly nearby, still standing.

"Where'd you go?" she asked. "I was worried you weren't going to come back."

"Sorry. I just thought it would be better if I got out of the way for a while."

That wasn't entirely a lie.

"Sit down so I know where to look," Denise said. Dutifully, I did. "We need to get you a phone or something," she went on. "Wait, do you *have* a phone?"

"No."

"I'm glad you came back," she said. "If you'd been much later, you would have missed us. Neely is coming by soon, and then we're heading out."

"You aren't grounded or something?" I asked.

"Larissa and Terrance don't really go in for that kind of thing." Denise leaned in conspiratorially. "Besides, they haven't found out about the party yet."

Footsteps on the stairs. I stood up, reflexively, moved toward the wall. But it was only Jules.

"Where's Neely?" they asked, looking around the room.

"Not here yet," said Denise.

"Oh, I thought I heard the door."

Jules walked over and plopped on the couch just as Denise was shouting, "Wait, don't!" but I wasn't sitting there anymore. Jules jumped back up, looked down at the couch, alarmed.

"I'm over here," I said.

Both heads whipped toward the sound of my voice.

"Sam!" said Jules, smiling in my general direction.

I felt warm, felt like I might burst. To be greeted, to be welcomed. As if I belonged.

"We had to clean up all the flour," said Denise, gesturing at the flour. "Sorry that didn't work."

"Don't worry about it," I said, thinking again about what my father had said.

"We can try to look for your mom again when we get back later," said Jules.

"Where are you going?" I asked, wanting to change the subject. I had no desire to explain what I'd discovered: that I may never find her, that she may not want to be found.

"Neely's band is playing again tonight," Denise said. "House show."

Neely's band. That meant Tess's band, too.

I'd barely thought about Tess at all today, which was unusual. Then again, this day was proving to be one of the most unusual in my entire life.

Knocking came from the front door. Banging, more like. Jules went to open it. At the same time, Larissa appeared on the stairs.

The door opened and Neely came in, followed by the skinny guitar guy whose name I'd never learned. I craned my head to see. Was Tess with them?

"Oh—Miss Larissa," Neely said, looking surprised. "I didn't know you'd be back."

"We had to cut things a little short," Larissa said.

I noticed Denise shaking her head at Neely, making small shushing motions. Probably worried she'd inadvertently spill the beans about the party. Behind Neely, the door opened again, and Tess walked in.

My heart sped up. But I had returned to my normal state. A fly on the wall. A nobody. Not even there, officially.

I backed quietly into the kitchen. Made quick work of transferring the newly acquired groceries from my backpack to the fridge and cupboards. Voices drifted in from the other room.

"You'll be home by eleven," I heard Larissa say, in a tone of laying down the law. "Don't do anything stupid, and watch out for one another."

An echo of agreement. Footsteps on the stairs again.

I peered cautiously into the living room. Larissa had gone back upstairs. Tess sat on one end of the couch, Jules on the other, Denise in the middle. Neely was squatting by an outlet, plugging in her phone. The guitarist leaned against the wall by the window, affecting an air of general disinterest.

Denise darted an occasional glance at where she believed I was still standing, over by the bricked fireplace. I crept into the room.

"Sucks about the fire," the guitar guy was saying.

"Keep it down," said Denise hurriedly. "My aunt and uncle can't know about that."

"And that headless girl," Tess said. "That was wild. Did you see my picture?"

A little chill ran up my spine.

"What picture?" asked Jules. Tess whipped out her phone. I inched closer, peered around the back of the couch.

Tess opened Instagram, held the phone out. I craned my neck to see the screen.

It was a picture of me.

Well, a picture of my clothes, but close enough. A surprisingly clear shot, given the low light. Only the slightest of motion blurs. My dress, my gloves, flailing in front of the mantel. Above the neckline, only wall, candle flames.

I leaned in as close as I dared. Tess had captioned the shot "this party is haunted #nofilter #nophotoshop."

There were almost a hundred likes. Which wasn't a huge number, I guess, but that still felt like a hell of a lot of eyes.

If my mother could see this, she'd be furious. This was worse than the Cathedral, maybe. Yes, there'd been a lot of pictures of that. It had been all over social media, local news.

But this was a picture of me. Actually me. Not just something I'd touched.

My heart was racing. I tried to take a slow, quiet breath.

It was the internet. The internet is full of nonsense. Most of it fake. A picture is nothing. Even if people believed the stupid hashtag, it wouldn't mean it was real. It could have been a mannequin. Could have been a clever angle, or something involving a mirror. Just today, Denise was showing me trick photos she'd created in exactly those ways. And hadn't I let Denise take a picture of me? This was no different.

"That was genuinely scary," Neely said. "Like, I thought for a second she'd fucking died. Like, her actual head had fallen off. Nightmare shit."

"You screamed right in my ear," said Guitar Boy.

"Maybe it actually did," said Tess. "I mean, none of you knew her. Do you believe in ghosts?"

Denise laughed.

"I'm dead serious," said Tess.

"*Dead* serious, eh?" Denise teased. She made a complicated but almost infinitesimal motion. Leaning toward Tess and then away, as if drawn by a magnet but resisting it. It was quick. I'm sure no one else noticed.

Just me.

"No," Tess said. "I mean it. A few years ago, a bunch of weird shit happened in my house. And then yesterday—well, I genuinely think my house is haunted."

It took me a moment to realize. But when I did, my stomach turned over.

She was talking about me again. Me and my mother. We were the weird shit that happened in her house a few years ago. Two, to be precise.

And yesterday I'd spoken her name aloud in the kitchen.

"Has anything else strange gone down here recently?" Tess asked.

Denise and Jules exchanged a glance. Panicking, I reached over the back of the couch, nudged Denise's shoulder. *Don't tell,* I wanted to say. She shifted, startled.

"Uh, no," she said. "Just that."

Tess was giving her an assessing sort of look. Denise noticed it and smiled and looked away shyly.

I felt something as I watched this, the echo of an emotion I'd felt once before. Two years ago, sitting in the cafeteria of

Tess's high school, I'd watched Tess as she in turn watched the girl she'd later kiss, Taylor.

I've learned a lot through observing what people say to each other without talking. Things they say with their eyes or their hands, the angle of their bodies.

This is flirting. A language I can't speak. Only decode.

I'm like a scientist who devotes her life to studying whale songs. She can interpret the patterns, she can understand them, but her throat could never make the sounds to sing back.

I didn't belong here, didn't fit in. How had I ever thought that I did?

This Side of the Ocean

I have seen both the Pacific and the Atlantic. Lived in houses overlooking them. Paced widow's walks and balconies. Felt the salt air. Heard the hush of the tide. Watched the water swell, surfers rolling under the tongues of waves, the tiny distant peaks of sails shimmering in reflected sun.

I cannot go to the beach when it is crowded. The craters made by my footsteps sinking into loose sand are too visible. But I can go when it is deserted, during storms, rain, the height of winter.

I can go at night, when the water is as black as the sky, the horizon line invisible, the two expanses melting into one another, indistinguishable, so it seems like the night sky itself is beating up onto the sand in waves, crested with a white froth of stars.

I have stood in both oceans up to my ankles, my thighs. Felt the undertow tug at the backs of my knees. I haven't gone farther than that.

This is a big country. I should know. It takes days to get across it.

But every time I stand at the edge of an ocean, my world feels so small.

31

I was pretty sure I hadn't imagined it, the way I'd seen Denise looking at Tess. Or, rather, not looking at her, which told me just as much.

I was good at watching people. It was basically my only skill, besides stealing.

"We should head out," Neely said.

"We can squeeze you both in the back of the van," the guitarist said.

"No," Denise said quickly. "You all go ahead. I'll take the bus. Meet you there. I need to get ready."

"You sure?" Tess asked.

"Yeah."

"I wouldn't mind a ride," said Jules.

The other four crowded out. As soon as the door shut, Denise stood and turned to the empty room.

"Sam?" she said. "You're still here, right?"

"I'm here," I said from beside her. She didn't even jump this time, just spun around to face my direction.

"Cool, let's go."

"Don't you need to get ready?" I asked.

"Not really. I just didn't think we could get you in the van without the others getting suspicious."

"Oh." I took that in. Maybe it was fun for her, to have a secret. An imaginary friend. I could be her ghost. It was more than I had ever dreamed was possible. It was enough.

It had to be.

"Thanks," I said, trying to keep my tone level. A lump had come into my throat.

"You'd rather they didn't know about you, right?" she asked me as she headed to the door and pulled on her jacket, a vintage neon windbreaker rather than black leather like the ones Neely and Tess wore.

"Uh . . ." I adjusted my backpack and followed. "It's just kind of risky. My mother always said . . ." I trailed off. Did I even believe in my mother's rules anymore? Denise and Jules knew about me. Nothing terrible had happened as a consequence of that. "She said we shouldn't tell people."

"It was kind of freaking me out after you left," Denise said, "thinking she might be somewhere in the house, watching us."

"No," I said. "She's not here anymore."

I said it without thinking. I didn't know that for sure.

Mostly, I was just trying to reassure Denise.

I should have learned my lesson after Christy all those years ago, learned never to get attached. I should have learned my lesson after Tess. We always had to leave in the end.

And yet here I was again with something to lose. If Denise got freaked, if she decided we were dangerous after all, this would be over. She'd want me to leave.

I didn't want to leave. Not yet. Maybe I could never truly fit in, never be a real person, but this was the closest I'd ever gotten to having a friend.

"She's not?" asked Denise, sounding skeptical.

"Uh, no," I said, improvising. "I figured it out while I was gone. She left. She does that sometimes, to get away from people. In the past, she's always taken me along with her, but this time she didn't."

It wasn't true. Or at least it wasn't the whole truth.

But the more I'd thought about it, the more I was becoming convinced that my father must be right. My mother had left me behind on purpose.

"Oh, I almost forgot," Denise said. "One second." She ran up the stairs, returned a minute later swinging a camera bag. She opened the front door and I followed her out, lost in thought.

Steve had said he never saw Felix ever again. Would I ever see my mother again? Did she even want me to?

"I'm really sorry about your mom," Denise said as we headed down the street. She didn't seem to care if anyone saw her talking to herself. "I can understand what you must be going through. I mean, it wasn't exactly the same with my mom. But she did kind of leave."

"What happened?" I asked.

"She had a break. A psychotic break." Denise kicked at a rock on the sidewalk. "That makes it sound really bad. But, well, I guess it *was* pretty bad."

"Sorry," I said quickly, "you don't have to talk about it if you don't want to."

We stopped at a corner to wait for the light.

"It's okay," said Denise. "Most people aren't very understanding. They hear 'psychotic break' and they just think, like, psycho killer. People are always afraid of anything they don't understand. But I don't think you're like that." She smiled vaguely to her left.

The light changed. Denise headed across. I hurried after her, resisting the urge to reach for her hand. My mother and I still held hands when we crossed busy streets sometimes. Or we used to. Before she disappeared. Or left.

"I try not to be," I said when we reached the other side of the street.

"Mom's doing a lot better now," Denise said, "with meds and therapy and shit. But we all just decided it would be better if I stayed with Larissa. Closer to school for me, and also less stressful for Mom. Sometimes I feel bad about that, like, did taking care of me make it worse? Is it my fault she had her break?" She shrugged. "I know I shouldn't think that way."

"I think I know what you mean, though," I said.

"Here's the stop," said Denise, pausing next to a signpost. She readjusted the strap of her camera bag.

"Are you working on your project tonight?" I asked, coming to stand beside her.

She turned her head in the direction of my voice, looked through me. "Nah, I'm taking pictures for the band."

"Do they do a lot of shows?"

"A decent amount. They've played at bars once or twice, but mostly it's just house shows. They play at the Church a lot."

"The church?" The band hadn't struck me as the ecclesiastic type.

"Oh, sorry, that's the name of the house. It's a proper punk house. Ed arranges shows every weekend. He's Neely's boyfriend. Unless they've broken up again. Hard to say with those two." She shrugged. "He's all right. Probably doesn't know how to boil an egg. Or what a sponge is. But he's well-meaning most of the time. And he's not hung up on normative bullshit. Maybe that's the best straight girls can hope for."

A guy walking past glanced at Denise, then glanced away. Maybe he assumed she was like Javier, hallucinating voices. Or maybe he just thought there was a Bluetooth device hidden under her mass of blue and purple curls.

"Is Neely straight?" I whispered. I was surprised. I guess I'd assumed since she dressed like Tess, hung out with Tess, she must be like Tess in other ways, too. But I didn't know. I guess I didn't know for sure about Denise, either. Only suspected.

Denise laughed. "Oh, right, I forgot, you barely know us, really."

I flinched. She was right, of course. Would she realize that she shouldn't be talking to me? Shouldn't be trusting me?

"Neely likes to joke that she actually had to come out as straight. Because everyone always thought she was a flamboyantly gay boy when she was growing up. But then she was, like, 'Psych! I'm actually just a lady.'"

"Oh," I said, "cool."

Denise leaned out from the edge of the curb, squinting down the road.

"I see the bus. So, how does this work? With you, I mean?" She was practically bouncing with nervous excitement. It was funny, as if riding the bus was a big deal instead of something I'd done a hundred times.

"Don't worry about me," I told her as the bus pulled up. "Just act normal."

She did not.

She fumbled with her card, chatted nervously at the bus driver. Turned around several times to glance at the door. Flinched when it closed. I had to poke her in the arm to get her to continue down the aisle.

I shuffled behind her. She stopped abruptly halfway, and I bumped into her.

"Where should I sit?" she said aloud.

The bus wasn't crowded, but several people glanced at her. I felt a flush of secondhand embarrassment.

I slid into the nearest seat, reached out, tugged ever so gently on her sleeve. She spun so fast in my direction that she nearly fell before taking a seat beside me. She scooted over too far and her thigh touched mine. I stiffened, shot through with a jolt of fear I was powerless to stop.

I pushed myself as far into the wall as I could, clenched my muscles so that the point of contact was gone. No touching. It was too much. Too much.

"This is wild," Denise said, making big eyes toward where I sat. I knew what she was seeing: her own reflection in the darkened window. Nothing else.

No one was really paying her much attention, everyone closed off in their own little bus worlds, but it still made me more uncomfortable than talking on the street. I should have told her about my father's phone trick.

She shifted in her seat, pulled her phone from her pocket, and I thought maybe one or both of us was psychic. But instead of holding it to her ear, she leaned it against the back of the seat in front of us, opened her Notes app.

I guess you probably don't want to talk out loud? she typed. She angled the phone so I could read it. I felt a funny little thrill. It reminded me of exchanging notes with Tess.

You should get a phone, Denise wrote. **Then you can text me.**

She typed with just her pointer finger. It flew over the screen, making loops and swirls, fast abstract gestures. I found myself watching her hand instead of the words.

It made me think of sign language. Made me think of my mother. Made the thrill I'd felt in the pit of my stomach turn sour.

Denise was staring at her phone. I realized she was waiting for me. I reached out with a gloved finger and awkwardly pecked out: **Yes sorry.**

Well we can talk as much as we want when we get to the Church, she wrote. **It will be loud and half the people will already be drunk.**

32

The full name of the punk house, it turned out, was the Church of Go Fuck Yourself, but everybody just called it the Church. The house was big, ramshackle, set into the side of a steep hill. We had to climb precarious concrete steps with rusty railings to reach it from the road.

We entered a cavernous space. Several walls had been ripped out between connecting rooms, leaving only the skeleton of load-bearing beams, scabs of torn plaster. At the far end of the space, a small stage sat beneath a large window, which had been made to look like stained glass with sheets of colored plastic, like theater gels. A gilded painting of an icon, Mother and Child, leaned on the sill.

"Sam?" said Denise.

"What?" asked a girl standing next to her.

"Oh, never mind."

I recognized one or two people from yesterday's party, though many were strangers and quite a few looked older, college-aged. Some were in costume. A band, not Neely's, was setting up on the stage.

Denise threaded her way through the crowd. I followed, trying not to be bumped into.

A doorway at the back of the room led into a small kitchen. An Exit sign leaned on the counter, arrow pointed at the refrigerator. I watched as a girl with feathered hair and big glasses opened it. We'd visited an art exhibit in Santa Fe once, *The House of Eternal Return,* where the fridge was a secret tunnel, and I half expected this to be the same.

This fridge held only beer. Still, this house was not unlike that one in some ways. Every surface was marked, decorated. The walls were graffitied. On the outside of the stove someone had painted in drippy red: BURN BABY BURN.

I drifted behind Denise, following her from one room to the next. The place was mazelike, something hidden in every corner. I'M SO GOTH I'M DEAD was carved into a banister.

We found Jules sitting on the staircase.

"Oh, thank goodness," they said when they saw us. "This crowd freaks me out. I think I might be the youngest person here."

"Where're the others?" Denise asked.

Jules shrugged. "I lost them."

I had pressed myself against a wall to avoid being bumped into. A laughing group squeezed past Jules and Denise on the stairs. Loud music started up in the other room. Denise looked worried.

She turned, peering down the hallway.

"Hey!" she shouted. "Hey, Ed!"

A short, muscular guy—Ed, presumably—came over. Snaking across his right arm was what I first took to be a tattoo but a closer inspection proved it was a scar, raised and knotty, the skin a shiny pink.

"Have you seen Neely?"

"Not since she got here," said Ed. "Squirrel Kill is up next, so she better not have bounced."

"Shit," said Denise as he moved on.

"What's wrong?" I asked, speaking for the first time since we'd arrived. The music from the next room was loud enough and no one was near us, so it was probably safe.

"She gets really nervous before shows sometimes," said Denise. "I hope she's not having a panic attack or something. We should find her."

"I'll help," I said. She had helped me so much. I needed to help her, too. Needed to make myself useful, so she'd want to keep me around.

Denise and Jules headed upstairs to look. I circled the downstairs again, weaving between groups of people, sliding along the walls.

I saw someone heading out the front door and thought I'd better check outside. Sure enough, I spotted Neely down the street a little ways, smoking and pacing in front of a white van.

I was about to go tell Denise when Neely kicked one of the van's tires hard, shouted, "Fuck!" At nobody. Watching her reminded me of watching Tess. They did look alike, a little bit. And Neely, it seemed, was also full of anger. She stalked back toward the house, breezing past where I stood on the front walk.

I ran along after her, around the side of the house, to the

backyard, where overgrown weeds were doing their best to break apart a concrete-slab patio. A group of people stood around a firepit. Neely marched up to two figures: Tess, who was smoking a cigarette, and the skinny guitarist, who was sipping from an actual metal flask. The firelight played on their faces, made demons of all of them.

I crept closer so I could hear.

"You were supposed to be out there ten minutes ago," Neely was saying.

"Chill the fuck out, Neely," said the guitarist.

"No, I will not chill. We agreed to meet at the van fifteen minutes before the set, and I've been—"

"No, we never agreed to that," Tess cut her off. "You just declared that it was going to happen. It wasn't even a discussion."

"Well," Neely shot back, "if you had a problem with it, you should have said so then. Now we aren't prepared. We need to go over the set. Warm up."

"I *am* warming up," said the guitarist. He raised his flask.

Neely knocked it out of his hands. It clattered to the concrete. Several people in the yard turned to look. I thought maybe I should go get Denise, but I couldn't tear my eyes away from Tess, the way the orange light of the fire reflected in her eyes.

"I don't think we want the same things anymore," Tess said simply. "For the band."

"Yeah," spat Neely, squaring her shoulders, drawing herself up to her full height, which was a full head taller than

Tess. "You're right. Sometimes it seems like I'm the only one who cares about this fucking band."

"Well, you don't have to anymore," said Tess, in a tone like broken glass.

"Have to what?" asked Neely.

"Care. About the band."

"What the fuck's that supposed to mean?"

The skinny guitarist was looking away, toward the shadows. I shifted sideways so he wouldn't be looking at me. Not that he could see me anyway.

"We talked," Tess said, "and we think it's best if we continue without you."

I sucked a quick, shocked breath in through my nose. Neely took a step back, shoulders sagging. She looked delicate all of a sudden, alone, made of matchsticks, the firelight accenting the hollows of her cheeks. It was silly—I hadn't known her nearly as long as I'd known Tess, and yet somehow my sympathies were entirely with her in this moment. I couldn't understand what she'd done to deserve this.

Tess must have had her reasons. She was stone-faced, features set in a hard blank.

"This is bullshit," Neely said. "You can't kick me out of the band. I started the band."

"Well—" Tess began.

Neely didn't let her finish. "Without me there is no band. I'm the one holding this whole thing together. I do everything. You guys just want to drink and party and take selfies."

"Now, hold it right there." Tess's cool façade cracked. She

blazed up, all the anger I knew was inside her rising to the surface. "I'm the lead singer. I'm the face of Squirrel Kill. I know how to promote shit. Okay? You say you care, but then you laugh at me for my 'social media bullshit.' That's how you get anywhere these days. You can cling to your grass-roots punk rock fantasy, but it is stupid and pretentious and you know it, Neely. You're not holding the band together. You're holding it back. You're trying to be so authentic, but you are more fake than me in every way."

The words lingered in the air for a moment, no sound besides the crackling of the fire. Neely looked as stunned as I felt.

"Fuck you," Neely spat finally. She wheeled away.

The guitar guy had retrieved his flask from the ground. He handed it to Tess. She took a swig, turned back to the fire.

I'd always admired Tess's anger, envied it, even. But I'd never seen her turn it against other people like this, and I had to admit, right now she just seemed cruel.

The Castle Tower

Tess's mother was obsessed with appearances. She'd had her on a diet since she was six. She bleached the fine hair on her daughter's upper lip when she was only nine. She took her to get electrolysis treatments at eleven. Dressed her up. Taught her how to do makeup. Taught her to suck in her cheeks for pictures. Made offhand remarks about the state of her waistline. I knew all this from Tess's journal.

I feel like one of her stupid dolls, she wrote. *Like a thing.*

For her, as for my mother, being seen was a burden.

And so once she grew up, once her anger had grown inside her for years, she tried to thwart her mother. She wore black clothes, ripped clothes, large and shapeless clothes. She wore no makeup or she wore sloppy dark eyeliner.

Punk uniform. Still a way of dressing to belong, but a changed allegiance. No more sweet dresses or neat slacks. No more preppy pastels. Tess tried to dress not to please the eyes of others, but to shield herself from them.

It was fascinating to me. A part of living I could never fully understand. I dressed myself in all sorts of fancy nonsense because it pleased me, but I never had to worry what other people would think about me. Nobody ever thought anything about me. They did not judge me as rich or poor, as slutty or demure.

And men's eyes, older men's eyes especially, never lingered on me. Tess wrote about that in her diary. How their gazes felt like unwanted touches sometimes.

Which is how it must have felt to my mother when her father looked at her the wrong way.

There's a lot she never told me, but I've been able to fill in some of the missing pieces. It's difficult for me to imagine my mother at my age, imagine her younger than me, even. My mother a teenage girl. My mother *visible*.

I know she didn't have many friends. She didn't talk much to the kids her own age, because she felt cut off from them, even though they could see her. Maybe she felt cut off from them *because* they could see her.

Maybe she felt cut off because she couldn't tell anybody what was happening to her. She's never told me, exactly, but I can guess.

My mother was poor. She didn't have lots of stuff, didn't have nice clothes. She's told me that. She's scolded me, when it seems I do not appreciate the luxuries of which we so casually partake.

Tess is rich. Most of the people whose houses we inhabit are rich. They have more stuff than they could ever possibly need. It makes them comfortable, clearly, but it doesn't make them happy.

33

I followed Neely, feeling oddly responsible for her now. I'd keep an eye on her, make sure she didn't do anything stupid. She wiped away tears with a sleeve as she stalked back around the side of the house, kicking at the weeds, and then headed down the hill to the van.

I thought she might get in and drive away, but instead she opened the back, wrestled a keyboard out from where it had been wedged next to a guitar case and some amps. She grabbed one of the amps, too, balanced the keyboard awkwardly under one arm, marched it toward the house, the plug dragging along the ground.

I picked the plug up, quickly, with a gloved hand, unseen, held it so it wouldn't spark on the pavement. A minor guardian angel. She didn't even notice.

The previous band were just bringing their instruments out. Neely shouldered past a guy carrying a guitar case.

Inside, she pushed her way to the front of the crowd in the main room, knocking into several people, who grumbled but gave way. I followed, still holding on to the plug. I let go a moment before she climbed onto the stage. She set up her keyboard hastily.

"I'm Squirrel Kill," Neely said into the microphone. It wasn't on. "Somebody turn on the fucking mic!" she shouted.

A few people toward the front heard her, but this was not a place with a fancy sound system. There was just a switch on the mic itself, which Neely had failed to notice. Without really thinking, I stepped up onto the stage, leaned over, and flicked the switch myself. The mic buzzed on.

"I'm Squirrel Kill," Neely repeated, amplified now. "Just me."

She stomped back behind her keyboard. Started to play. Banging out chords angrily.

I recognized the tune from the party last night. But it was only part of it. No lyrics. People seemed to be treating it as background music. A few glanced over at the stage, but most continued talking, as loudly as before.

I remained rooted to the spot, standing by the microphone.

Here I was. Onstage.

It wasn't the first time. In fact, I'd been on much larger stages than this. It was one of the great ironies of my life: that I could stand in front of hundreds of people, all of them looking right at me, and remain completely unseen.

I spotted Ed, way in the back of the room, gesturing expansively to some girl, leaning a little too close to her as he talked, and I felt awful for Neely. Her playing was fine, but I understood why people weren't paying attention. She was just banging away angrily at the keyboard, staring down at her own hands. *She should sing,* I thought. Could she sing?

I'd hardly finished the thought when she opened her mouth and began to mouth words. Was she singing silently? I moved closer, trying to hear.

No, she was singing, but quietly, and her voice wasn't carrying at all.

Well, here I was.

Guardian angel, right?

Before I could think it through, I was pushing the microphone stand, the one set up near the front for a lead singer, slowly toward Neely.

She was still looking down, cheeks red with anger, so focused on her hands, she didn't even notice.

But other people did. Not everyone. Just a few people up front. I heard a *Hey, look,* heard a subdued *Whoa,* heard someone laugh, amused, heard a susurration of whispers traveling outward, away from me, a wave.

A shiver washed over me, scalp to heels, running down my back. People were looking at me. They couldn't see me, though. I was sure of that. I was safe. They merely saw the microphone stand moving on its own. Some straight-up *Fantasia* shit, as Jules would say. I didn't stop until I'd scooted the microphone close enough that it picked up Neely's voice.

She wasn't singing the lyrics from the song she was playing. Not that I actually knew them, but I was pretty sure I remembered them sounding different than this. She wasn't even really singing. Just talking. Chanting, almost. Low, nearly under her breath, though with the microphone, it took on an interesting loud-soft quality.

"*Go fuck yourselves,*" she was saying. "*Go fuck yourselves. Go worship at the Church. Beg forgiveness. It will never come. You will never get it. Never ever get it.*"

She was improvising, I was almost certain. Ranting at her ex-band, riffing on the name of the house we were in, but it kind of worked. It was raw.

She was managing to rant with a certain hypnotic rhythm, with a definite intensity.

I looked out at the crowd. More of them were paying attention now. A girl up front was saying something to the boy beside her, pointing at Neely.

No, at the microphone stand.

It wasn't that dramatic, what I'd done. Onstage in a stadium, that kind of effect would have been absolutely nothing amid pyrotechnics, lasers. So what? The microphone could move on a track, or via magnets, whatever. But this was a grungy punk house. They weren't expecting anything fancy.

Neely had gotten quieter again, her voice breaking, like she might cry.

"*You are nothing. Without me, you've got nothing. Empty bottles. Empty songs. Go get fucked up if you want to.*"

People in the back were still talking. I heard someone laughing loudly. Too loudly. Neely's eyes flickered for a moment up from her hands, to the crowd, back down. Tess was there now, I saw, toward the back, scowling.

I reached out for the microphone stand, to scoot it closer. But there were cords on the floor blocking the way. So instead, I popped the microphone itself free from the stand, lifted it into the air.

There was a collective intake of breath from the crowd. Someone whistled. This wasn't like last night. No one screamed. They thought this was planned. Thought this was on purpose.

They fucking loved it.

Loved me?

No, but almost. I was like an actor disappearing into a role.

All I was doing was holding the microphone. But to them it seemed like magic. I could almost feel it, in a way I usually couldn't, feel the way my power must appear to other people.

I moved the microphone closer to Neely's face.

Floated it, from the crowd's perspective.

"*I don't care,*" she sang/chanted, "*go away if you want to, leave me alone, I am better alone.*"

Everyone was staring at the microphone, whispering. Neely's eyes flicked up again, glanced at the crowd, the microphone. She blinked hard at it. Her voice faltered for a moment, but then she kept going.

"*You can worship at the Church, I am my own fucking church, I am a chapel, I'm the pope, I am a burning bush on fire with the power of go-fuck-yourselves.*"

Her voice rose at the end of the last line, getting louder, almost a shout. She banged out some new chords on the keyboard, a key change. I was pretty sure she wasn't sticking to the old song anymore. This was something new.

She let out a whoop, a wordless yowl.

Neely reached out for the microphone. I held my breath, timed it just right. An instant before her hands would have encountered mine, I yanked them away. The microphone dropped. She caught it. The crowd went wild.

New York, NY

My mother and I had gone to many Broadway plays. All of them, even an opening-night sold-out performance, were free for us. If it was a very popular show, we sometimes had to stand, or sit in the aisles, but that was fine.

I loved the theater, couldn't get enough of it. We could go wherever we wanted, so I got to see behind the scenes, too. The cramped corridors and little rooms under the stage, the sandbags and lighting rigs.

We watched one play, the whole thing, from the wings. A strange sideways view. I was fascinated by the moment each actor exited the stage. Many of them stayed in character for several feet past the bright lights, and then their body language would shift subtly. They would collapse back into themselves.

Another night, which I will never forget for as long as I live, my mother let me watch from onstage. I had begged her to let me do this. She'd told me it was too risky, but I insisted I'd be careful. Insisted I just wanted to see what it was like up close. As close as I could get.

It would be educational, I told her. That was her

weakness. She felt guilty sometimes that I never went to school.

And so there I sat, in the middle of the set, perched on the edge of a table that I knew no one would touch until the end of the third act. I could see the actors, see their makeup, the little droplets of sweat beading along their foreheads. They passed within inches of me. It was like I was in the play.

My secret stupid dream. More stupid, perhaps, than the idea that anyone could ever love me.

How I wished I could be one of those actors. How I wished, idiotically, that I could stride to the front of the stage and stand there, arms outstretched, face turned up to the light, and have all eyes on me.

In the final act of the play, I hopped down from my table. Weaving around an actor declaiming a monologue, I made my way slowly downstage, let the footlights fill me. I spread my arms, pretended the audience was looking *at* me, not through me.

And then my mother's hand clamped on my arm. She'd been waiting in the wings, but this must have scared her. Like an old vaudeville cliché, she dragged me from the stage.

34

I stood beside Neely, every nerve in my body buzzing. Sweat trickling down my forehead. There was sweat trickling down hers, too. Our hands had come very close to touching when she reached for the microphone, but I had been careful, precise. A fine performance.

"Thank you," Neely said into the microphone. "This next song is called 'Fried Eggs.'"

She replaced the microphone in the stand, moved the whole thing closer to her keyboard. She was feeling confident now, in her element. Partially thanks to me.

She flexed her fingers. The crowd was watching, waiting. She played a pretty, almost baroque trill up the keyboard, then hit a pedal with her foot and the notes fuzzed into distortion.

"*YOUR HEAD IS AN EGG,*" she shouted.

I had achieved my purpose. People were paying attention. I could stop now. I could leave the stage, fade away.

I didn't want to.

Neely was still just one girl alone on a stage. She'd found her energy now, was practically spitting her words out.

"I WANT TO BREAK IT."

But she couldn't move much. She had to stay behind the keyboard. The stage wasn't big, certainly, but she still looked small up there without the rest of her band.

"FRY IT UP WITH SOME BUTTERRRRRRRRRR."

She dragged the last word out and then spun it into a sort of yelp, and as she did so, I knelt and grabbed the nearest thing I could find, which was a cord running across the stage, and lifted it.

Murmurs of approval ran through the crowd. The cord was attached to an amp near the edge of the stage, but the end I held was loose, not currently hooked into any instrument. I shook it in time to the music, sending tremors and waves up and down, made the metal end dance like a charmed snake.

"EAT IT ON TOAST."

It was simple. Stupid, even. If they could have seen me, they would have all been, like, *Who is this stupid girl playing with a damn amp cord like she's a toddler?* But with me out of the picture, it looked like the cord had a mind of its own. Like it was alive, enchanted.

"SALT AND PEPPER, HOT SAUCE."

I whipped the cord so it slapped against the stage. I glanced over at Neely. She was staring at the cord now, eyes wide. Someone in the crowd cheered. I whipped it again, harder.

Neely screamed into the microphone. Not a terrified scream but a powerful one, starting low, getting louder, running up the scale.

I yanked the cord so hard it flew out of the amp, which toppled over. Disconnected, the cord whipped across the stage, nearly hit me in the face. I lost my grip on the end I was holding. The cord whacked against the opposite wall, slithered down onto the floor of the stage.

"YOUR HEAD IS AN EGG," shouted Neely, her voice raw from the scream. I wanted to do something else. Something better. I was intoxicated from the attention.

I saw the golden icon painting behind her, ran to it.

"I'M GOING TO EAT IT."

She smashed out one final massive chord on her keyboard. Right on time, I grabbed the painting of Mary and the baby Jesus. Lifted it and ran forward. Held it, my hands shaking with adrenaline, over Neely's head.

The notes of her last chord faded. The crowd erupted. Clapping and cheering and hollering.

"Holy mother of Jesus!" someone shouted.

Neely looked up, flinched as she saw the icon hovering, shaking, above her head. She reached for it. I let her take it the same way she had the microphone, pulling my own hands away quickly just as hers reached it.

"Thank you," she said, hugging it to her chest, though you could barely hear her.

She rushed off the stage, clutching the icon. The crowd was still clapping. I heard one or two shouts of "Encore" and "Go on, do some more."

I stood on the stage. Stood at the center of it. Soaked it in.

They didn't know it, but they were cheering, at least a little bit, for me.

Raton, NM

After the Broadway show, the one where I'd gone onstage, my mother said she was done with the city. We got on the train the next day, got off two days later in New Mexico, at a tiny station in a town with hand-painted store signs. There was a Boy Scout ranch in the area, a few miles out. A whole pack of scouts got off the train along with us, and we followed.

We raided their base camp that night, grabbed backpacks filled with supplies for scrawny twelve-year-olds to carry on a grueling multiday hike into the mountains. Which is what my mother planned for us.

"I don't want to do this," I told her.

"Okay," she said. "You can stay here." She gestured back at the Boy Scouts' campsite, the rows of canvas tents. I think she meant it.

But I didn't want to be alone, so I followed her into the wilderness, though I knew she was going there for the silence.

Look, it was beautiful. Haunting. The Sangre de Cristo Mountains painted red by the sunset. Aspen and ponderosa pine. Cinquefoil and blue columbine. Ancient petroglyphs carved into cliff walls. Barren rocky canyons as empty and echoing as the surface of the moon.

I hated it.

My legs ached. My lips cracked and peeled in the summer sun. I pulled at a dry flake of skin, I remember, let it float away on the wind. It popped into full visibility as soon as it left my body, left my hands.

I can be seen only when I'm dead, I thought.

But my mother loved the dry heat, the cold nights with so many stars that the sky looked fake, like a mural some rich person would paint on his ceiling. She seemed to be healed by it. She didn't speak to me for three whole days.

When she finally gave in, when she spoke to me, when she agreed to return to civilization, I could see how sorry she was to leave the wilderness.

I wondered what would have happened if I hadn't gone with her. Would she ever have come back?

35

Once it became clear that Neely wasn't coming back, somebody jumped on the stage, picked up the fallen cord to inspect it. Somebody else came to check out the microphone.

Reluctantly, legs rubbery with adrenaline, I left the stage.

I was full of it, still, the feeling I'd had when I was up there. Floating off the ground with it. Feet not touching the grimy, splintered floor.

Had Denise and Jules seen the performance? They alone would have known it was me.

I knew Tess had been in the crowd. What had she thought?

I should leave, I told myself. I've gone insane, I have gone too far, and I need to get out of here and not look back.

I ran to the front door, pushed my way out.

Three figures stood on the front lawn: Jules, Denise, and Neely.

"I'm a witch," Neely was saying as I approached. "I have magic powers. I can move shit with my mind."

She was pacing in a tight circle. Her hands were shaking.

"What happened with Tess and James?" Denise asked her.

"Those fuckers dumped me," Neely answered. "I'll curse them. Turn them into frogs or some shit."

"You're not actually a witch," said Jules.

"What am I, then? You saw that, right?"

"We saw it," said Denise.

"I've got powers. I've got mad powers."

"You can tell her," I said. Neely spun around, searching for the source of the voice. I was getting used to that. It was almost fun.

Denise grinned. I felt full of myself. I wanted credit. I wanted praise.

"Who said that?" Neely asked.

"Neely," Denise said. She took Neely's shoulders, spun her back around so she could look into her eyes. "I'm sorry, but you're not a witch. Sam is."

"Who?" Neely said.

Good question. Who was I?

Who the hell was I?

I didn't even know anymore.

Denise grabbed Neely's wrist and pulled it out in front of her, so her hand dangled in the air.

"Go on," said Denise, still grinning, enjoying being in on the joke. "Shake hands. Make friends."

With a twisty thrill of fear—I was getting used to that, too—I made the simple, monumental gesture of grasping Neely's limp hand with mine. Gloved, of course. But still.

Her eyes went wide, and she yanked her hand away.

"Remember the headless girl?" said Jules, their voice

soothing rather than teasing. "From the party? That wasn't a trick."

Neely didn't run or scream. She looked down at her hand, wiggled her fingers experimentally, looked up at the empty space. Then she thrust her hand back out, held it outstretched in the air, a determined look on her face.

She waited.

Cautiously, I reached forward again. Just rested my gloved palm against hers. She moved quickly, grasped at the air frantically until she'd caught hold of my arm.

"Holy shit!" she declared. "There's something here."

"Someone," Jules corrected her.

"Hello," I choked out, panic-stricken.

Neely flailed another hand out, coming straight for my face. Visions of Slots, the party, flashed. I yelped, dropped to the ground with a thump.

"Sam?" Denise said, in the general direction of the ground. "You okay?"

I managed a vague noise of positive confirmation.

"What's going on?" Neely asked.

And once again, Denise did the explaining for me. Jules had been calm when they found out this morning, accepting. They were calm now, too, a small knowing smile on their face.

Neely, on the other hand, was freaking out.

"Holy shit-balls," she said, and "What the fuck?" and "Are you serious?"

She kept squinting at the air, trying to see me. She kept reaching out her hands, trying to touch me.

I'd backed myself against the front of the house, the fear

I should have felt this whole time having finally caught up with me. Would she be angry? Would she start screaming? Would she tell everyone?

"Well, tell her thanks, I guess," Neely said finally, once Denise had convinced her that she was telling the truth. "That was the most amazing thing that's ever happened to me in my entire life."

"She can hear you," said Denise.

"Oh. Um, *thanks*!" This last bit she shouted at an empty spot I'd long since vacated.

"You're welcome," I said very quietly. Three heads swiveled my way. I sagged against the wall, weak with relief. This hadn't gone too badly.

A burst of fuzzed-out guitar came from the house behind us.

"Ugh," said Neely, scowling. "That's them. They're playing without me. The goddamn nerve."

"Maybe you can get the band back together," suggested Denise.

"Never. I hope they rot." Neely brightened suddenly. "Sam, can you, like, mess them up? Unplug their amps or something?"

I was startled to be addressed. Neely was staring at the wall several feet to my left.

"She doesn't have to do that," said Denise. Then, to the air: "You don't have to do that."

"If I actually had witch powers, that's what I would have done. How about it, Sam? You and me, huh? You can be in my new band. We'll be way better than them."

Neely stomped back up to the house. She turned at the front door, waiting.

For me.

She'd accepted me that quickly. How could I not repay her? And Tess really had been a jerk to her—I'd seen it myself.

"I don't know if that's a good idea," Denise said.

"Come on, Sam," Neely said.

I must have still been high off my performance. Because Denise was right. Of course, it wasn't a good idea. But I followed Neely as she pushed through the front door and headed inside.

I'd be willing to do far worse than what she was asking in exchange for what she was willing to give. *How about it, Sam? You and me, huh?* I had done worse for less, hadn't I? Those paintings in their golden frames.

"Sam?" Neely hissed once she'd reached the back of the crowd. She craned her neck up to see Tess and the guitarist, who I guess was called James. "You with me?"

"Yeah." I was with her. How odd, to be *with* anyone.

Her eyes were shining in the dim light. Her face was full of mischievous glee.

"I'll owe you one hell of a favor if you do this," she said. "You don't mind, do you?"

"What?" said someone standing near us. "Are you talking to me?"

I pushed up through the crowd without answering, wove my way to the stage, climbed up onto it as I had before. But I was careful this time, quick. Just knelt beside an amp and popped the cord out very gently. The sound of the guitar dropped out. James shook his head, confused. Tess shot him a dirty look.

James picked up the fallen cord and hurriedly plugged it back in. Kept playing.

My heart pounded in my ears. My hands were sweating in their gloves. I moved slowly, so slowly, toward Tess.

She hardly looked real under the stage lights. Or maybe she looked too real. Strands of her hair were plastered to her forehead with sweat. A few drops of spit flew into the air as she shouted the song.

She was still beautiful to me, still made my stomach turn. Did I really know her? Was she the girl I'd fallen in love with two years ago, through notes, through reading her secret words? Or the girl I'd seen being cruel to Neely in the yard?

I put out a shaking hand, my eyes flicking back and forth between it and Tess. My stupid Jell-O mold hand. See-through, still in the same silk gloves that I hadn't even had a chance to wash. The silk was going gray with grime.

What if I just reached forward? What if I touched her face?

I reached forward, switched off the microphone. Tess's voice went quiet and then cut out completely as she stopped singing abruptly.

"Fuck this," I heard her say. She snatched up a beer bottle that had been sitting near her feet and stomped off the stage, brushing right past me, so close I could smell the alcohol on her breath.

James stood openmouthed for a moment, as alone as Neely had been before, but he didn't try to keep going. He shrugged, then said, "Show's over, folks."

Tess could have simply switched the microphone back on. She hadn't even tried.

Regret rushed through me. I'd gone too far. I needed to follow her, needed to apologize.

My loyalty should have been with her, shouldn't it? I'd known her first. I was in love with her, wasn't I?

I pushed through the crowd. Overheard murmured snippets of conversation. *Is Neely coming back on? That was wild. Such a cool trick. How did she do it? I thought I was just too high at first. Yeah, same.*

I bumped into people but didn't care. Ripped black jeans, vests with patches. Black boots. Thrift store T-shirts. But none of them Tess. I didn't stop, couldn't stop.

If I could do what I had just done. Could do what I had done on the stage earlier. If I could be that brave. If I could be that stupid.

Then I must be ready to do something even braver, even stupider. Something I'd been dreaming about doing for two years.

I was going to find Tess. I was going to tell her everything.

It was the reason I'd made my mother come to Pittsburgh. Maybe the reason she'd disappeared. If I didn't do this, then it was all for nothing. All my selfishness, all the lies I'd told.

I couldn't tell you before, I'd say. *But it's me. I'm the one who left you all those notes. It's me. I'm invisible. I exist. I'm sorry.* And she would realize, wouldn't she? Realize how wrong she'd been two years ago. She'd remember the connection we had. All those notes we'd written. She'd forgive me. She'd accept me, just as Denise and Jules and Neely had done.

I raced through the rooms. The kitchen with the EXIT sign by the refrigerator, a growing stack of empty cans and bottles in the sink. No Tess.

The stairwell, crowded now with people lounging, talking, smoking. No Tess.

Out the front door. The sky a dark blanket. Around the side, to the back.

On the ground, bits of broken bottle caught the flickering light of the dying fire. I paused, picked up one of the shards. A green-brown jewel. It nicked my thumb with a sharp edge, and my blood oozed out, translucent.

The glass wall. Broken. Dangerous. What was I doing?

And then I saw, at the edge of the dying fire's light—Tess.

Her back to me. Arm raised to the side of her head. I moved toward her.

Tess, far away.

Tess, closer.

Tess, right beside me. A breath between us.

Tess on the phone. Her voice quick, ragged.

"It's here. Right now. I swear, the ghost is here. It must be the same one."

I stopped short, my heart stuttering.

"I think it's angry. I think it's haunting me. This is just like the bullshit that happened in my house two years ago."

She meant me. She was talking about me.

"So can you help?" she asked. "Like, do an exorcism or something? Make it go away?"

It felt like the ground had dropped out beneath me. Felt like I was falling.

I didn't need to tell her about me. She already knew, didn't she? Already knew she wanted to get rid of me. There'd be no acceptance here.

"Oh, thank goodness," she said. "Yeah, no, sorry, it's not a real church. Do you have a pen?"

The darkness of the sky was pressing down on me, melting, dripping into the yard, blotting out the trees, blotting out my view of everything but Tess. The world going dark. Nothing but her. Leaning into the phone, one hand cupped around it, conspiratorial, giving the address.

"Thank god you contacted me," she said. "I just want this to be over. Can you please hurry? I don't know what the ghost will do next."

The Castle, Crumbling

There is something I haven't told you about the last time we lived in Pittsburgh. Something I don't like to think about.

Something I did that day before we left town. The day I saw Tess kiss Taylor.

Touching the wall was bad enough. Blotting out a whole building with my careless jealousy.

But I didn't stop there.

I kept thinking how stupid I was. What a pitiful loser. My idiotic bubble of hope shattered. It seemed so unfair that Tess could have this much power over me when she didn't even know I existed.

I was angry.

At myself, mostly. But at her, too. I'm not proud of that. None of it was her fault, not even a little bit. I can see that clearly now. How selfish my love had been.

I went back to her house. Got there well before she did. She and Taylor probably got frozen yogurt and ate it while cuddling on a park bench or something stupidly cute like that. I let myself in the basement window. Tess's parents were out. I could tell because the house was dark. So I called, aloud, for my mother, but she was out, too. If she'd been home, I don't know what I would have done. Burst into tears? Confessed everything?

Instead, I broke shit.

Didn't think. Just let it all out. Every feeling I'd been holding inside for the last few months. I let it all bubble out, and I picked up a decorative glass bowl that sat on the kitchen island to hold fruit and I hefted it above my head and I smashed it on the ground. Once I'd started, I couldn't stop.

36

In the dark backyard, my first instinct was to run.

That's what my mother had taught me.

That's what we did in situations like this. When people called the exterminators or the exorcists, we left. Who had Tess been calling? A friend? A priest? I thought of the paranormal researcher lady that the girl at the grocery store had mentioned. Was someone out there trying to track me down?

No matter what, it felt dangerous. The reality of what I had done tonight was hitting me hard, a fast hangover.

But I forced myself to take a deep breath, to go back inside. I found Denise. Tapped her on the shoulder. She turned, eyes searching for something they'd never find. Would she be mad at me after what I'd done? I hoped not.

"I need to go," I whispered urgently.

"Is everything okay?" she asked. I was relieved to see only concern in her eyes.

I thought about telling her the truth—about Tess—but it was too big, too messy.

"Yeah," I said. "I'm sorry. It's just—I shouldn't have done all that. It was too much."

She checked her phone. "We probably need to get back anyway. Hold on a second."

She interrupted Jules and Neely, who were nearby, chatting.

"We're heading out. You staying here with Ed?" Denise asked Neely.

Neely toed at the floor with her boot. "Could I crash at your place?"

"Of course," Denise answered.

We all left, headed down the hill, waited for the bus back. I was starting to feel sick to my stomach. Actually sick, like I might throw up. Was I catching the same thing as my mother?

I imagined her standing on the front stoop of the house when we returned, furious as all get-out, ready to ground me for a month in a tent in the woods to think about what I'd done. I would go willingly, would savor the silence. I deserved it, and it would mean she was back.

During the ride, Neely filled Denise and Jules in on the fight she'd had with her former bandmates. I stayed silent, even when we got off the bus. My boldness earlier in the night was having a kickback effect: I couldn't even bring myself to speak.

The temperature had dropped, and I had no coat. I can't really wear winter coats. Not easily. If I layer my clothes too much, I risk having the top layer show. That's part of why my mother and I usually stick to warm places. After New York, we'd probably have headed down to Florida or maybe back to the Southwest. I hugged my arms around myself, shuffled behind the others, head down.

Larissa came padding down the stairs when we came in

the front door of the house. She was in a robe and slippers, her hair wrapped in a scarf.

"Cutting it close," she said.

"Sorry, Ma," Jules answered.

"Sorry, Miss Larissa," Neely said. "Is it okay if I sleep here tonight?"

"Of course, Neely. You know what I said, any time you need to."

"I'll make up the couch," Jules offered.

I realized suddenly what it meant that Neely was staying over. She would sleep on the couch. Of course, she would. Somehow I'd just assumed I'd sleep there again. But I had no reason to think that. It wasn't mine.

Would I need to find somewhere else to go? I could sleep in the graveyard.

But no, Denise and Jules were kind. I'd acted foolish tonight, but they'd probably still let me sleep on the floor somewhere, wouldn't they? Maybe in the basement?

"Sam," Denise said, startling me. "You here?"

Her aunt had headed back upstairs.

"Oh," I said. My voice came out a whisper—all I could manage. "Yeah, sorry. I can go if you want."

"What? Why?"

"Just, uh, if the house is full."

"Oh, right." She glanced into the living room. "You probably wouldn't have been able to sleep there tonight either way, now that Larissa and Terrance are back. They might try to sit on you."

Or notice the depression my body made. She was right.

I was even stupider than I'd realized. Was it even safe to stay here at all? I should have been thinking ahead. Should have just run away after I overheard Tess on the phone. Run like my mother taught me.

The graveyard, then. I could borrow a blanket, maybe, break into a tomb and sleep beside a corpse. I was about to ask Denise about the blanket, but she spoke before I could.

"You'll just have to sleep in my room."

I was too stunned to respond. I'd never even thought of that as a possibility.

Which was stupid. I know it was. I can see that now. But even in all the time we'd stayed with Tess, I'd never slept in her room. Not once. Sleeping in the same room as other people was risky. I hadn't done it in years.

I followed Denise upstairs.

"The futon is big enough," she said once we were both in her room with the door shut. "I've shared with friends before." She pulled an extra blanket from her closet, set it on one side of the futon. "You don't mind, do you?"

Mind?

Well, I was freaking out.

This wasn't dangerous the way my brain was telling me it was. Denise already knew I existed. There was no risk that I'd make a noise in my sleep and give away my presence.

But at the same time, I had never, ever shared a bed with anyone other than my mother. Like I said, I'd barely shared a room.

What if I accidentally touched her foot with my foot? I might die.

"I don't mind," I said.

"We can even make a wall, see." She rolled up a third blanket and laid it down the middle of the futon. "I did that when my friend Kylie stayed over in sixth grade, because she was, like, *Don't try to lesbian me or anything* and I was, like, *Bitch, please, I do NOT like you that way*."

Denise rolled her eyes.

"Right, yeah," I mumbled. "It's not a problem."

Denise slipped off to the bathroom to change and brush her teeth. I didn't have pajamas. My mother and I usually just slept in our clothes. I took off my shoes, at least, and my backpack, set them in the corner. I crawled awkwardly onto my allotted half of the futon and burrito-wrapped myself tightly in the blanket. It was invisible now, as was the pillow where my head rested, but I arranged it so I wouldn't make the whole futon disappear.

Denise returned and switched off the light. The futon shook as she slid onto her half. I held myself rigid, stiff, terrified of moving.

I doubted I'd be able to sleep.

"Tell me a secret," Denise said.

"What?" I flinched, startled in the silence.

"When I was younger and I used to have sleepovers, we'd always tell secrets before we fell asleep. With everybody lying awake in the dark, not being able to see each other, it felt like you could say anything. It was freeing, you know."

"Oh, right," I said, but I had no idea what she was talking about. Secrets aren't for telling people. They're for keeping. That's what makes them secrets.

"Well, go on," said Denise.

"Uh."

"It doesn't have to be a big secret," she prompted. "At sleepovers we mostly just told each other who we had crushes on that week."

I already told her the biggest secret there is. The biggest secret was hello. The biggest secret is that I exist.

"Okay, fine," said Denise. "I'll start. You know Tess, the singer in Neely's band? Or I guess maybe she's not anymore."

"Yeah," I said. I wanted to tell Denise to stop. I was pretty sure I knew what she was going to say, but for some reason, I didn't want to hear her actually say it.

"Well, I have a crush on her."

"Oh," I said.

Denise laughed uncomfortably. "It's part of why I was so eager to throw that party at our house. To impress her or something. Which is so stupid. Like she's ridiculously rich, and she's kind of a party animal. I don't think she'd even give me a second glance if I didn't take pictures for the band."

It was strange to hear Denise talking this way. Almost as if I was listening to myself.

Maybe it should have made me feel better, like solidarity or something, like we had something in common. But it didn't.

Denise actually knew Tess. Actually talked to her, interacted with her. They lived together in a world I was not a part of. They were both real.

"You don't go to the same school as her, do you?" I asked. Not that I could possibly remember everyone I'd seen at

Tess's school two years ago, but for some reason I thought I'd have noticed Denise.

"No, she goes to Catholic school. Jules and I go to CAPA."

"To what?"

"Oh, sorry. It's like a magnet school for artsy shit. Neely went there for music before she dropped out. We take math or whatever in the morning and then spend all afternoon on art stuff."

"That sounds cool."

"It's fine, but it's also your turn. Don't think I've forgotten."

I could hear her turning over to look at me. The glow of a distant streetlamp through the window was enough to outline the room in gray. But I didn't dare look at Denise. I was far too aware of how close she was. I squeezed my eyes shut.

"Go on," she said. "Any secret."

What could I tell her?

That I've watched people have sex right in front of me?

That I'm almost certain my mother once killed someone?

"Do you have a crush on anybody?" Denise asked, teasing. I almost laughed.

"I did, I guess," I said. "There was a girl my age whose house my mother and I stayed in a few years ago. And I had a crush on her. But she didn't know I existed, and I never actually spoke to her."

"Oh," said Denise, sounding disappointed. "That's really sad."

It was.

And it felt dangerous to say it out loud like that, even

281

with all the details stripped away. It made me uncomfortable, desperate to change the subject before Denise asked any follow-up questions.

"Also," I said, "my name isn't actually Sam."

"What?"

I opened one eye, regretting my words already. Denise was leaning up on an elbow. In the darkness, I couldn't see her expression.

"Um, yeah, I'm sorry. That was just a name I gave at the party."

"Well, shit, what's your real name?"

"Pietà. But I go by Pie."

"Huh. Well, I guess I'd better call you Pie."

She was silent then. We both were. The futon jostled as she rolled over. I could hear her rustling the blankets. She hated me now. Regretted letting me stay. Regretted letting me share her room, share her bed.

"You okay?" Denise asked into the silence. "Pie?"

I wasn't. Not by a long shot.

But the fact that she had asked me that—the fact that anyone was asking me that—well, it made me so happy for a moment that I wasn't entirely lying when I said yes.

I lay as still as I could, not daring to move. Even with the blanket wall, I was aware of Denise's terrible, wonderful proximity. I could hear her breathing. Even when I closed my eyes, I could almost make out the shape of her, as clear as day, beside me. I drifted, finally, her words echoing in my mind.

Memphis, TN

I woke to the scent of burning. Opened my eyes to see a young woman in flowy pants and a wrap shirt, both dyed in sunset ombré, waving a bundle of sticks above the couch where I lay. The sticks were on fire. Sage-scented smoke snaked upward.

She was, I realized groggily, smudging out the bad spirit: me.

I clutched my backpack—which had spent the night on the couch with me, one strap looped carefully around my wrist so it would stay invisible—and rolled off the couch.

My mother, who'd been sleeping on an oversized bean-bag chair in the next room, appeared in the doorway. "Time to go," she signed. I was used to this. Getting up. Getting out. Never getting quite comfortable before it was time to move on.

We drifted away, the two of us, as insubstantial as the purifying smoke that curled toward the ceiling and disappeared.

37

I woke to the scent of burning. Jolted upright, still mummi-fied in a blanket. I didn't move much when I slept, a habit from years of sleeping in small train compartments.

Denise, on the other hand, was sprawled, one arm flung across the blanket wall, one leg sticking out of her quilt onto the floor.

I rolled inelegantly off the futon with a thump and stumbled to my feet, disentangling myself from the blanket. Sleep-addled, I was certain that the house was on fire. I had to run. Had to get out. No firemen would save me. No one would even look for me.

Denise blinked her eyes open in time to see the blanket pop into existence as I finally wriggled free of it.

"Morning," she said.

"What's that smell?" I whispered urgently.

She sniffed. "Someone must be making toast."

"Over a bonfire?" My nerves were calmed slightly by her complete lack of concern.

"Our toaster is half broken," she explained. "Sometimes it works fine. Sometimes it demands a sacrifice."

I could go to the store, grab a new toaster. One that looks kind of like their old one. Switch it out. A benevolent ghost.

Maybe that was what I should have been doing all along. Staying in smaller, run-down houses. Sneaking in gifts. Making them nice.

But smaller houses didn't have room for ghosts.

How long would I be able to stay here? I would wear out my welcome any minute, I was sure of it.

Still jittery, I trailed Denise downstairs. Neely was snoring gently on the couch. Denise's uncle Terrance was up, making scrambled eggs to go with the burned toast. He'd grated some of the cave-aged Gruyère I'd picked up from Giant Eagle onto the eggs.

"Did you kids get all this?" he asked Denise, indicating the cheese.

She squinted at it. "No."

"Huh. Well, I sure don't remember buying it."

Denise blinked hard, frowned over at the wall to her left. I was behind her. "Maybe Neely brought it," she said.

"Neely?" Terrance sounded surprised, a little doubtful. "She didn't have to do that. Well, tell her thanks from me."

He served up a steaming plate of eggs. I wanted some but didn't feel right sneaking a plate like I normally would at a restaurant or the house of a stranger.

Denise was on it. "Hey, can I have another plate to take up to Jules?"

"Sure."

About five minutes later, we were heading up to the attic.

Denise had poked Neely awake, and she came up with us, balancing three cups of coffee (one for Jules) on a small tray.

As soon as we made it to the third floor, Neely burst out, "Is Sam still here?"

Instead of answering, I reached out, grabbed one of the coffee mugs with a gloved hand, floated it to my mouth, took a sip.

Neely shrieked with delight, which woke Jules, who'd still been in bed.

We settled ourselves on the floor, sitting on pillows, surrounded by plants, and shared our breakfast. Bathtub the cat trotted up the stairs, tried her best to steal a bite of eggs.

"Sam," Neely said, "you've got to be in the band with me."

I laughed. "I can't play any instruments."

"Just bang a garbage can lid or something," Denise suggested. "Neely digs experimental shit."

"Yeah," added Jules, "sounding terrible is very punk."

"Fuck you." Neely threw a pillow in their direction. Jules dodged neatly. "But, yeah, I don't think it matters if you're, like, classically trained or whatever. Jules, where's your laptop?"

Jules groaned but pointed to a computer. A minute later, Neely had pulled up a song on YouTube.

It . . . wasn't good. It sounded like a song taken apart and then put back together in the wrong order. Or like each instrument was playing a different song. A girl started singing in a monotone about her pal, whose name was Foot Foot.

"The Shaggs," said Neely, grinning. "Grandmothers of punk."

"You are such a hipster," said Jules.

"So are both of you," Neely shot back. "Anyway, yeah,

they can't really play. It isn't *good*"—she mimed air quotes—
"but it isn't mediocre, you know? It's bad in this really intense, unique way. It's got the invisible needles."

"The what?" I asked.

"Oh," said Neely, "no offense to, like, the invisible community or whatever." She made a cringing face, and I honestly couldn't tell if she was kidding or not.

"Uh," I said, "don't worry about it. But what did you
mean, 'invisible needles'?"

"I don't know. It's just something I used to think about
when I was younger."

"When you would get really stoned?" Denise asked.

Neely threw a pillow at Denise, too. It hit her in the face.
I laughed, clapped a hand to my mouth. But it was fine—
I was allowed to make noise.

"No," Neely went on, "before I ever did that. There were
some songs that I listened to and they were fine, they'd just
wash over me. But some songs, I didn't know how to describe
it, they got under my skin. Gave me chills. It was almost too
much. Like how can a simple progression of notes make me
cry? So I thought of it as invisible needles. Stabbing me all
over. Getting at the meat of me."

"You're weird," said Jules.

"So are you," said Neely.

"If we weren't all weird, we wouldn't be friends," said
Denise.

"That's why we like *you*," said Neely. I realized that she
meant me when she jabbed one finger out at the empty air to
my left. "That's why you belong in my new band."

I smiled so big it would have been embarrassing if they could see me. Hid my face in my hand.

To be liked. To belong.

That was something meant for other people. Not me.

And yet here I was. With sun pouring through the dormer windows, pooling like honey on the broad green leaves of a vining philodendron above the heads of my friends. My friends.

How dare I be so happy? When my mother was missing. When I was breaking every single rule that I lived by. When I was being an idiot every second of every day.

This was so much worse than Tess. Worse than notes.

I was in love with everyone. In love with the whole house, maybe. I wanted to compose odes to the philodendrons. Wanted to adopt Bathtub the cat, swaddle her in floral silk robes, rock her like a baby, sing her off-key lullabies. Wanted to kiss Cindy the mannequin on the mouth, like my mother told me she had done with the statues in museums once.

My happiness was almost too much. Like Neely had said. Needles. A happiness sharp and dangerous. I felt electric with it, this knife's-edge ecstasy. Balanced on that thin blade, everything felt perfect.

A millimeter to either side, though, disaster.

I knew it. I could feel it, lurking just out of sight: how easily this might all go wrong.

Winona, WI

We lived for a month and a half in an assisted-living retirement home. Every hallway was beige, featureless, identical, which seemed like a poor choice for a building full of people with dodgy memories.

I felt very tall when we lived there, although I was only eleven. There were all these tiny old women, some hunched over walkers, others upright but diminutive nonetheless. They moved slowly through the hallways, running stiff fingers along the handrails.

We stayed with the same woman the whole time we were there. Her white hair clung like wisps of cotton to her head. Her pants hung loose around her legs. I never saw them bare, but I imagined them as actual bones.

I didn't like it there, and I asked my mother many times if we could move on. *I'm bored,* I said. *The food from the café here is bland.* But my mother didn't listen. We stayed.

One afternoon, the woman collapsed.

Just fell to the ground a moment after standing up from the sofa. My mother and I had been sitting on the floor, watching *Jeopardy!* along with her, signing answers to each other.

When the woman fell, my mother jumped up, ran, and pulled the emergency call cord on the wall in the bathroom.

Then my mother did something I've only ever seen her do once: she broke her own rule.

She held the woman's hand. Grasped it in her own. I don't know if the woman was conscious or not. Couldn't even tell you if her eyes were open. I was too scared, had backed up against the wall.

My mother leaned down, whispered something into the woman's ear.

Members of the staff opened the door a few moments later, and my mother got up and moved away from the woman, whose hand grasped at the empty air.

38

"What about a surgical mask?" asked Neely. "That wouldn't draw too much attention."

"Those only cover half the face, though," Denise pointed out.

They were trying to fix me. After the Shaggs, Neely had played me more music. Poly Styrene and X-Ray Spex. The Raincoats. Bikini Kill, which her own band's name was a nod to.

Neely asked me questions, too. Did I go to school? What was my life like?

Every answer I gave seemed to delight her more. *You are so lucky,* she said. I found myself arguing, trying to convince her my life wasn't so great. How I had to be careful not to get found out or else I might get captured, studied, exploited. I told her I was jealous sometimes of kids who could live a normal life. Who had the option of going to the store, going to school.

And now this.

"Well, she could wear sunglasses, too," Neely said. "Ooh,

or how about one of those head covering things, what are they called? A hijab?"

"I think a niqab is the one that covers your face," said Jules, "but also that would probably be super disrespectful."

"Yeah, yeah, you're right. Okay, what if we said you had a terrible skin condition and you had to be wrapped in bandages?"

"Like a mummy?" Denise asked.

"I'm just brainstorming here."

"Paint," said Jules. "What about paint?"

"Oh," said Neely. "Or what about just super thick foundation?" She touched her own face.

Jules jumped up from the floor, went over to the vanity table, rummaged around in a drawer.

"Anything that touches my skin disappears," I said. It was kind of funny, the way they were fussing. Kind of sweet, too.

"Well, if you put it on thick enough, some of it would show up, right?" Jules held up a fistful of makeup—lipstick, foundation. "We saw your dress and your skull mask at the party, didn't we?"

I shrugged, which was stupid, because none of them could see.

"I have to layer," I explained. "Two pairs of gloves. Two masks. Two dresses. The bottom layer will be invisible. The top layers will show."

"So two layers of makeup would work, right?" Neely said.

"No, they are . . ." I struggled. "They are too similar. They'll count as one thing."

I knew there was no simple rule. It was my own brain, my own understanding of the boundaries of things that made my power work. If I could convince myself, truly, on a subconscious level, that blue paint and red paint were different things, truly separate entities, then layering them might work.

But I don't believe that. No matter how hard you pretend to believe something you don't, some part of your mind will know the truth.

No matter how hard I pretended to believe I could belong here, I knew I didn't.

"What if it was two different brands of makeup?" Jules asked. "Or, like, eyeshadow on top of concealer?"

It wouldn't work. I'd tried it all before. I'd tried everything. I'd even painted myself, once, when I was four or five, squeezed out a whole rainbow of acrylics, rubbed them into my skin like lotion, left smudges all over the house, and of course my mother was furious and of course it didn't make a difference.

But I didn't want to disappoint them. I didn't want them to give up on me. I wanted to keep pretending I belonged.

"I don't know," I said instead. "You could try."

So they did.

I sat in front of Jules's vanity, Neely hovering eagerly nearby. Jules rubbed a round brush onto a palette of coverup, reached it haltingly forward into the air. I held my breath. Finally, the bristles grazed my skin, and the whole brush went translucent—to their eyes, vanished.

I flinched away, involuntarily. Jules snatched the brush back, eyes wide.

"Wow," Neely said, "that's so cool."

"Are you okay?" Jules asked me. "Do you want me to stop?"

"No," I said. It was strange, to have the two of them so intensely focused on me. A little overwhelming. But I liked it, too. I was an actress, in the makeup chair before a performance. "Go ahead."

They tried layering different kinds of foundation. Tried putting blush on top of that. I tried to concentrate on how blush is a different kind of makeup. But it was still makeup. I knew that. I couldn't un-know that. They tried eye shadow, a shimmery highlighter. Neely ran downstairs, returned with a tube of her own foundation.

"This has really good coverage," she said.

But all of it vanished. In the mirror, I could see the chaos of my face, the streaks and smears of pigment, muted and diaphanous. But they couldn't see a thing.

"Ooh," exclaimed Neely, digging through the drawers of the vanity table. "Glitter! What if we tried glitter?" She held up a tube.

"Holy shit," said Jules. "Imagine if that worked, Sam. You could be a being of pure glitter. That would be killer."

"It wouldn't help her," Denise cut in. She'd been quiet for a while now, sitting against a potted fern, scrolling on her phone.

She sounded annoyed, though I didn't know why.

"What about papier-mâché?" asked Jules.

"She's not a piñata," said Denise. She heaved herself up and headed downstairs.

"Papier mâché?" I asked, watching Denise go.

"Well, I guess it would still just be a mask," said Jules. "Oh, or I have these plaster strips I could use." Jules went and dug through a stack of supplies in the corner of the room, returned a moment later with the roll of plaster strips. "I bet I could do like a realistic cast of your face. And then you could wear that. Like in *Mrs. Doubtfire,* though not quite as good as that, maybe. It would be something. Do you want to try that?"

"Yeah, maybe," I said. It sounded promising, actually, but right then I couldn't focus on it. "Just give me a minute."

I excused myself and went downstairs. Denise was in her room, hunched over her desk, clicking through pictures on the camera viewscreen. I knocked lightly on the doorframe.

"Hey," I said, thinking of the night before, when she'd asked me the same thing, "are you okay?"

She turned. "Yeah, I'm fine," she said, but in the kind of tone my mother had used two days ago. The kind of tone that made it clear she wasn't.

I wavered in the doorway, unsure whether I should say more. How would a normal person act in this situation? A person with friends?

The stairs creaked. Terrance and Larissa were coming up. Larissa said something and Terrance laughed, his voice deep and resonant, echoing up the stairwell. I froze.

Denise jumped up from her desk. "Pie," she whispered urgently, "where are you? Come in my room."

I shuffled in. Denise reached carefully forward, wary of hitting me, and pulled her door shut.

"Are *you* okay?" she asked me, still speaking quietly.

"Me? Yeah."

"It didn't bother you, the two of them messing with you up there?"

"Should it have?" I asked. They'd only been trying to help.

She shrugged. "Maybe I was just projecting. But it's like, all three of us get flak sometimes for not being the way society says we're supposed to be, you know? And like, you're different, but that's cool. We should just accept that and not try to change or fix you as if there's something wrong with you."

"Oh," I said. Probably I should have thanked her, or told her she was cool, too, because she was, but I was stuck on the rest of what she'd said. I'd always felt like there was absolutely something wrong with me.

I mean, there was, wasn't there?

Broken. Insubstantial. Less than real. Barely a person at all. These were all ways I'd described myself in my head. For all his peculiarities, though, I would never apply any of those words to the man I met the other day—Steve. He was different but happy, functional, solid in his own way.

So was it wrong, that I'd so often wished I could change?

"I don't think it's quite the same thing," I said. "I'd still be different, even if people could see me. And I'd like to be seen, sometimes."

"Yeah, sorry. I guess it was more about me." Denise returned to the desk, sat down. "Do you want to know something terrible?"

"Um . . . sure?" I said, still thinking about myself. Denise laughed, not a full laugh but a strained half laugh. "So the other night, when you tried to talk to me, I thought for sure I'd gone crazy. And there was a moment when I felt relieved. Like, I thought: *Okay, I can stop trying now. I can just give up.* Isn't that terrible?"

I made a noncommittal noise, uncertain what to say.

"It's wrong, anyway," Denise said, suddenly serious. "My mother's never given up. She's struggled a lot, yeah, but she keeps on trying. She has to try harder than most people, too. Maybe she's not 'normal' or whatever, but that doesn't make her any less valid." She sounded almost angry now, brows furrowed, both hands clenched.

"You're right," I said.

Denise shrugged, relaxed. "Sorry, I get kind of heated up about this stuff."

"No," I said, "that's cool."

"I'm going to visit her later today, actually. I always go Sunday afternoons. Um, I'd invite you, but it would probably be better if you didn't come. Just, like, no offense." Denise offered a slight smile in my direction. She got close, her eyes staring only a few inches to the left of me.

"None taken."

Now I was thinking about my own mother.

She'd become invisible because terrible things happened

297

to her when she was young. Because they kept happening and she couldn't make them stop. Disappearing was the only way her body knew how to escape.

It worked for her. She got away.

And yet she never really stopped. Her whole life, she kept running, trying so hard to keep us safe. Trying to outrun the danger that, in her mind, was always just one step away.

Winona, WI

"What did you say to her?" I asked my mother after the old woman in the retirement home had been taken away by the EMTs.

"I told her that I forgave her," my mother said.

"What?"

I stared at her, in the musty carpeted apartment, not understanding. My mother sighed, her forehead creased deeply.

"That was my grandmother," she said.

"Your . . ." I trailed off, unable to process what I'd heard.

"My father moved us far away from my mother's family when I was eight or nine. He cut off all contact with them. But later I found my grandmother's number. I called her and I tried to tell her . . . I wanted her to come get me, to take me away. But she didn't. She couldn't, or wouldn't, or didn't believe me."

I tried to wrap my head around that. The woman was my great-grandmother. And the whole time I hadn't known. If

I'd only had some idea, if my mother had only told me . . . "Is she coming back?" I asked.

"I don't know."

"Will we wait for her?"

"No," my mother said.

39

In the bathroom, I scrubbed at the wasteland of my face. As soon as the paint and makeup dripped off my skin into the sink, the colors returned to their full brightness, ran down the drain a garish mess.

When I was done, Denise and I headed out. We'd agreed that the house was too crowded. She called up the stairs to tell Jules and Neely she was leaving to work on her project but then hurried away before they could try to join her.

We walked together down the street, Denise holding her camera.

"So what do you think about being in some more pictures?" she asked me.

"Well," I said, "I admit I had never considered modeling a likely career prospect."

Denise laughed. "You're basically my muse now."

Not for the first time, I was glad she couldn't see my expression. My cheeks would no doubt have been red if they had any color at all.

"What happened to that dress?" Denise asked.

"Dress?" I asked, not sure what she was talking about.

"The wedding dress. From the party," she said.

"Oh." I thought back to my desperate, stumbling run. My panic, my hopelessness. It was not a flattering memory. "I kind of . . . threw it away."

Denise abruptly stopped walking. "You threw it away?" She sounded appalled.

"Uh, sorry."

She shook her head. "Well, damn. I'd been hoping maybe I could re-create a version of the photo like Tess had on her Instagram."

This gave me conflicting feelings. On the one hand, I wanted to help Denise. Wanted to make myself as useful as possible so she would continue to like me.

On the other hand, did Denise want to re-create Tess's picture because she had a crush on her? Would I be helping her win the heart of the girl I liked?

The former feeling won out, and Denise and I spent the next fifteen minutes or so scouring the alleyways.

The trash hadn't been picked up yet, luckily, and we found the dress. Denise pulled it from the can where I'd crumpled it.

"I can't believe you threw this out," she said. "It looks like it cost a fortune."

I didn't have a good response to that. It had cost me nothing, of course.

She shook the dress out. The hem was ripped and muddy from my escape, but it was no worse off than it had been when I'd thrown it away. The other trash in the can had been sealed safely away in a bag.

"You don't mind, do you?" Denise asked me.

"No," I said, because I knew that was the right answer.

I wasn't sure whether I minded. What did that even mean? All of this was still too new. Too strange and terrible and wonderful all at once.

I followed Denise back to the main street and down several blocks. She stopped in front of the brick house with the painting of the bride on the wall behind it.

"So I was thinking you could stand here," she said, pointing, "in front of the mural. Two ghost brides."

It would probably look cool. But I hesitated, looking back and forth between the wall and the nearby road. "It's kind of busy here," I said. "There's lots of cars."

"Oh." Denise sounded a little put out. "But you did that whole stage thing last night."

And she had a point. I'd thrown all the rules away, hadn't I?

That's why people liked me now.

Neely had accepted me because I'd been useful to her. My father seemed to primarily value me because I stole for him. I needed to stay useful to Denise. I had to keep her happy. That's what friends did.

"Right," I said. "Never mind. Wait here a second."

I took the dress from Denise and walked around behind the house, for privacy. Which was silly since she couldn't see me. I pulled the dress on over my other clothes, made some adjustments so it wasn't touching my skin anywhere. Once I was sure the dress was fully visible, I walked back out.

"That's so damn cool," said Denise, and I couldn't help smiling. I mean, it wasn't like she was really giving me a compliment. I hadn't done anything. But still.

I posed the way she told me while she snapped photos, tried not to think about the passing cars. Hopefully no one would notice, or if they did, they'd think nothing of it. My mind returned to the paranormal researcher the deli girl had spoken about, to the unknown person Tess had called to dispose of me.

"These look great," said Denise, peering at the viewfinder. "Come look."

She held out the camera, and I shuffled over, dress rustling, to see.

"Are you going to use these for your project?" I asked.

"Definitely," she said. "With the pictures we took yesterday, I have a full series. Just in time, because I've got to show them in class tomorrow. You totally saved me, Pie. You're the best."

No, you saved me, I wanted to say, but I felt too shy to speak all of a sudden.

I'd done it. I'd made her happy.

We were friends.

Denise's phone buzzed. She let her camera fall on its strap and pulled her phone from her pocket.

"Oh," she said, surprised, when she read the text. "It's Tess."

She went quiet as she exchanged several texts. A slow smile spread on her face.

My heart sank.

"She's in the neighborhood," Denise told me. "She wants me to meet her at Spak Brothers pizza. You want to come?"

"No," I said quickly, shucking off the wedding dress.

"That's okay. I think I'm going to head over to the art museum. There were some paintings Jules told me about that I wanted to see."

It was a lie, of course. Or a partial lie. I did need to go to the museum, to meet my father.

Denise gave me directions for catching a bus to the museum. She reminded me she was visiting her mother later that afternoon, so depending on when I got back to the house, she might not be there, but I should make myself at home. We said our goodbyes, and I walked away.

Then turned and walked back.

I knew I shouldn't. Knew I should just head downtown. But I had to know. Had to see for myself.

I followed Denise at a distance, trailing her for several blocks. Tess was leaning against the heavily graffitied side of a one-story brick building, eating some sort of hoagie. She waved when she saw Denise.

I crept closer as they greeted each other. Spying was easy for me. I had no need to hide.

"Yeah," Denise was saying, "it was pretty wild."

"And you really don't know how Neely did it?" Tess asked. "She didn't tell you or anything?"

"Uh, no." Denise looked down at the ground, not meeting Tess's eyes.

"I'd ask her myself, but we had kind of a falling-out. Do you want something from Spak?" Tess asked, smiling in a way that reminded me of my father somehow—too big, too sincere. "My treat."

"No, that's okay," Denise said.

"I mean, like, no way Neely just threw all those effects together out of nowhere," Tess said, launching right back in. "She would have told us if she'd been planning something like that for the performance ahead of time. I mean, it seemed straight-up supernatural, you know?"

Denise shrugged. She looked a little uncomfortable. I was uncomfortable, too. Tess was fishing for information about *me*.

I guess I should have been flattered, but after the phone conversation I'd overheard, I wasn't sure I wanted her knowing anything about me.

Which was, I realized, a pretty big change.

"I guess I'm, like, extra aware of weird stuff like that," Tess said, "because of the totally haunted shit that's gone down in my house. What about that headless trick? It can't have been a coincidence. Two weird things in as many nights."

She was right. It was no coincidence.

Denise looked away again, chewing on her bottom lip. "Uh, yeah, I guess."

She wasn't going to tell, was she? She couldn't.

I wanted to jump out and shout at her. Tell her not to say anything. But, of course, that would be completely self-defeating.

"And you were there both times," Tess prompted. She leaned forward, her face perilously close to Denise's. A breath between them. "If you know something, you can tell me. I'm good at keeping secrets."

Tess reached out, put a hand on Denise's arm. Actually put a hand on her arm!

Did Tess know that Denise had a crush on her? She must. She was probably using it, trying to get the information she wanted. Denise glanced at Tess. She looked like she might swoon.

I made a small noise of disgust. Barely audible, but Tess turned her head.

She wasn't quite looking at the spot where I stood, but she was looking in my direction, eyes searching the empty space.

With a jolt of panic, I ran down the sidewalk, away from the two of them.

I just had to hope that Denise wouldn't tell Tess about me. Never mind that just yesterday I had been considering confessing everything to Tess myself.

I headed toward the bus stop, quietly seething with worry.

And with jealousy. I wasn't sure if I was jealous because Tess had been flirting with someone else and I still liked Tess. Or if I was just jealous because flirting was an option for her. I could never do that. It took me so much effort to interact at all.

I wasn't even sure how I felt about Tess anymore. If you'd asked me just two days ago, I'd have said I'd love her forever with a white-hot burning intensity and nothing could ever change that. I'd have said that the letters of her name were carved into my heart with a knife, bloody and raw. I'd have been a sappy fool.

It's not that I'd been wrong, exactly.

Maybe it's just that I was more in love with the idea of her. In the years since we'd left Pittsburgh, I'd built Tess up in my mind to near-mythological status. She was a legend, a dream, a symbol of everything precious, everything unattainable.

Now that I was actually here, I'd had to confront the fact that she was an actual person.

It wasn't that the real Tess didn't live up to my expectations. She was just different.

I guess I didn't know her anymore. Maybe I'd never really known her in the first place. She certainly hadn't known me.

Could you build love, or even friendship, on lies?

I brooded on all this as I caught a bus to Oakland. My father was in front of the museum, leaning against the sheet-metal statue.

"I'm not taking any more paintings," I told him, once I was close enough.

"That's fine," he said.

"I need a favor from you," I said.

He grinned. "What a coincidence. I was going to ask for a favor from you, too."

40

I sat in the front seat of the van this time but kept my hands in front of my eyes. As my father drove to the Giant Eagle, I explained what I wanted him to do.

"And don't make it seem too obvious," I said.

"You don't need to tell me how to do my job," he scoffed.

When we got there, I followed him in and discreetly directed him to the deli girl from the other day. I waited by the pickle bar while he went to strike up a conversation. I could have stood closer, I suppose, but I could tell even from a distance that he was being disconcertingly flirty. The girl was older than me but certainly a lot younger than him. Gross.

After a charade of American cheese slicing, he left the deli counter, grabbed a soda, and paid. I hovered impatiently behind him, unwilling to call any attention to myself.

Finally, he headed back out to the van. He opened the passenger-side door for me and spoke.

"Pie?" he said. "You here?"

"I'm here. Did you get it?"

"Of course." He pulled out the package of American

cheese and showed the phone number written in pen on the label. "Shall I try it?"

"Yes," I said, "but be careful. I don't want this so-called researcher, whoever she is, getting suspicious."

"Leave it to me," said my father. Once we were both in the van with the doors shut, he dialed.

I chewed on a fingernail, watching him. Even though he was on the phone and no one could see him except me, he adopted a blandly pleasant expression.

"Yes, hello," he said, his tone upbeat but entirely unlike him. He sounded guileless, a bit dim. Acting.

My father was an actor. I took after him more than I realized. More than I wanted to, maybe.

"My name is John. I got your number from my friend Penny— Yes, she said she met you at Giant Eagle, where she works."

I could only hear my father's side of the conversation. I should have asked him to put the call on speaker, but it was too late now.

"See, I was telling her about this weird thing that happened to me the other day, and she said you might know something about it— Well, I couldn't say, exactly. I was just sitting there in the park near my house when the bench across from mine completely vanished. Craziest thing. And then about twenty minutes later, on my way home, I was passing by this one house and I swear I saw the front door vanish and then reappear. Now, maybe I was just hallucinating, but— Oh, really? Huh, now isn't that odd. I mean, I've always thought it was possible— Oh? Is that so? Well, yes, I'd be happy to show you."

He set up a time to meet, a place.

"Did you get a name?" I asked once he'd hung up.

"Cynthia," he said.

"That's all? Any other information?" I'd told him I wanted to know who this paranormal researcher was, wanted to know whether she was dangerous, whether she was looking for real ghosts or if she somehow knew about people like me.

"You told me not to make her suspicious. I'm going to meet her tomorrow. I'm much more charming in person." He flashed a grin.

I snorted.

"Don't worry, kiddo," he said. "I won't let her track you down."

Of course, he wouldn't. Not when I was finally useful to him.

He had turned out to be somewhat useful to me as well. But not in the way I would have liked him to be. Not as someone to care about me.

"Well," he said, a twinkle in his eye, "seems like it's time for my favor now."

"Show me the note first, the one from Mom. Or I won't do anything." I hadn't forgotten about it, the bait he'd thrown out the other day to ensure I'd come meet him. Lie or not, I wasn't going to let him off the hook.

"All right." He reached across me, popped open the glove compartment. From the midst of a jumble of registration booklets and ketchup packets, he extracted a small envelope. He pulled out a piece of paper, unfolded it, held it out.

I took it.

With a jolt, I saw that the paper was indeed covered in my mother's cramped pen scratch. It was stationery from a hotel we'd briefly stayed in a few months ago, where we'd moved from empty room to empty room.

Dear J, the letter said, *I hope this reaches you.*

That was the same wording she'd used in the note I found in the floorboards. My breath caught.

I've been thinking about Pietà. I want to know, would you take care of her—could you?—if anything happened to me? Would you be a father to her? I know I haven't exactly given you the chance before. But I hope you would try if you had to. I'll call sometime. Maybe we can meet up on the coast before the winter.

Love, Annette

"What is this?" I asked. I didn't understand. It was all too strange.

"It came a few months ago," he said. "To my mother's place. I admit I didn't think much of it at the time."

"You didn't—" I faltered, still reeling. "How could you not think much of it? Why didn't you mention this right away?"

He shrugged.

"Weren't you surprised to get a letter from her?" I demanded.

He gave me a funny look. Or, rather, he gave the passenger-side door of the van a funny look.

"No," he said.

I stared at him, too confused to think of a response.

His expression softened. "She always sends me letters," he said. "Half a dozen a year, usually. Didn't you know that?"

No. No, I didn't. She never told me. She must have written them when we were apart or when I was sleeping, slipped them into postboxes without my noticing. She had kept this from me. She'd kept so much from me, it seemed.

If anything happened to me. She had known, or at least suspected, months ago. She had planned for it.

"Did you write back?" I asked.

My father snorted. "How could I? There was never a return address."

Would you be a father to her?

"Did she call? Like she said in the letter?"

"Nope. Didn't hear anything else until I got the call from you," he said. "Anyway, it sounds like she was planning something. So it's probably just me and you for a while, kiddo. You want to ride in the back?"

I sighed. That was probably the best I was going to get from my father. It was almost affection, if you squinted. He remembered how I felt about cars, was looking out for my comfort. It was something.

Better than my mother could give me now.

I crawled over the gearshift, settled myself among the stolen canvases and their golden frames. Painted faces staring out at me. Bowls overflowing with fruit. Brushstroke trees on burnt sienna hills. Cerulean seas bathed in cadmium-yellow light.

Chicago, IL

My mother took me to museums whenever she got the chance. As a kid, I delighted in climbing into off-limits exhibits, scaling model dinosaurs, sitting on historical furniture.

When I got older, I began to appreciate the art as well. Once I took my glove off and ran my bare fingers over the rough brushstrokes of a van Gogh. My mother noticed, slapped my hand away.

"No one saw," I said, thinking she was merely worried about being caught. The painting had vanished for a moment, of course, but I'd made sure I was alone in the gallery.

"The oils in our skin damage the pigment," she said. "Don't be selfish."

"At least I wasn't stealing it," I shot back.

She grimaced. I thought she might get really angry then. Or even give me the silent treatment. But she just sighed. "Be better than me," she said.

My mother could spend hours wandering art museums. Maybe I simply wasn't sophisticated enough, but after a while, I have to admit, the endless white galleries would wear me down. I'd stare at the planes and angles of a 1940s all-night diner and think: *The man who painted this is dead. All these people are dead.*

Loneliness would wrap her arms around me and squeeze.

41

Ten minutes or so later, the van pulled to a stop. I poked my head back into the front. Through the windshield, I could see we were in a neighborhood that looked a lot like Tess's, parked in front of a sprawling Tudor-style house set back from the street, shielded by towering oaks.

"Just a quick in and out," my father said. "Grab anything that looks valuable. Easy peasy."

I was not surprised. Neither was I particularly thrilled. "Who lives here?"

My father shrugged. "Does it matter? Somebody rich."

It wasn't that I minded taking things. Especially not from people who so clearly had more than they could ever need, who could easily replace what they lost. I took things all the time, from houses and from stores. I took things without thinking about it.

I'd never even considered whether there was another way to live before I met Steve.

But taking things this way, for my father, for a profit, made me feel like a criminal. There wasn't really any difference, when you got right down to it, though. So maybe I'd been a criminal all along.

"I know this guy who does landscaping around here," my father explained. "He tipped me off on the best houses to hit."

"I'd rather not," I said quietly.

My father laughed, as if I'd told a great joke. "We'd all rather just sit around and do nothing, wouldn't we? Now, look, kiddo, I'm more than happy to help you get rid of this 'paranormal researcher' who's been breathing down your neck, but I need money to stay in the city. Unfortunately, that's just a fact of life."

"What if the doors are locked?" I asked. "I can't walk through walls, you know."

My father tapped the side of his nose. "Landscaping."

So it was that about five minutes later, I found myself rooting around in the perfectly coiffed garden, until I found the one false rock with a hidden compartment in its plastic base.

I let myself in, quietly, through the side door.

The floors here barely creaked at all, padded as they were with lush carpet.

I made a quick sweep, collected some cash from atop a dresser, one iPad, a jeweled brooch, and then headed back out. I returned the key to the rock. It all took very little effort.

My father had moved the van a block away. I deposited my haul on the passenger seat, where it blinked into visibility.

"That's all you got?" he asked, regarding it.

"Yes." He'd told me to look for cash, small electronics, jewelry. I'd done exactly that.

"Well, next time look harder. And take the duffel."

So this was a spree. My father was going to wring every last drop he could out of me. His golden goose.

Maybe this was just how it worked. Maybe this was at the heart of every relationship. People using each other. I thought of Tess leaning in so close, clearly taking advantage of Denise's feelings for her to get what she wanted: information. And what about Denise? I had begun to think of her as my true friend, but for all I knew, she was giving me up right now to get what she wanted.

Well, if she did, I'd need my father's help more than ever.

The next house made even Tess's house look like a humble cottage. A broad stone staircase lined with hedges led up to an arched doorway absolutely smothered by ornamentation. I went around the back, used a sliding glass door that Dad's landscaping guy had said was usually unlocked.

Inside, the floors were cold white marble, while dark wood beams crossed the ceiling in ornate patterns.

The paintings on the walls had little individual lights pointed at them as though this were a museum, not a home. A grand piano in the corner of one room almost looked small, dwarfed by the scale of the place.

We'd stayed in places just as lavish plenty of times, but I guess I'd spent too long at Denise's, because this house felt too big to me, too empty. That used to be the kind of house I loved.

I wandered into a room with dark wallpaper and a heavy pool table, the wooden legs crowded with carvings. I pulled an Oriental rug from beneath a side table. Rolled it up, tucked it under my arm. It was just about the right size to replace the burned one from Denise's house. If she hadn't betrayed me yet, I'd need to make sure I stayed in her good graces. Stayed useful.

This house had an elevator. The elevator had a chandelier. Upstairs was equally ornate. In the first bedroom I checked, an enormous gold cross hung above the bed. I took that, too. I'd give it to Neely—perfect décor for the Church of Go Fuck Yourself.

The walk-in closet of the next bedroom held row after row of gorgeous dresses. I shoved several into my bag. Hidden beneath a folded silk scarf, I found a small ring of keys. One fit into a jewelry box in the bedroom. I opened it, put on all the necklaces, layering them one after another around my neck until I was laden down, my neck heavy with cold metal, all of it translucent now. Every finger got a ring. I gilded my arms with bracelets.

I clinked with each step now, so I took the quickest exit available. Front door. Opened it, closed it, ran down the long lawn. A bracelet flew off and lay in the gutter. I left it. Whatever.

My father had parked even farther away this time, and I was cold by the time I reached the van. I almost wished someone could see me, to admire my finery. My mother would have laughed. Called me Your Majesty and asked if I thought I might be underdressed for the occasion.

Except if my mother was actually here, I wouldn't be doing this.

I tapped on the van window, and my father opened the door. I deposited most of my haul on the seat. My father was pleased, oohing over several rings and a necklace he pegged as genuine diamonds.

"That's enough, right?" I asked, though I had a feeling I already knew the answer.

"One more," he said. "Just one more house, okay, kiddo?"

"Fine." I was resigned to it now. And besides, I'd found a way to make it work for me, too. I crawled into the back of the van, still holding the carpet under one arm. I hadn't shown it to my father. I'd also kept back some dresses and jewelry that I thought Jules might like and the gold cross, all of which I hid in the back of the van.

The third house my father took me to was cold and modernist. Open metal staircases. Walls of windows. One of those human aquariums, as my mother would call them.

Finding valuables was trickier here. Everything was tucked away, neat and faceless. Every surface flat and smooth and shining. Well, I didn't mind a challenge, and I certainly didn't mind making my father wait.

I was making a search of an upstairs office, had just slipped a laptop into my bag, when I heard a man's voice calling from another room.

"Dan?"

I froze. I hadn't realized anyone was home.

"What?" another man called back.

"You're making too much noise. I told you I have a head-ache."

"Is shouting good for your headache?"

"Don't start with me, Dan."

"I'm not making any noise. I'm being entirely silent like you asked."

"You're opening and closing drawers."

"I am not."

"Well, *someone* is."

They were both quiet. So was I. The moments stretched. Carefully, I crept out of the room I'd been in, started down the stairs. I was just thinking how this was an upside to industrial-style modernist houses: no old wooden creaky stairs.

But then the duffel bag clanged against the metal railing.

"Did you hear that?" called one of the voices.

"Yes."

"Oh, Lord, I think there's someone in the house. I'm calling the police."

"You're overreacting. I'll go look."

Here is where, if I was a normal thief, I'd be screwed. What would I do? Hide? Make a mad dash? I would need to be lucky. Fast.

Me, though? I just stood very still.

A tall, broad-shouldered man passed by the top of the stairs, clutching an abstract statue—a swirl of polished stone—in one hand, eyes searching.

He couldn't see me, but I was still afraid. Invisible wasn't invincible. I could still be hurt.

Once the man had moved past, I reached down, tugged off my sneakers so I could move more silently. I wore no socks, as usual, out of necessity, so I padded barefoot down the stairs, each step vanishing as my foot touched it. I dashed across the pale wood floors toward the door. But I stopped before I reached it.

Through the floor, now, which had gone translucent at the touch of my bare soles, I could see into the basement. I hadn't been down there yet. It was where all the mess in the house was hiding. Tangles of cords. Stacks of video games. Open bookshelves lined with little statues. A mirror-walled home gym.

My bag was nearly empty. If I came back this way, I would bet anything that my father would make us go to a fourth house. A fifth, maybe.

The first two houses had been easy—fun, even, as bad as that sounds. But this one had been too risky. Better to give my father what he wanted, get it over with if I could.

So I found the entrance to the basement. Put my shoes back on, went down. I worked quickly, filled the bag with electronics. There was a camera down there, a nice one, which I took to give to Denise.

By the time I came back upstairs, police lights were flashing outside.

I took a deep breath. Held it. Squared my shoulders, hugged the bag close to my chest, pushed open the door. And, heart pounding, walked straight out between the cops as they marched up the lawn.

42

I was shaky with adrenaline in the van. Sure, the cops couldn't see me, but you didn't need to see to shoot. I knew that from experience.

This time, I let my father drive me home, though I gave him an address a few numbers off from Denise's real one. I shoved the treasures I'd hidden into my backpack, picked up the rug. He made a half-hearted appeal for me to stay with him—said he'd book a motel room—but I declined, and he didn't push too hard. We made plans to meet again tomorrow, after he'd scoped out the paranormal researcher.

The house was dark when I reached it. No one home. Denise must have been visiting her mother, like she'd told me. I wasn't sure where everyone else was.

I let myself in with my key, unfurled the new rug on the living room floor. It looked good, better than the old one.

Everything else I took up to Denise's room. Laid it all out on the futon. Glittering jewels and gold and the camera and some cash, even. It all looked wonderful. Like Christmas morning.

I dozed off a bit, sitting in the midst of my spoils, waiting for everyone to come home.

I was woken by the noise of the front door, downstairs, voices. I put my ear to the floorboards, like I used to do in other houses, with other voices. I could just barely make out a few trailing snippets of conversation.

"She is doing much better, though, you have to . . ."

"I don't care, I wish she'd just . . ."

A few minutes later, the sound of someone climbing the stairs. Denise walked into the room and froze, taking in the heaped treasure.

"Pie?" she asked.

"I'm here."

"What is this?" Her eyes flicked between the piles on the futon. She seemed suspicious, which was a fair reaction to mysterious treasure, I suppose.

"It's for you," I said. "All of you. Here."

I held out the camera I had taken, with a gloved hand, so it floated in midair. She quickly closed her door before plucking it from the air. She turned it on, flipped through images on the viewscreen. I grinned, remembering how she'd complained during the party about not being able to afford a camera of her own, waiting for her face to break into a smile.

"There's pictures of a family on here," she said. "Where did you get this?"

"I picked it up," I said honestly.

Denise looked up, her forehead deeply creased. She opened her mouth to speak but was interrupted by Larissa shouting her name from below.

"Hold on a second," Denise said to me. She set the camera down and ran back downstairs.

Unease gnawed at me while she was gone. This wasn't the reaction I'd been hoping for. Maybe this meant she had in fact told Tess all about me, and now she was feeling guilty.

When Denise returned, she didn't look any happier.

"Was that you, too?" she asked. "The rug in the living room?"

"I got it to replace the one I ruined," I explained.

"Did you steal all this?" Denise hissed. She almost sounded angry.

Could I tell her I'd found it on the curb, the way they'd found their couch?

I mean, I *had* found it.

I was starting to get annoyed, too. I'd tried to do something nice. It hardly felt fair that I was being yelled at.

"I'm invisible," I said, a touch defensive. "I can't just turn that off. How do you think I got my stuff? How do you think I got that wedding dress?"

Denise pushed some jewelry out of the way and sagged down onto the futon. "Well, fine," she said, deflated slightly, "but I didn't think you'd keep doing it." She picked up a ring and scrutinized it. "Is this a fucking diamond?"

"Um, maybe." I honestly couldn't tell real ones from cubic zirconia, though my mother had tried to show me the difference once.

"Are you the one who got that fancy cheese?" Denise asked, in a tone far too accusatory for cheese, if you asked me. "Did you steal food and put it in our refrigerator?"

"I was being a good guest," I said.

"You don't need to steal for us. We're not your charity case."

I knew Denise and my father were wildly different people, but still I hadn't expected their reactions to be so opposite. My father was delighted when we took things for him. His face had lit up with joy in the van when he laid eyes on the diamonds.

I thought Denise would be happy, too. She'd been happy enough when I helped Neely perform. Happy when I posed as a ghost in her pictures. Happy when I was useful.

"I'm not your charity case, either." My throat felt tight. I was worried I was going to start crying. This wasn't how this was supposed to go at all.

I was out of my depth. I'd never fought with anyone other than my mother before. I stood up, backed toward the wall.

"Did you even think about how much trouble we could get into if we got caught with stolen things?" demanded Denise, staring at the ring again. "I could get arrested. I could get *shot,* Pie."

"I didn't—"

"Not everyone has the luxury of being invisible." She glared at where she thought I was.

"It's not a luxury." I was angry now, too. My face felt hot. My throat burned.

"You've got to understand how it is for other people." She shook her head. "We have to deal with consequences that you don't. You'll probably just leave some morning and not tell any of us and we'll be stuck dealing with all of this."

"That's not true," I insisted.

But she had a point. I was my mother's daughter, after all. I'd spent my whole life learning how to leave.

Thinking about my mother made me angry all over again.

"You don't have to deal with half the shit I do," Denise said. She threw the ring back onto the bed. "You can just do anything you want: steal a necklace, unplug people's microphones. It's not like that for me. If I mess up, I can't just hide."

"You don't know anything," I said. I started grabbing the treasures I'd laid out on the futon, stuffing them into my backpack. All I'd done was help her.

Well, after I broke into her house, I guess. After I'd used her to get to the girl we both had a crush on.

"You're just mad because I messed with Tess," I said, "and you're obsessed with her."

"That's got nothing to do with this."

I spun on her, jabbed a finger toward her face—a gesture totally lost on her, since she couldn't see it. "Did you tell her about me?" I demanded.

"No." Denise scowled. "I haven't told anyone."

Was it true? I wanted to believe it, but I couldn't shake the doubt.

"I bet you did," I said. My turn now for accusations. "You seemed like you were going to tell her."

Denise sat back, her expression more confused than hurt. "What?"

"She was manipulating you. Flirting with you to get information. That stupid trick with the arm. She thinks she's so smooth."

"Oh my god," said Denise, her eyes widening.

I realized, too late, what I'd just admitted.

"Were you spying on me?" Denise jumped to her feet. "Did you follow me?"

"No, I just overheard—"

She was the one backing up now, her mouth twisted, eyes filled with revulsion, with horror, with all the worst emotions I could imagine. "That is so fucked-up, Pie. Normal people don't do that."

It must have happened gradually, our voices rising a little at a time without either of us quite noticing, but we were both nearly shouting now. I took a breath. I felt dizzy, like the floor wasn't quite holding me up.

I was really going to cry now. Probably my period was about to come. That always made it harder to push down the damn tears. "But it's true," I insisted, my voice ragged at the edges. "She wanted to use you to get to me."

"That doesn't even make sense," Denise said, and then her eyes drifted to the middle distance as if she had seen something, and when she spoke again her voice was quieter. "Wait a second. That girl you told me about, the one your age, whose house you lived in a few years ago. The one you said you'd had a crush on. I'd almost forgotten."

"Shit," I said, too quiet for Denise to hear.

"Pie," she said, her voice suddenly even, serious. "Did you used to live in Tess's house?"

I could have lied. I should have lied.

"I—yes."

"So, you were the one using me," Denise said.

It was scarier, how flat her voice sounded. I wish she'd yell at me again. I felt tears coming, couldn't hold them back anymore.

"I'm sorry," I said. My voice sounded small, far away. "It wasn't like that." But she was right. That's exactly how this had started.

It wasn't like that anymore. It was so far from that now.

"You are a stalker," she said flatly. "You are a creep."

"I'm not," I said weakly. I felt dizzy, sick. The room swam, watery.

"It's worse: you're a coward. Sneaking around, lying. I trusted you, you know? I guess that makes me stupid. You made me feel sorry for you." Her voice finally rose again, ragged with emotion. "You made me fucking care about you."

That hurt so much worse than if she'd never cared at all.

She was right. I was a monster. I slid along the wall, feeling that without it I would collapse. I tripped on a pile of books, tried to set them right. My hands were shaking.

What had I been thinking? I'm not the kind of person who can have friends. I'm not the kind of person that anybody likes.

What a fool I had been. What a sad-sack sorry loser, so desperate for any scrap of affection that I would throw aside every principle I had lived my life by up until that point. I would forget everything I knew about living, about the rules of How Things Worked, because someone was a tiny bit nice to me.

I was invisible not for my own protection but for the

protection of everyone else in the world. So no one had to look at me. No one had to know about me.

I should disappear better. Disappear harder.

"Get out." Denise's face was a wall. A closed door. "Get out of my house."

What would she do now? She would call Tess, and they would both turn me in. Or she would shout for her aunt and uncle.

I was in trouble, really in trouble. I reached for the doorknob. I thought I was going to faint.

My vision was going black at the edges.

I tried to do what Denise told me. I turned the doorknob, wanting only to get out. I turned the doorknob, hand shaking. I blinked.

I blinked and when I opened my eyes the room was gone. The futon was gone. Denise was gone. I was nowhere.

Darkness. Nothingness. Blank.

I'm dead, I thought.

A Complete List of the Ways
I Always Thought I Would Die

Hit by a car because the driver couldn't see me.

Hit by a bus or a truck or a motorcycle for the same reason.

Hit by a cyclist or a skateboarder or someone on one of those odd little electric scooters and knocked into traffic, where I'd be hit by a car because the driver couldn't see me.

Something heavy dropped on me by a construction crane because the operator couldn't see me.

Burned up in a house fire even if the firefighters arrived in time, because they wouldn't know I was in there, wouldn't even try to save me.

Not like this.

43

I couldn't see my hands. I couldn't see anything. A darkness so complete that the word seemed inadequate.

I couldn't even feel my hands. Couldn't feel anything at all. It was like my body was gone. Or *I* was gone.

Thankfully, all the fear and anger and hurt that had been consuming me just moments ago was gone, too.

My heart didn't race. I couldn't feel my heart.

The darkness was an ocean. And I was a wave—just another part of it.

As soon as I thought that, I did feel something. Though "feel" is the wrong word. "Sense," maybe.

The darkness was not perfectly still. There were currents, eddies, vibrations. Gradations in depth. Places where the darkness had a sort of warmth, or where it was harder or softer.

The darkness was rich with detail, if I could let go of trying to see.

I began to recognize edges to the darkness. An area of currents and flat planes, perhaps an open window. A cold still darkness in the shape of a mannequin. A warm, flickering darkness in the shape of a girl sitting on the floor.

I was still in Denise's room.

My body still existed, another quality of darkness, though I remained unable to feel it the way I normally would. I was able to move through space. I tried speaking, which created vibrations but no sound.

I reached out to touch the darkness-that-was-Denise, but the darkness-that-was-my-hand passed right through her shoulder.

The world and I had fallen out of sync with each other. I was truly a ghost now. Seemingly without mass, without substance.

The floor, I thought. *Why is the floor even supporting me?*

The instant I thought this, I fell, the darkness below me giving way, a rush of movement.

Would I fall straight through the earth? Keep falling forever through the vacuum of space? I cried out, soundlessly, and abruptly my descent stopped. I crumpled to the plane of darkness below me, which, I was pretty sure, was the floor of the living room.

I was not alone.

The shape in the room here with me was different from the darkness-that-was-Denise. More distinct. Sharper. It moved, and I could perceive the shape of the face.

Mom! I tried to shout, but there was no sound here.

She lifted her hands and signed, "Hello."

I felt the shape of the signs instead of seeing them, the movement of her hands through the air.

My mother reached forward, touched my arm. I could

almost feel it, like a buzzing. I got this sense of joy and sadness radiating from her, an orchestral swell.

"Is that really you?" she signed.

"I think so. Are we dead?"

She laughed. The sound waves made ripples in the darkness. "No," she signed.

"Where are we?"

In reply, my mother made a sign for the world and a sign for place, and then brought her hands together, almost touching.

Somewhere close to the world but not quite the world. Denise was right there, upstairs. If I concentrated, I could still sense her, all the way through the floorboards, a dazzling darkness.

We'd slipped through the cracks. Fallen.

Or jumped.

A shred of the emotion I'd left behind slid back into my mind like an electric shock: anger.

"Why did you leave me?" I asked.

The darkness pulsed around me—a mix of emotions so overwhelming that I reeled back. Regret, sorrow, guilt, relief, anger, uncertainty.

My mother twisted the sign for "mistake" across her chin. It wasn't clear whether she meant that it had been an accident or that it had been wrong of her to leave.

This was the strangest conversation I'd ever had, and yet in some ways, this was the most open my mother had ever been with me. Somehow, in this place, I could sense much more than words. I could sense her emotions.

"I was so scared," I signed, and I could feel my anger pulsing in the air around me like something alive, a herd of strange animals stampeding through the dark. I tried to calm them.

My mother held her hands out at her sides, palms up. It was the gesture that the carved Mary was making in Michelangelo's statue the *Pietà*.

It meant my name. It meant *I'm sorry*. It meant *I have failed my child*.

"I didn't know what to do," I said. "I called Dad."

She nodded. "Good. Did he come?"

"Why didn't you come back?" I asked instead of answering.

She paused, too long for the answer to be as simple as *I don't know how* or *I tried so hard and I couldn't*. She didn't want to. I was sure of it.

My mother must have been able to feel my anger then, because she moved away from me.

"You're hiding," I said. "Like you always do. You're running away." I signed this forcefully, dismissively, each "you" a pointed finger, an accusation.

She sagged, her outline sinking slightly into the floor. I was worried for a moment that she would fall right into it. I reached for her.

When my hand touched her shoulder, I realized, with a jolt, that I could feel my hand. See it, almost. I blinked, and for an instant, as if far in the distance, I thought I heard a low hum. I pulled my hand away. The sensations faded.

"Do you know how to get back?" I demanded.

"I think you're already going." She pointed at my chest.

I was flickering, I realized. Like she had been, but in reverse. For a moment, my body would fade into partial visibility, and then it would be gone again.

"Come back," I said, with the first glimmer of fear I'd felt since I got here. I didn't want to lose her again. I reached out for her.

"I . . ." She waved her hands, faltering.

"Please, Mom," I signed, my desperation growing as the real world flickered in and out around me. "I need you to come back."

I reached out farther, almost frantic now. To my relief, she moved forward. She took my hand.

She took my hand and I pulled her back through.

There was, first, a feeling of separation—the air and my skin peeling away from each other. I became aware of my edges. I became aware of the flow of air against my skin. I hadn't fully realized how strange it was for this sensation to be gone until it returned.

Sound was next. An odd hum, a sort of thrumming, almost deafening for its previous absence. I realized that the thrum was my blood rushing through my veins. The drum of my heart came next. And then a thousand hushes and murmurs and creaks of the world outside my body.

Light was third. I could see, but only gradations of shadow and brightness. Pale and dark, patchy and alternating. Even that was shocking after so much nothing. Like walking out of a movie theater into a sunny day. I blinked and blinked.

My mother was a shape I could see suddenly, standing next to me, a blur of dark and light.

Color came last.

My mother's face resolved into something like one of Jules's paintings, blobs of color, and then finally the face I knew, as pale and glassy as ever but bright with the hues of a poster behind her.

"You're back," I said, out loud this time, overwhelmed with sensory input, flooded with relief. "We're back."

The room was empty. No sign of Jules or Denise or Larissa or Neely. I didn't know how much time had passed. It had been dark outside when I vanished. It was dark out now. Did time pass differently where we'd been? It wouldn't have surprised me.

My mother's eyes flicked here and there around the room. She squinted and blinked, as though everything was too bright.

"Is your father here?" my mother asked, her voice hushed.

"No, he's in town, but I didn't tell him where I was staying."

"I taught you well." She smiled at me, rueful. "Maybe too well. I'm sorry, Pie. I didn't mean to hurt you."

"I know," I said, but I didn't know. Not really. I wanted very much to believe her. Maybe she hadn't actually meant to leave. Maybe it had been an accident. *I* hadn't done it on purpose.

A floorboard creaked upstairs. We'd been whispering, as we always did.

"We should go," my mother said. She looked tired, less substantial than usual. But she was here. I could see her, faintly but definitively. "This house isn't a good place to stay. There are too many people here."

"Uh, yeah," I said, thinking of Jules, of Denise. Would my mother and I go back to normal now? Go back to our old lives? Running from city to city. Living in the houses of the rich. It was a fine life. It was all I knew.

It was enough.

"Come on," she said, moving toward the door. I should have been happy. I should have been thanking my lucky stars. My mother was back. Everything was okay now.

I hesitated. "Maybe I . . . could just say goodbye."

My mother turned sharply.

"What?" From her tone, you'd think I had just suggested setting myself on fire.

"No, never mind, sorry," I mumbled. It had been a stupid idea. Denise hated me, anyway. And for good reason. Maybe Jules did, too. Neely wasn't even here, as far as I knew.

I'd just leave a note. An apology, maybe, for what I'd said.

"Say goodbye to who?" my mother asked, urgent, her whisper tinged with an edge of something. Fear? She reached out and grabbed my arm, gripped it too hard.

Had she grown fainter?

"Um, the people who live here," I said. "They . . . they helped me."

"They know about you?" She flickered, so quick I almost missed it. But she was gone for a second, then back.

"Mom," I said, my voice getting louder, a little too loud, desperate again. "I'm sorry, but you were gone. I was freaking out. What was I supposed to do?"

"You can't just tell strangers," she said. She seized me by the shoulders, shook me so hard it was frightening. "Why would you do that? It's so dangerous." She was flickering more, flashing like a dying lightbulb.

She was pulling me with her, I realized as darkness tinged the edges of my vision. I could feel her fear again, the way I'd been able to in that other place, like emotion was just another sense.

"It's okay," I said, trying to calm her down but pulling her hands from my arms as I did so. "I swear. They aren't strangers anymore, Mom."

"You can't trust anyone," she gasped.

"No, really," I insisted. "This girl Denise and her cousin Jules, they're both really nice. They wouldn't—"

"No," my mother said, her voice anguished. She took a step back.

And she was gone again.

New Haven, CT

We have seen some awful things.

Sometimes, when they're behind closed doors, people do funny things, normal things. They dance and sing, unashamed. They fart freely. Pick their noses. Scratch their butts. Watch TikTok compilations on YouTube for hours. Laugh until they can't breathe. Touch themselves. Talk to themselves. Pretend that their cat is a contestant on a game show.

But sometimes they do other kinds of things, things I'm afraid to mention, afraid to think of.

They hurt themselves. Hurt each other.

When I was eight, we stayed in a house with a girl my age. She had long shining hair, which I was jealous of. I thought she was pretty, though back then, thinking a girl was pretty simply meant wishing I could look like that. Wishing I could look like anything.

My mother and I slept in the guest room, but some nights my mother let me go stay in the girl's room, like a sleepover. Her room had a white carpet, soft and thick, so I slept on the floor in the corner by the ladybug nightlight.

One night, late, her father came into the room.

I watched what happened next. Yes, I watched it. I didn't understand it. I wish I'd stopped it. But I didn't know what to do.

So I stood there, my back pressed against the wall, and watched what he did.

I told my mother in the morning, after the house had emptied out. I told her what I'd seen and she asked if I was sure and I said yes, I'd seen it, though I didn't understand, and my mother gripped my hand so hard it hurt.

She told me not to think about it. We went out and lifted a whole pizza from the rack at the Pizza Hut, and we ate it sitting outside in the park. We went to a library. My mother sat me down in the kids' area and told me to wait there and she'd be back in an hour. I picked at the peeling spine of *Goodnight Moon*. An hour passed. My mother didn't return.

I got scared, so I wandered the half mile back to the house we'd been staying in. There were police cars and an ambulance out front. Had my mother called the police and told them what I'd seen? Were they going to arrest the man?

My mother found me standing outside. She had changed clothes—borrowed a dress from the woman who lived there. Her hands were wet, like she'd just washed them, and her hair was disheveled.

"Come on," she said. "Hurry."

As she hurried me along the sidewalk, I turned back, saw the shape of a body, obscured by blankets, being loaded into the back of the ambulance.

It was many years before I understood what happened that day, before I realized what my mother had done.

44

"Mom?" I called.

Panic gripped me. No. Not again. I had just gotten her back, and she was gone again. Desperately, I flailed at the air around me, trying to grab at the place I'd last seen her hands.

She hadn't truly left. She was here. In the room, just out of sync with me. She had to be.

"Mom?" I tried again, but I didn't dare shout. Larissa or Terrance might be home. Faint creaks came from the upper floors.

My mother wouldn't be able to hear me, anyway, would she? Not if she was in that other place. I tried signing it, over and over: "Mom, come back."

I blinked and blinked, trying to return to that strange darkness. I tried to access the emotional state that had pulled me there before. Betrayal, sorrow, fear. The rug of the world being pulled out from under me.

But no matter how I tried, I couldn't make myself feel afraid. I couldn't even feel despair, really.

All I could feel was angry.

I didn't want to be angry. I should try to be sympathetic

343

to my mother. Fear, clearly, is what pushed her away—I'd felt it from her before she vanished. And isn't that what Steve had said about that guy Felix, that he'd been afraid?

But all I could think was: *She's done it again. She's left me.*

I'm not sure how long I sat there waiting, hoping something would happen. Hoping she would come back or that I would vanish again.

I heard voices upstairs. Muffled.

I got up and climbed the staircase, pressing my feet as close to the wall as possible to avoid creaks.

Denise's bedroom door was open. I crept over and peered in. Denise was sitting on the edge of her futon, knees up. She looked like she'd been crying. I could tell from the lumps in the duvet that she'd hastily hidden the stolen stuff under there. Did that mean she hadn't told her aunt about me yet?

Larissa sat in the chair by the desk, leaning over with her hands on her knees, expression soft, sympathetic.

"I wish everything was easier," she said. "For both of you."

"She's too stubborn," said Denise thickly.

For a moment, I thought she meant me.

"You must have gotten that from her," said Larissa with a smile.

Her mother. Of course.

Denise hung her head, hunched farther into herself. Larissa moved to kneel at her side, put an arm on her back.

"She loves you, you know," she said.

"Yeah," muttered Denise.

"I'm sure she'd love to have you living with her again."

"Then why won't she just—"

"Denise," Larissa said softly, cutting her off. "She doesn't want you to have to take care of her. That's not your job."

This wasn't meant for me to hear. Denise's words from earlier echoed in my mind: *You are a creep. A stalker.*

I went back downstairs. Carefully, quietly, I eased the front door open just far enough to slip out, then shut it behind me.

I sank down on the front step. It was cold. Cold enough that normally my mother and I would think about moving south. My breath came out as a small cloud. The instant it left my body, it became visible.

I watched it for a moment or two. Then I put my face in my hands.

Don't trust anyone, my mother had always told me. *Don't fall in love. They'll only betray you. You'll only get hurt. You'll only lose everyone and everything and find that all those years you spent thinking you were lonely, thinking you were alone—you didn't even know the meaning of the word.*

A hand closed around my arm.

A hand.

With a spike of fear, I tried to jerk away, but the hand gripped harder. Whoever it was grabbed my other arm, too, from behind, so I couldn't see them

Was it Tess? Denise? Jules? My father?

I struggled, twisted, too shocked to think anything beyond simple visceral thoughts, instinctive, reactive.

I was so used to being quiet. It didn't even occur to me to scream.

Was it my mother? Had she come back after all? The thought sliced through my animal panic a mere second before the person spoke.

Spoke in a voice I did not recognize at all.

"Stop it," the voice said. "I can see you."

Denver, CO

"I think there's someone in the house, Patricia," the man had said. A different man, a different house, years ago.

"You're drunk," Patricia said. He was.

My mother and I were in the room with them. We'd paused on our way from the kitchen, our arms full of food we'd just taken from their refrigerator. The man and his wife lounged on their leather sofa, mere feet away. They'd been watching television a moment ago, but the man had turned it off.

"No, really," he said. "I think someone is in here with us. I heard noises."

Patricia sat up. Her eyebrow was quirked, skeptical, but unease crept into her tone. "Well, what do you want me to do about it?"

The man kept small bottles of whiskey hidden around the house. These two were well-off but not mega rich. They had a once-a-week cleaning service rather than a maid. They had a bar well stocked with fine liqueurs, but the whiskey he hid was the kind that came in plastic. He hid it so it was always within reach, so he could drink it without Patricia's knowing.

"Nothing," said the man, "nothing. Just tell me, Pat."

"Tell you what?"

I don't know if it is necessary to mention that I had seen Patricia with another man one morning when she was supposed to be at work. I'd seen him slide a hand up her skirt. Seen her reach for his pants, her mouth latched onto his neck like a leech. And then my mother appeared beside me and I turned away quickly, so she would not see that I had been watching.

This couple was not happy. I don't know if that matters.

"Is it him?" the man asked Patricia.

"Who?"

"The one you've been fucking?"

And then they were both standing, shouting at each other. My mother made big eyes at me. We didn't even need to sign. It was time to leave. We paused long enough to shove some of the food we'd been carrying into our backpacks. The man stormed off.

We were weaving our way quietly out of the room ourselves when the man came back. With a gun.

"Get out of my house!" he screamed.

"Jesus Christ, Ron," Patricia said. "Stop it."

My mother and I ran. In the next room, I tripped, knocked into a side table. The man heard and came running after us.

He couldn't see us, couldn't see anything, but he fired

anyway, shot wildly in the direction of the noise. We ran for the door, threw it open. The next shot thunked into the wood of the doorframe.

I stumbled out into the darkness, terror following close at my heels. So close I could feel it, like icy hands on my skin.

45

Caught there on Denise's front step, I froze. My heart fluttered and snapped in the wind. The person holding my arms behind me tightened something around my wrist. A click. Cold metal.

My hands had been cuffed. Was it the cops from that rich person's house? Had they found me somehow? Did they know what I'd done? How was that possible? How could they see me?

I was pulled to my feet, pushed. I stumbled.

A car was parked up the street with the driver-side door hanging open, dim light spilling out like breath. It wasn't a cop car. Just a plain sedan.

My assailant yanked on my arm, pulled me toward the sidewalk. I finally got a look at her.

It was a woman, taller than me, her hair pulled back in a tight ponytail. She was wearing a winter jacket, gloves, black pants. She was solid, not translucent. I couldn't see her eyes. They were covered by the strangest goggles I had ever seen. Like two camera lenses, one mounted over each eye, sticking out stalklike, attached to a black metal framework, with a chin strap, a head strap.

The paranormal researcher. She must be.

I stumbled on the grass, glanced back toward Denise's house. Should I shout? But what hope of rescue was there? Denise must have called or texted Tess after all. Must have told her everything. And Tess must have sent this lady after me.

I opened my mouth, but the woman shoved a gloved hand over it.

"Don't," she said.

Looking into the flat black disks of her goggles made me feel like I was being stared down by an alien. A monster.

"It's not you," she said, "is it?"

I didn't understand the question. It sounded like she wasn't really asking, like she knew the answer but was hoping maybe she was wrong. I blinked at her, too bewildered to answer, even if she hadn't been covering my mouth.

She pulled me to her car. She was strong. She yanked open the back door, pushed me in, slammed it closed. With my hands bound behind me, I couldn't reach for the lock. Twisting my head, I could see that the cuffs had gone translucent, but that didn't make them any less effective.

All those years of being careful, of trying not to be discovered, and I had thrown it all away. I was being kidnapped, stolen the way I stole things.

Why the hell hadn't I listened to my mother?

The car pulled away. I craned to look back out the window

at Denise's house, tried to pay attention to where we were going. Which way we turned. Would that help me?

"Who are you?" I asked.

The woman didn't answer. Just drove.

"What do you want?" I asked.

This wasn't a sleek black government-looking car. Surely if I was being carted off to Area 51 for experimentation, there would have been more than a lone woman sent to capture me. Or at least she'd be wearing a nice black suit.

Although what did I know? That's only how it was in movies.

"How can you see me?" I tried.

"Infrared," she answered.

That explained the goggles.

"Where are you taking me?" I asked.

She didn't speak again.

I had thought I was dead just an hour ago, sure, but now I thought I was going to die. Those might sound the same, but they are not. One is much worse.

If you are dead, it's over. There's nothing more you can do. Might as well relax.

But if you *think* you're going to die, your animal brain is screaming and flailing and doing everything in its power to carry out its one primary directive: to survive.

What could I do? I was in a moving car, my hands locked behind my back. The woman still wore the goggles. I couldn't see her eyes. I could hardly see anything.

My breath came as fast and shallow as it had when I wore the skull mask two days ago. Shallower, even. I wasn't getting a full breath, though there was nothing obstructing my lungs but fear.

No one would come look for me. If I died, no one would miss me. Not even my mother. She wouldn't know, safe in her world of darkness.

Denise would merely think I had left, just like she told me to.

Denise.

We'd been friends. We really had, hadn't we? And I'd fucked it up.

It was too much. All too much. I squeezed my eyes shut.

The woman slammed on the brakes. I slid forward off the seat, unable to catch myself.

She twisted around to stare at me through her goggles. It was unnerving, almost painful, to have those grim black disks glinting at me.

"What did you do?" she demanded.

"I didn't do anything," I said, struggling back onto the seat.

"Yes, you did," she said. "In the rearview—I saw it. You disappeared."

"I'm invisible," I said, confused. And then it hit me. I must have flickered. The way my mother had done on the train. I hadn't been transported completely to that other place, but this was the first step.

Could I go the rest of the way? Could I escape that way? Into darkness? Nothingness? I needed to focus on my fear, let it crescendo.

The woman turned back around, thumped the wheel with an open hand. The car horn gave an abortive bleat.

Her hand, I saw, was shaking.

I closed my eyes again, tried to get back to the same pitch of desperation I'd felt a moment ago, right before I'd flickered. All I could see, though, was the image of the woman's shaking hand. Somehow, that let all the air out of my panic.

I opened my eyes.

"Please let me go," I said. My voice came out calmer than I'd expected.

The woman jerked in the seat as if I'd poked her instead of spoken. *I was right,* I thought. She was scared, too.

"I'll get you money," I said, thinking of my father. She must be like him, hoping to use me as a tool. "Or drugs. Whatever you want."

"I'm not a junkie." She twisted around to look at me again.

I flinched from that flat gaze.

The woman stared me down for a long moment before speaking again. "There's only one thing I want," she said. "My brother."

Somewhere South of Glenwood Springs, CO

For weeks after the man shot at us, I'd wake up in the middle of the night shaking, sweating, body ready to run. My mother would smooth my brow. Tell me we were safe, that we got away, that she would never let that happen again.

We stayed away from people for a month. Went silent together, hiked two days down the Rio Grande Trail, set up camp in a ghost town of drafty wooden shacks, the Rocky Mountains standing sentinel in the distance.

I was so lonely. So scared.

I couldn't stop thinking about how, if those bullets had hit us, if my mother and I had been killed, no one would know.

We would have died, invisible. Our bodies would rot, unseen. No one would come looking for us. No one would report us missing. No one would wonder why we hadn't shown up to work or school. No one would even care.

46

The strange woman had parked at the end of a dark street.

"I don't know anything about your brother," I told her, eyeing the car door. I couldn't tell if it was locked or not, didn't know enough about cars.

"You're like him." She waved a hand in my direction, twisted around in her seat. "He's like you. Invisible."

Just days ago, this would have been radical news, but my worldview had shifted.

"Oh," I said simply.

This woman was like my father, in a way. He'd been looking for me and my mother, after all, when he stumbled across Steve.

I made a move for the door, but the woman saw me do it. In an instant, she had reached through to the back seat, grabbed my arm. Not hard, but the sheer strangeness of being touched sent shock waves all through me, nerves crying out in alarm.

"I'm not letting you go," she said. "I was watching that house for hours. I would have kept watching for a week if I had to."

"Why?" I gasped out, yanking my arm away. The cold metal of the cuffs dug into my wrists.

"I pay attention," she said. "Things have been happening around the city. Things most people wouldn't understand. But I did. I hoped it was him."

"But the house," I said. "Why were you at that house?"

Maybe it shouldn't have mattered. But I wanted to know. What if it had been Denise? Did she get the phone number from Tess? Did she bring this woman here directly? Somehow that felt worse than just telling Tess about me.

"An informant," the woman said simply.

"Who?"

"Does it matter? Some girl. You're going to help me find my brother."

"I don't know anything about your brother," I said, annoyed, distracted. Some girl. The most likely answer was Tess, but I wished I knew for sure. Had Denise sold me out?

Why should I even care? It didn't matter anymore. Everything had fallen apart. This was still dangerous. I needed to focus on getting out of here alive, not on whether Denise had betrayed me.

"I can't wear these all the time," the woman said, indicating her goggles, "but you can see each other, can't you? Other invisible people, I mean."

"Just let me go," I said, pulling at the cuffs, trying to squeeze my hands free. My fear was coming back. The simple fear of a trapped animal. "Please."

She shook her head. "I can't let you go," she said, and my

heart sank. "I'll do whatever it takes. He's my little brother. Nothing could ever change that. I have to talk to him."

"Is his name Steve?" I asked, feeling desperate.

"No." Her tone was guarded. "It's Felix. Why?"

Felix. With a jolt, I realized I actually did know about her brother. He was the one who disappeared.

Could I just tell her that? Would she even believe me?

"Look," I said. "If I take you to someone else, another invisible person, will you let me go then?"

She stared at me.

"He's the only other invisible person I know," I added. On this plane of existence, anyway. "Maybe he'll know where your brother is." I wasn't sure if that counted as a lie or not.

"Fine," she said.

I gave her the address.

Ten sickening minutes later, we pulled up in front of Steve's house.

"Will you take off my handcuffs now?" I asked. "I'm co-operating. I'm helping you."

"No," she said as she helped me out of the car, one hand holding on to my arm just firmly enough to let me know I wasn't free. Her manner was brusque, businesslike. "Not yet."

She was taller than me. Stronger, it seemed. I didn't know if I could squirm away and make a run for it. Her hand on my arm was setting off every alarm bell in my nervous system. My heart thudded. A door slamming shut over and over, to no avail.

"He's here?" the woman asked, eyeing the house as she led me up the walk to the door.

"Yes," I said. "He's paranoid, though. He might not come to the door if he sees you. So you should uncuff me and I can knock and you can hide."

If I was free, I could run. She let go of my arm—relief, the pressure gone—and uncuffed me, but before I could so much as shake my cramped arms, she grabbed my wrists and relocked the cuffs, just in the front now.

"I'll be right here," she said. She moved slightly to the left and pressed herself up against the front wall of the house.

"You said you'd let me go," I said.

"I will," she said, "once I know you aren't trying to trick me."

Seeing no better option, I knocked on the door as best I could with my shackled arms.

"Hey it's me," I called. "Pie. Please let me in. I need help."

It was late. He was probably asleep. My whole body was tense, waiting for the right moment to get away.

The woman motioned for me to knock again. I did, but it was awkward with my arms stuck together. She made a noise of disgust, stepped in and pounded on the door. Loud. Over and over.

"Go away," crackled the speaker.

I tried to take a step back, but the woman nudged me, gave a sharp nod.

"Uh, I'm sorry to show up like this," I said into the intercom. "But I really need your help. My father isn't here."

"I told you never to come back here," Steve said. He didn't sound angry so much as uncomprehending. Why hadn't I done what he'd asked?

The woman pushed me aside and spoke into the intercom.

"I'm looking for my brother, Felix," she said. "Do you know him?"

There was a long pause. I thought Steve wasn't going to answer. But then the intercom crackled on. "I used to."

I chose that moment to run.

I made it down the steps, onto the grass. But the woman was faster than me. Next thing I knew, I was on the ground. Her knee was in my back.

"Let me go," I shouted, panicked.

"You are causing a scene," the loudspeaker crackled. "Stop it."

The weight on my back lessened. A moment later the woman was hauling me up by my arm, dragging me back to the door. She pounded on it with a fist.

"Where is he?" she shouted.

The light in the house next door flicked on. I tried to cover my face with my hands, but they were still shackled.

"Please be quiet," said the loudspeaker.

The woman pounded louder. "I'll scream," she shouted, "at the top of my lungs."

I heard some inaudible grumbling, and then the lock clicked.

"This is absurd," Steve said as he opened the door. "If you must shout, come do it inside."

The woman dragged me after her. Steve stood against the

wall, holding himself stiff and still, a look of absolute fury on his face.

The woman, whose name I still didn't know, swiveled her head and then stopped, staring at him. He stiffened even further, turned to me, his eyes wide.

"She can see us," I said, miserable.

"You are only a smudge," said the woman, "a blob of heat."

Steve looked as miserable as I felt. "What have you done?" he asked me, voice tight.

"She kidnapped me," I protested feebly. "I had no choice."

"Where is my brother?" the woman demanded.

Steve closed his eyes, pressed his hands against them. He slid down the wall until he was sitting, hunched over, hiding from the woman's gaze.

"Don't shout at him," I told the woman. "Or he won't tell you anything."

She lifted her own hands to her goggles. At first, I thought she was adjusting them, but then I realized she was wiping her face where tears had leaked out beneath them.

She was crying. All her anger. It was desperation, grief. The three of us were just trading our misery around, multiplying it, throwing it at each other like some idiotic game of hot potato, burning our hands, burning each other, burning everything.

Was *this* how it truly worked? The absolute rotten heart of all human interaction? Is this why my mother always said never to trust anyone?

I took a step backward down the hallway. The woman turned toward me.

She could see me. Both of them could see me. The terror of being trapped in the car crashed back down on me in a sudden wave, the way the sound of those gunshots from Colorado had chased me for months. Showing up out of nowhere. A danger with no escape. Just pure fear.

I had no one. No one on my side. My mother was gone, my father cared more about paintings than me. To Tess, I'd never been more than an angry ghost.

Worst of all, I'd lost the only true friend I'd ever had.

And I was still trapped.

I took another step backward.

And plunged into darkness.

47

I'd returned to the void, disconnected from myself and from the world. I could just barely sense the room I'd left, though not with sight. I wondered whether this was how bats or dolphins understood the world. Some type of mind's-eye sonar. A map of the room but inside my head and without colors, without light. Just shapes, edges.

I sensed a shape moving toward me. A darker darkness, a darkness with a certain electricity.

The shape was Steve, I was pretty sure. Or the woman.

I felt the vibrations of their speech, the way you might feel the deep bass of a speaker, but I couldn't understand it.

The Steve shape moved again.

He reached toward me. I tried to back up, but I was awkward at moving through the strange nothingness here. The handcuffs had traveled with me, so my hands were still bound. The shape of his arm came at me.

It reached my shoulder.

A sensation. Not of touch. Not of pain.

Something like cold and heat at the same time. A feeling like very gentle razors peeling off your skin in strips as thin as tissue paper, whittling you down so gradually as to be nearly imperceptible. A feeling like a gust of wind stirring the small hairs on your arm but from the inside.

Steve had not touched me. The shape of his arm had met the shape of my shoulder and kept going. Right through me.

With muted horror, I perceived that his arm was piercing my shoulder. The freezing/burning/razors/wind feeling (but gentle, so gentle, like the memory of a feeling) pulsed at the point of overlap.

I was frozen. Pinned by the blade of his arm.

Or was I?

I moved away. There was no resistance. I found that if I thought of my movement as swimming rather than walking, it was easier.

The Steve shape straightened, withdrew his hand. It took me a moment to make sense of my perceptions. There was a low plane near where he had been reaching. A table. He'd been picking something up. He hadn't known I was there at all.

I didn't exist.

I found the shape of the doorway to the room and moved out. I was navigating more by memory than by my poorly developed shadow sense. The front door was closed, bolted, and chained.

I moved close to the plane of the door and reached out, but my hand passed through the chain. Overshot, went part-way through the door. It tingled slightly, fainter than when Steve had stuck his hand through my shoulder.

This was maddening. I couldn't see. My brain was

struggling to process this new way of perceiving my surroundings. I was on the point of crying in frustration when I realized what an absolute idiot I was being.

I'd become what I always felt like: a ghost. Ghosts don't need to bother with locks. Ghost don't even need to bother with doors.

I moved forward. Some small part of my mind was resisting, sending frantic instinctual signals to stop, holding on to my notion of walls. But I shoved it aside, stepped into the plane of the door, stepped past it, a faint chill moving through me.

I was outside. The boundaries of my senses expanded. There was an enormous expanse of nothingness above me and a cacophony of shapes around me.

As I focused on the shapes, they seemed to multiply. I could perceive not only the outsides of houses but the insides, too.

My mind went wandering. I think that's the best way I can describe it. There were no apparent limits to how far I could sense the world around me. Buildings didn't block my line of sight, because it wasn't really sight. Distance didn't dim it, either. I searched so far that I lost track of my point of reference. Lost track of myself.

I'd already lost touch with my body, but now my identity grew distant, too. I was just an observer. I was not even an I. The lines between the world I observed and the point from which I observed it were gone. No way to tell where I ended and it began. The glass wall dissolved entirely.

It wasn't painful. Wasn't sad or lonely. It was peaceful, easy.

More than anything, it was safe. Nothing could harm me. Nothing could reach me at all.

I could have stayed that way forever, maybe. Floating, unburdened, untroubled. But something caught my attention. A figure. Different from the shapes around it. More distinct.

My mother? The memory tugged at me. Observing closer, it became clear that this was not my mother. This was someone else.

Felix? I thought the name with my whole strange incorporeal being and somehow—don't ask me how—the figure seemed to understand. Understand and respond.

Yes.

It came to me not as a word but as a wave of sensation.

Your sister. I didn't speak these words, or sign them. I'd lost track of my mouth, my limbs, myself. But I sent them somehow in the direction of Felix. *She is looking for you.*

The reply I got was even less like words.

A refusal. Sadness. Pulling away. An overwhelming feeling of rejection, aloneness. I recognized those feelings. I'd felt similar things so many times before myself. The deep well of loneliness. Endless. Overwhelming.

And I pushed back against it.

I didn't know Felix. But I knew that feeling. And maybe that simple fact—the two of us connected by the same aloneness—made us no longer alone.

Besides, he had a sister who loved him so fiercely she would do anything to reach him.

I sent all this to him without words. I didn't even really do it on purpose. Just a big burst of thought, like a flash of light.

Oh, came his reply, a tiny spark. And a tendril of his being reached out toward a tendril of my being, trying to see who I was, I think. Trying to touch in whatever way was possible in this world.

I was so startled that I pulled away, the whole shadow world retracting.

And all at once I came rushing back into myself.

I was still in the safety of the shadow world, not the real world. My body still felt distant, a strange numb shadow puppet, but I was unmistakably in it.

I puzzled over what had just transpired. As dreamlike as the events seemed, I had no doubt that I'd genuinely communicated with Felix.

Things felt clearer here, simpler, less clouded by the complications of the regular world.

I would find my mother, I decided. I would tell her she'd been right about everything.

I moved along the street, following what I thought was the sidewalk, though I might very well have been walking in the street. Eventually I found myself heading up a hill. At the top, I turned my perception to the horizon, seeking out distant shapes, sensing the skyline, the peaks and valleys of rooftops.

At length, I found it: the Cathedral of Learning. I knew that shape, the way it stuck up higher than the shapes around it. Once I knew where it was, I could orient myself.

I headed in the direction of Denise's house, taking the

shortest route, moving through walls, through houses. I sensed other people sometimes. They were in the real world, so to me they were nothing more than moving shadows emitting odd energy.

At some point, without quite noticing it, I had begun walking. At the beginning I just moved, floated. But instinct kicked in, I guess, and after a while I became more aware of my legs and feet—though they felt distant, as if they belonged to someone else. The farther I walked, the more I felt my body.

I felt it in the form of an ache. First in my feet and legs and then in my stomach, because I hadn't eaten in many hours. My wrists and shoulders ached, too, from the cuffs, which I'd failed to escape. My tongue was dry. I was cold.

And the more I felt my body, the more I felt the world around me, too. There were moments, brief flashes, when I thought I could almost see something. But I resisted those flashes, turned away, didn't try to bring them into focus.

I didn't want to go back.

The world had thrown me out, or I had jumped free of it, a burning building. I was where I belonged.

I sensed my mother before I even reached Denise's house, a shivering darkness flitting in the distance.

I think she sensed me, too. She went very still as I approached. And then she came toward me, through the flimsy planes of the walls, out into what I was pretty sure corresponded to someone's front yard. I couldn't tell whether this was Denise's street or not, but it didn't matter.

"Pie?" my mother signed, spelling my name in the air with her hands. "Why are you here again?"

In reply, I held out my arms to show her how they were bound.

She was still wearing her backpack. She dug around, withdrew something. She bent over the handcuffs.

There was no click, not audible, but there was a lessening of the pressure as she picked the lock, and then the shape of the handcuffs fell away from me. As they did, they changed, became less distinct.

They had fallen through to the other side. The real world. For an instant, I thought I saw them glint, thought I saw the patch of grass where they'd fallen, but I blinked it away.

I didn't want to go back. I wanted to be here, where I truly belonged.

A dull sadness radiated from my mother's direction.

"Aren't you glad to see me?" I asked.

"I'm surprised."

"Don't worry," I said. "I'm not going to try to talk you into going back. I want to stay here."

My mother shook her head. "You don't want that."

I felt a pulse of anger. The strength of the emotion was like a beam of light, piercing into the other world, pulling me through. I tried to stay calm, to return to a state of nothingness.

I had to stay.

"Let's stay here," I said. "The two of us together. I understand why you came, now. It's safe here. It isn't safe back there."

Images flashed through my mind: that man shooting at us years ago, the woman's hand closing around my arm, Denise's expression of repulsion and disgust. Here, I could hold all those things at a distance. They couldn't hurt me.

My mother sighed, rippling the darkness between us.

"I'm sorry," she said. "I failed you."

My surprise must have been palpable, radiating off me. She went on.

"It's easier to see things objectively here," she said. "To look back and see how I was always afraid. I wanted to keep you safe. Keep you from ever getting hurt. But in trying to do that, I held you back. I've known for a long time that you wanted more than the life we had."

I wanted to protest, but she was right, of course. I had wanted more. Wanted it so badly that I'd made a complete mess of everything.

"I was so scared for you," my mother said. "Scared of what I knew I had to do."

"What? Run away?" I could feel the anger pulling at me. Feel the world pulling at me, too. I pushed them both away.

"No," my mother said. "Let you go."

I couldn't tell if the sadness was mine or hers. They ran together. I ran toward her, too, pushed her hand away. I didn't want to be let go. I wanted to stay.

I threw my arms tightly around my mother, hugging her, holding on to her like an anchor. She could keep me here.

A strange thing happened then. Instead of emotions, I got images. It was a bit like how I'd communicated with Felix but more overwhelming. I saw things, but the way you'd see a memory, inside your mind. Indistinct. Some parts blurred, others too bright, too distinct. Weighted with feeling and context.

I saw my mother grabbing a small hand, a child's hand—my hand—and running. I saw her watching me as I played alone with some rich kid's toys. I saw that moment in the Broadway play when I had stepped downstage, saw it from her perspective as she reached out a hand to stop me.

I saw her writing a letter to my father. Gazing at herself in a mirror, flickering in and out of existence. A sick feeling as she resisted the urge to escape entirely, to dissociate into safety. The strain of holding herself down in the real world.

And fear. Writhing, like insects under her skin. Where my constant companion had been loneliness, hers had been fear. Following her everywhere. Inescapable.

In the present, she pulled away from me, broke the connection. Her hands formed the sign for "sorry."

I reached for her again, grasped both her hands with mine.

Concentrating hard, I sent her an image. A series of impressions. Me watching her. Me at four, at seven, ten, sixteen, just a few weeks ago. Watching as she retreated into silence. Wanting nothing more than to know what was in her head.

In reply, my mother sent me an image of a closed door in a house I'd never seen. A hand, her hand, closing it. Her hand as I had never seen it. Solid.

She closed the door again and again, desperate to keep something out.

In the darkness, she pulled her real hand away again so she could speak in signs.

"I . . ." She faltered, let her hands fall to her sides for a moment. "I never dealt with what happened to me when I was younger. I never talked to anyone about it. Not even your father. And I had no one else."

"You had me," I protested, a little hurt.

"But you're my daughter. I'm meant to protect you and comfort you, not the other way around. You need to go back. Live your life."

"How can you tell me to live my life when you won't?" I felt angry again, though I tried to resist.

"Your life is your life. Mine is mine. I'm trying." She hesitated. "There are others here, you know. I can"—here she made a sign that was halfway between "see" and "feel"—"their presence. I met one. We spoke. Not words. At a distance."

Had it been Felix? I raised my hands to ask, but how would I even begin to explain who he was, how I knew about him?

So much had happened to me since my mother had vanished.

So many terrible wonderful things.

"Did you know?" I asked instead. "That there were other people like us in the world?"

What I meant was: Did you lie to me?

"No," she said. And then, "Yes. Maybe. I wasn't sure."

Anger was leaking back into me, disturbing the peaceful nothingness. "So, what?" I asked. "You're just going to stay here?"

Her shape moved in a funny way, which I think was a sort of shrug.

"I'll stay too," I insisted.

"No," she said. "You're flickering. Even now."

It was true. I tried to ignore it. I willed myself to stay still, to stay in the shadow world, where I belonged. But some part of my mind resisted, some part of me was straining toward substance. I got brief flashes of sound. Color. My hands would tingle. My heart would beat.

"Do you just want to get rid of me?" I asked my mother.

"No! Never that. Look, we can send letters."

She pulled something out of her pack. A notebook, a pen. These objects, since they existed here with us, were more distinct than the shadow outlines of things in the normal world. She opened to a blank page, wrote on the paper, ripped it out and handed it to me.

When I ran my fingers over the page, I could sense where the ink was and wasn't. I could read it that way.

"I love you," she had written. "No matter what."

Tears came to my eyes, and I could feel them as they trickled down my cheeks. I was struggling to stay.

"Watch." My mother ripped out another page, dropped it, and it winked into a shadow blur. It had fallen through into the real world now.

I feared I would follow it any moment. I was flickering

373

more and more, kept catching fragments of sight out of the corner of my eye. A blade of grass. A single brick on the façade of the house. A window. I wanted those things. There was no use denying it. I wanted the world.

"Will you ever come back?" I asked my mother.

"Someday," she said. "I hope."

48

I was back, standing in front of Denise's house.

I felt unimaginably heavy. It reminded me of the few blissful times my mother had allowed me to go swimming. Not the swimming itself, but the moment after you get out of the water, when gravity reasserts itself with a vindictive glee, dragging you down.

I couldn't say I was sorry to be back, though. The world was bright and crisp, the streetlamps shining like spotlights on a stage. Every blade of grass hammed it up.

The shadow place had smoothed out the world, made it simpler and calmer, but I'd missed this. Missed the jagged details, the grit and extravagance.

The handcuffs glittered on the lawn by my feet. I picked them up, stuck them in my pocket.

My mother had said she failed me, but I didn't think that was true, not entirely. She'd given me a far better childhood than she'd had. Maybe I was kind of messed up and lonely, but at least I'd been loved.

I could face my problems.

At least, I hoped I could.

I wandered down the street, found my way back to that bar from the other day. Slipped in, invisible. Found the most obnoxious drunk guy there, helped myself to his cell phone and wallet. I took the cash and left the wallet on the floor by his feet to find later.

Somehow, I had to fix every single thing that had gone wrong. Had to put it all back together.

Out front, I called my dad, asked him to come get me. I left the cell phone for the drunk guy to find later, too.

"It's late," my father said groggily, after he'd pulled up across from the bar and I'd tapped on the window.

"I found the paranormal researcher," I told him as I slid into the passenger seat.

"Oh." He looked genuinely caught off guard by that, which gave me a little spark of joy. "Do you still want me to meet up with her tomorrow?"

"No need," I said. "Can you take me to Steve's?"

"What?" My father was blinking at the passenger-side door handle.

"You know, the invisible guy."

"At this hour? Why?"

"Here," I said instead of explaining. With a gloved hand, I reached into my pocket, pulled out the wad of cash I'd taken from the guy at the bar. As soon as it cleared the pocket, the cash flashed into existence. His eyes widened, ever so slightly but I saw it.

He reached for the cash.

I quickly transferred it to my left hand, which was ungloved. It vanished.

"I'll give this to you when we get there," I said.

"We make a great team," my father said with a smirk, "you and I."

I climbed into the back of the van and sat there while my father drove. When we arrived, I handed over the cash as promised, asked him to wait outside while I went to talk to Steve.

My heart beat faster as I approached the door. He might be furious. He might be asleep. He might be dead, for all I knew.

I knocked.

I didn't even have to wait very long. The intercom didn't buzz on. Steve must have seen who it was on his cameras, because he opened the door. His face registered more emotion than I was used to from him. Surprise, mostly. Curiosity.

"You vanished," he said. "I didn't think I'd ever see you again."

"Well, I'm back," I said, flooded with relief that his first impulse didn't seem to be anger. "That woman still here?"

"Cynthia. She refuses to leave."

Steve waved me inside.

The woman was sitting on the couch, her goggles on the cushion beside her. I wondered whether Steve had convinced her to remove them. They'd pressed an imprint into her skin. Her eyes were red, her face was puffy, from crying.

She was clutching a mug, staring down at it.

I took a step toward her. "My name is Pietà," I said.

She startled, flung out her arms, dropping the mug. Without her goggles, she hadn't even realized there was anyone in the room.

Behind me, Steve made an exasperated noise. He knelt to pick up the mug and dab at the spilled tea or whatever it was.

"You never asked," I said, "but that's my name."

She reached for the goggles. Her whole manner was different than it had been earlier in the car. She seemed exhausted now, a little scared.

"Don't put those on," I said, "or I'll leave."

She hesitated.

"I found your brother," I said.

She jumped to her feet, eyes desperately scanning the room. A hint of her previous recalcitrance came back into her tone. "Where is he?"

I took a step back. "Are you going to apologize?" I demanded. "For kidnapping me?"

She sat back down, her face set as if in pain. "I'm sorry," she said, but I could tell she didn't mean it. I could tell that she'd do it again in a heartbeat. "Will you take me to him? Please?"

"How do you know he wants to see you?" I asked.

She hung her head. She really did seem sorry then.

"Our parents," she said haltingly, "they couldn't accept him for who he was. They made him feel evil, they tried to change him. I should have stood up for him then. I didn't. I need to make up for it now. Please, I'm sorry about the way I approached you. I was desperate. Please take me to my brother. I'll make it up to you."

"I can't take you there," I told her, and saw anger come down over her face like a window shade. "It's not a place you can go."

I gave her the most basic explanation I could manage for something that I didn't fully understand. I told her how there was another step beyond invisibility, a place only people who were invisible to begin with could access, and even then only in extremes of emotional distress. I wasn't even sure Steve could get to that other place—he seemed to have found his peace.

"But you can write him a letter," I finished. "I'll make sure it gets to him. And if he replies, I can get that to you, too. But you have to promise to leave us alone otherwise."

She squeezed and unsqueezed her fists.

"Yes," she said. "Okay."

Steve found paper and a pen. While the woman wrote, I told Steve more about my experience in the other place. He asked if it was okay if he took notes, kept asking me questions about things I had failed to adequately observe—gravity, for instance, and power lines. But his eyes were shining. He was fascinated, and I got the sense that he had forgiven me.

Sometime later, I left with a long letter and an address for the woman, Cynthia. She and Steve, to my surprise, exchanged contact info. He wanted updates.

I would write my own letter, to my mother. Send them both through to her.

Already I was exhausted, physically and emotionally, from all I had faced.

But this was only the beginning.

I'd asked Cynthia one last question before I left. How had she known to wait outside that particular house? What exactly did the girl she mentioned earlier, her informant, tell her?

"She told me this was the house where the headless girl had been," Cynthia told me. "She told me the girl who lived here—Deborah or something—claimed to know nothing about it, but that she seemed like she was lying."

Denise hadn't sold me out.

49

The driver's seat of the van was empty, so I banged on the back doors. My father, looking bleary, opened them a few minutes later. He'd rolled out his blankets on the floor of the van, been sleeping in the center of his gold-framed hoard.

"It's me," I said, though he must have known that.

My father moved aside so I'd have space to climb in the van. "So you didn't talk him into adopting you, huh?"

I ignored this. "I need to make another stop," I told him.

"Really, Pie? What is it, three in the morning?"

"I'll stay with you," I said. Give the mark what he wants.

"Huh?" He rubbed his eyes. He didn't seem to be acting. He was just him, a tired middle-aged guy who wanted to go back to bed.

"You want me to, right?" I searched his face, hoping for a sign of something real, some genuine emotion. "Mom's not here. She wanted you to take care of me. You asked me to stay the other day. Said we'd make a great team."

He switched on, his charming smile appearing light-switch quick.

"Of course," he said. "We would. I'm glad you finally came to your senses."

"Just take me to the Cathedral of Learning," I said with a sigh. "I don't want to explain why."

"This can't wait until the morning?"

"No."

My father rolled his eyes. Muttered something under his breath that might have been "Women," I wasn't quite sure. He climbed out, got into the driver's seat.

While he drove, I quietly stacked all the paintings, wrapped them carefully in the blankets.

My father parked on the far side of the building, not the side facing the museum, which was fine. I didn't want to tell him where I was actually going.

"Can you get out of the van?" I called up to the cab. "And help me with something?"

He walked around on the sidewalk, shuffling and yawning. I hopped out of the van, tiptoed over beside him.

"Dad," I said.

He picked his head up. "Yeah?"

"Would you still like me if I wasn't invisible?"

"Of course," he said. "You're my daughter."

I stared closely at his face, trying hard to detect any hint of insincerity. But I honestly couldn't tell.

Well, no turning back now.

I touched his sleeve. He tilted his head, uncertainty flitting across his face. He didn't entirely trust me. And he was right not to.

I snapped the invisible handcuff around his wrist. Quickly, before he could react to the cold bite of metal, while the cuffs were still invisible, I snapped the other cuff around his right wrist. Then I let go and stood back.

His eyes widened. He flicked his eyes back and forth from me to his wrists, the cuffs now visible.

"Wh-wh-what . . . ," he stammered.

"Sorry, Dad," I said. "I'm robbing you."

His eyes went even wider. I saw horror, realization. I thought he was going to scream, to yell. I expected fury to break through his careful mask.

But instead, he started to laugh.

"Jesus," he said, wheezing. "Oh god. You really are my kid. Sometimes I wasn't sure. But you really are."

I paused, taken aback. "You weren't sure?"

He gave a halting shrug, the movement hindered by his cuffed hands. "Never saw your face. Could have the mailman's nose for all I knew."

He was still laughing as I walked away.

He'd left the door of the van open, the keys still in the ignition. I got behind the wheel. I only had a block and a half or so to go. I thought I could manage it.

I shut the door and turned the key. I'd only ever seen this in movies and TV. The van squealed to life, and my stomach turned over.

"Hey," my father shouted, "hey, what are you doing? You can't drive!"

Was this safe? Absolutely not.

I could have had my father drive us right to the museum, but I wasn't certain he would have cooperated. I didn't want him messing anything up. And I didn't want him to see what I was going to do.

I barely pressed the gas. Just enough to make the van roll slowly down the street. My father came running after, so I had to speed up. There were hardly any other cars around this late, which was good, because otherwise I'd have lost it for sure. I glided down the street, heart racing, finally worked up the nerve to turn.

My father fell behind, unable to keep up. I was in the belly of the beast, but I was in control, my hands gripping the wheel, eyes nailed to the road. I breathed in and out, worked to stay calm.

I parked, sloppily, by the back of the museum.

At first, I thought I might try to break in. This wasn't the way I normally did things. For me it was all daylight, easy, walking right in, taking whatever I wanted.

This must be how normal thieves felt, my heart in my throat, pulse pounding almost as hard as it had when I got kidnapped.

Though I wasn't here to steal anything.

I wondered whether my father held on to the paintings because they reminded him of my mother. Maybe they were proof, in some way, of his devotion. Looking at it that way, it was almost sweet.

But it was selfish, too. When my mother had chided me for touching the van Gogh, she'd told me to be better than her. Other people deserved to see these paintings. And if my father really wanted to show that he cared about my mother, about me, he needed to care a lot less about his stuff. People were more important than objects. Always.

In the end, unsure how to truly break in, I simply crept into the sculpture garden behind the museum. I propped the three paintings I'd stolen gently against the back wall.

I'd thought about adding a note—*Here you go, sorry for the bother* or *Oops, I thought this was the library, sorry*—but I didn't have any paper.

I ran back and forth from the sculpture garden to the van, nervous the whole time that at any moment a security guard or my angry father would burst out of the dark. The rest of the paintings from my father's collection I left in the middle of the sculpture garden, covered with his blankets to protect them from the elements. If my suspicions were correct, most of these originated from across the ocean, but I couldn't very well take them all the way back there.

This would have to be good enough.

I drove the van four blocks away from the museum before my fear caught up with me and I bailed. I had to spend a few minutes sitting on the curb, head between my knees, breathing hard. At least the van wouldn't be right next to the museum, though. I didn't want my father to get caught. We just both needed to think about other people and not only ourselves for a change.

I loaded up the duffel bag with everything from the van that I'd stolen the night before—electronics, jewels, cash—and started walking. It was a long way, mostly uphill, but I kept going, driven by a glassy-eyed determination. Sleep could wait.

At the first house, I was still nervous, so I left the stolen goods on a back patio. At the second house, I got braver, fetched the key from where I knew it was hidden, put things back inside. Same for the third. From that house, I did also take something: a scrap of paper and a pen. It wasn't a nice pen or anything, though, so I figured no one would miss it.

It was nearly dawn by the time I made it to my final stop: the castle. Or, rather, the playhouse behind it.

I crawled inside and wrote a note. I didn't confess all my feelings. That would only have been selfish. I wasn't sure whether this note was selfish, too, but all I could do was try.

Tess, I wrote, *I'm really sorry for haunting you. I am going to leave you alone forever now. Sincerely, the ghost.*

It wasn't really enough. But nothing ever would be. All I could do was move on. All I could do was be true to my word.

50

The sun blazing through a small grubby window woke me. I'd fallen asleep curled up on the floor of the playhouse behind Tess's house. By my best guess, only a few hours had passed. I'd had a long night, but I still wasn't done.

I left the note I'd written in the center of the floor, weighed down with a rock.

My final task would be the hardest. Denise had called me a coward, a liar. I had to prove to her I could be better than that.

I walked the now-familiar route to her house, my legs aching dully. It was Monday. Denise and Jules would have left for school already. Hopefully, Larissa and Terrance would be at work. All I needed was the plaster strips from the attic. The ones Jules had almost used the other day to make me a mask.

I let myself in with the key I'd taken that very first night. The lights were off. I ran up the stairs, not bothering to go quietly.

But when I reached the attic, I stopped cold.

Jules was sitting up in bed, staring wide-eyed in my general direction.

"Sam?" they said.

I let out a breath. No hiding. "Yeah."

"Oh, thank goodness," they said, visibly relaxing. "You scared the shit out of me."

My mind was already scrambling for an excuse, but I made myself spit out the truth. "I'm sorry, I didn't think anyone was home. I thought you'd be at school. Is it a day off or something?"

"No, Mom let me stay home." Jules shrugged. "I said I wasn't feeling well, but honestly, I just didn't feel up to it. Lucky you, you never have to go to school."

It reminded me a little of the things Denise had said to me before I fell out of the world, though Jules didn't sound angry.

"I'm sorry," I said. "I can leave."

I turned. A stair creaked beneath my feet.

"No, wait, Sam, come back." Jules hopped out of bed, grabbing their floral robe from where it hung off a plant, pulling it on.

"I'm still here," I said.

"What happened yesterday?" Jules came toward the stairway, eyes scanning anxiously. "Denise wouldn't tell me. She just said you had to leave suddenly."

"Uh, yeah. We had a fight. She told me to leave."

"Shit, she did?"

I hung my head. "It was all my fault. I'm really sorry I tried to sneak in here. I just wanted to borrow—" I stopped myself. It wasn't really borrowing, was it? "I was going to take those plaster strips you mentioned the other day."

"Why?" Jules still didn't sound mad, just curious.

It made it easier to tell the truth.

"I want a face," I said.

Jules offered to help immediately. Insisted, in fact. They didn't seem to care that I'd been planning to take their things without asking. They were just jazzed about the challenge.

We used the plaster strips to make a mold of my actual face, covering my skin with Vaseline and then layering the strips across it. The plaster was cold and wet but soothing in an odd way. When the mask had dried, we lifted it away, and there it was. A face. White, blank, but more solid than my real one.

While we worked, I told Jules everything that had happened since yesterday.

I stumbled over the moment where I had turned back to spy on Denise and Tess. I found myself, almost instinctually, trying to soften it, play it off as an accident.

But I made myself tell the truth.

I told Jules about my father. The heists. The things I'd stolen. I told them that my name wasn't really Sam. Told them why I'd come here in the first place. About how I'd lived in Tess's house two years ago.

If Jules changed their mind, cracked the mask in two, kicked me out, I wouldn't blame them.

I told them about the fight with Denise. The things she'd said. The things I'd said.

"She was in a bad mood last night," Jules said. "She'd just been to visit her mother. That always puts her in a weird place. Don't take it to heart."

"No," I said. "She was right to be angry at me. That's what this is for." I indicated the mask. Jules was painting it now, in their own style. Beautiful, rich colors. Blues and pinks and purples and reds. "I want to go talk to her. Face to face. Tell her I'm sorry."

Jules checked the time on their phone. "It'll be hours until school lets out. She's still in morning classes."

"I'll go meet her there," I said. "Show her I'm not a coward."

"The doors are locked during the day, though," Jules said, "for security. You can't just walk in, even if you are invisible."

"Oh. Right. I hadn't thought of that." I was disappointed. It was silly, I guess, but waiting outside didn't seem as dramatic a gesture.

"Well, some of the teachers come in late—around lunchtime," Jules said. "Oh, and I know a guy who told me he snuck in through the eighth-floor boys' bathroom once. You can reach the window from the roof of the next building over, apparently. . . . Or the whole top floor is this warehouse space where they host events for fancy people sometimes. We're not allowed up there."

"Why—" I started, then hesitated.

"Why aren't we allowed up there?" they guessed.

"No. Why don't you hate me, too?" I'd told them all my worst secrets. Let them see me for who I really was. A thief. A liar.

Jules snorted. "Okay, so you're kind of weird and messed up? So what? You're nice, Sam. Or sorry, Pie. I have no

390

reason to hate you. Denise probably doesn't hate you, either. Not really. She just got mad, sounds like. Here."

They held out the finished mask. A version of my face as it had never been before: solid, kaleidoscopic, full of life and color.

"I hope you're right," I said.

Jules told me where to go, what bus to take. I wondered, if they hadn't been home, if they hadn't been kind to me, if I'd still have had the courage to go through with this. I made a few stops on the way, to gather supplies.

CAPA, the school of Creative and Performing Arts, was downtown near the river, one of the city's many bridges looming just beyond it. It was all glass and concrete, very different from the old-fashioned brick of the Catholic school Tess went to.

I walked into the law firm next door to CAPA. All the buildings on this block shared walls, so once I reached the roof, it was easy to cross over. I located the bathroom window Jules had told me about, squeezed through.

In one of the stalls, I changed. Pulled on a second pair of gloves, a second pair of tights, a dress borrowed from Jules over the one I'd been wearing. A ski mask. And over that, a wig and the mask Jules had painted for me.

A face.

It wasn't realistic, exactly, but it was beautiful. Jules had even painted eyes, glued fake lashes to the mask. We'd cut small, neat circles for the pupils so I could see. I wore a pair of lightly tinted sunglasses over the mask.

Down the hallway, down the stairs.

I couldn't see well at all through the mask. My hands shook. But if I was going to do this, I wanted to do it all the way. I passed rooms with music seeping out, rooms with doors through which I could glimpse bodies moving, dancing.

It was afternoon now, which meant Denise would be in her art classes. Jules told me which floor the photography classrooms were on, though they didn't know which room. I hoped no teacher or hall monitor would stop me in a hallway. I had no clue what I would say.

I peered through a glass-windowed doorway: students bent over desks, drawing. Peered through another: an empty classroom. Peered through a third.

And there, projected on the far wall of the classroom: a picture of me.

I felt my knees going weak, felt the pull of darkness, the desire to give in and vanish completely.

It was one of the shots with the yellow curtain. You could barely make out an indistinct suggestion of my profile beneath it, a hint of shoulders, one arm raised. Denise stood at the front of the room, talking.

Through the glass of the door, I couldn't hear what she was saying.

I couldn't go in.

This whole plan was idiotic. I moved backward until I found the wall, pressed against it. I could run. Or just throw off my second layers where I stood, return to invisibility.

A bell rang.

Doorways all along the hallway flew open, and students

poured out. I turned, ducked my head a little. Most students who passed by ignored me, too focused on their rush to the next class. One or two gave me curious looks.

Somebody muttered, "It's not Halloween anymore, weirdo," as he passed.

Denise was the second-to-last to leave her classroom.

She froze when she saw me, her eyes fixed on my mask. The person behind her bumped into her. Denise dropped the armful of photographic prints she'd been holding.

And she swore, much too loudly.

51

I knelt to help Denise gather her fallen photos.

"Is there somewhere we can talk?" I whispered.

I was worried she would say no. Maybe I should have launched right into it, the things I wanted to say.

"Yeah," she said, blinking at me as if she couldn't quite believe what she was seeing, "okay."

She led to me an empty art studio at the end of the hallway.

"I'm so sorry," I said breathlessly as soon as the door closed. "About everything."

"I can't believe you're here," she said. She reached out a hand toward my mask, then let it fall. "Where did you get this?"

"Um, Jules helped me." Was she mad? I couldn't tell.

"I'm sorry, too," she said. "I shouldn't have called you a coward."

"You were right, though, completely. Everything you said."

She frowned. "I was kind of upset. I don't know. I'd just been to see my mom. And, like, I want to support her and everything, but sometimes it makes me feel bad."

"Yeah," I said. I'd been to see my mother, too, now. Sure, she was staying in an alternate dimension rather than an apartment, but both our mothers were dealing with their own darkness—darkness that we couldn't fix for them, that was not our fault, but that cast its shadow on us sometimes. "I get it."

Denise's phone buzzed. She checked it. I hoped it wasn't Tess. She spent a while reading, then held the phone out to me to see.

"Was this you?" she asked, eyebrows raised.

It was an article on a local news site with the headline MUSEUM REPORTS REVERSE HEIST.

I skimmed the first few lines. The Carnegie staff had apparently been pleased but confused to find, upon reporting to work that morning, not only the paintings stolen from their own museum a few days prior but also works of art from many other institutions, including some pieces that had been missing for seventeen years.

"Yes," I said, unable to keep a hint of pride out of my voice. I'd pulled it off.

"Jules just sent me the link," said Denise, sounding baffled.

"There are some things I didn't tell you," I admitted, and then I told her about my dad. A short version, but I tried not to hold too much back. No lies. I told her about the art I'd stolen from the museum, the art my mother had stolen with my father before I was born.

"But I put it all back. I put the stuff I stole from the houses back, too." Most of it, anyway. "I can put back the stuff I gave you, too. Or you can keep it. But I'm so sorry I brought it into your house. You were right, I wasn't thinking. I just wanted you to like me, wanted to be useful."

"You don't have to be useful," Denise said.

She was frowning a little. I was worried I'd said the wrong thing. "Well," I clarified, "helpful, you know. Like being in your pictures. That was something I could do that was of value to you. I wanted to be of value. So we could be friends. I'm sorry I messed it all up."

Denise shook her head. "Shit, I think I must have messed it up, too. You didn't need to help with my pictures to be my friend." She looked down at her phone again. A smile crept across her face, and my heart soared. "Pie, did you seriously do all this last night?"

"Yes." And then I couldn't help myself. Words were tumbling out, and I was telling her about the paranormal researcher. The shadow place. My mother.

"God," she said, forehead creased with concern. "I can't believe you were straight-up abducted. I had no idea."

"It's fine," I said, grinning despite myself.

"No," she said. "I'm sorry. I guess I didn't really understand the danger you might be in."

"It's okay, honestly," I insisted. "These last few days. They've been the most amazing time of my life. Meeting you has been the most amazing thing that has ever happened to me."

I realized as I said it that it was true. I used to think that meeting Tess was the most amazing thing that had ever happened to me, but I was wrong.

Maybe that's what life was. A series of increasingly

amazing occurrences, each new one making all past experiences pale in comparison.

That sounded both exciting and exhausting.

"Yeah," Denise said. "Same here."

I scoffed. Well, more like snorted if I'm being honest.

Denise quirked an eyebrow. "What?"

"There's no way that our meeting has been even a fraction as big a deal for you as it's been for me."

"It *was* a big deal," she insisted. "I had no idea invisible people existed before I met you."

"I'd basically never even talked to anyone before I met you!"

Denise laughed. "I wish I could see your face."

"I know," I said. "That's why I made this." I touched a glove to the mask.

"But your real face."

"Oh."

This was stupid. Terrible. The worst idea I'd ever had.

But maybe the glass wall was a window I could open instead of break. I pulled the gloves free from my right hand. Both pairs, outer and inner layers. Dropped them to the floor.

The bell for the next class rang.

"Do you need to go?" I asked.

"It's fine if I'm a little late," said Denise.

So before I could think too hard about it, I reached out and let my fingertips brush, ever so slightly, against the back of Denise's hand.

Like the wall of the Cathedral, like so many things I'd touched before, she went transparent. She still looked like herself, round-cheeked and curly-haired, but see-through, drained of all but a hint of color, a suggestion of brown and black and purple. Drained of solidity, as if I were a vampire.

I was stunned. I'd never touched anyone visible with my bare skin. Not once.

Her eyes were wide. She'd felt it, felt something change. She looked down at herself. I let go of her hand quickly, took a step back, horrified at what I'd done.

She reached for my bare hand, grabbed it, clumsily because she couldn't see it, could only see where my sleeve ended, but as soon as her skin touched mine, she went glassy again, the window behind her flashing into view, light flooding through. Shock waves up my arm.

I was tearing up, but at least I still had the mask on.

And then she reached out with her free hand, and gently, she pulled my mask away. First the painted plaster, which she set gently on a table beside us, and then the ski mask.

She was invisible now, too, which meant she could see me.

She could see my face.

She was looking me in the eyes.

It felt like jumping into water, cold water, a shock and then your body adjusts.

"So that's what you look like," she said, smiling.

I couldn't speak. It was all I could do not to look away, not to let go, to run.

I remained acutely aware of the feel of her hand against mine. A warm pressure. Soft landscape of hills, valleys. A rough callused spot on her palm. I could feel her blood pulsing there. Our heartbeats, slightly out of sync.

It was too much. Everything I had always feared. Everything I had always wanted. This was so much more than the picture on Instagram. So much more than the pictures projected up on the screen in front of everyone. This was no performance.

It was just me. No mask. No filter. Nothing between us. Only air.

I let go of Denise's hand, took a step back.

"Wait," she said. She reached for my hand again. Her skin slid against mine. So warm and so strange.

This time when she touched my hand, she stayed the same.

I was the one who changed.

Only for an instant. But we both saw it happen. As quick as a camera flash.

For a moment there, I was solid. Visible. For a moment, anybody in the world could have seen me.

52

My hand wasn't translucent. No soap-bubble skin, no glass-shard fingernails. It had flushed taupe, tan, olive, a hint of blue-green under the skin where my veins lay. Denise let go.

"Oh my god," she said. "That was . . . that . . . did you . . . ?"

My stomach lurched. I felt the darkness tugging at me, trying to pull me out of myself. "I'm sorry," I said hurriedly, backing up. "I've got to go."

"Hey, wait a second." Denise reached out a hand as if she wanted to grasp mine again. "I'll skip after next period. I can meet you out front in an hour. Okay?"

"Yes," I said.

And then I ran. Out into the hallway, up the stairs, pushing past a few stragglers who hadn't yet made it to their next class. To the eighth floor, the boys' bathroom. A birdlike boy was leaning halfway out the window, smoking a cigarette. I pushed him aside. He yelped. I hefted myself up, squirmed through the window, dropped to the roof, rolled.

Crouched out of sight farther along the roof, I pulled off

all my second-layer clothes—the overdress, the tights, the mask and wig.

I stayed down, kneeling on the tar paper, dry-heaving.

The image of my hand kept flashing in my mind. My solid hand. Heavy, irrefutable, suddenly vivid. A flashing red flag of a hand. Anybody could have seen it. Anybody could have seen me.

In some ways, it was what I'd always wanted.

But it was a lot. It was so much more than I'd expected. What if it had been permanent? What if there had been no way back?

I felt the darkness of the other world pulling at me. I wanted to run and hide more fully. To be safe. That was what I should do.

It wasn't safe to be seen. It wasn't okay to be solid. To be out there, vulnerable. Everyone's eyes all the time. My pulse raced. My breathing was shallow. It was the same as those months after we'd been shot at. This was the same fear I'd felt, the same way my body had reacted out of nowhere to a danger that was in the past.

I forced myself to take slow deep breaths. No one could see me now. I was safe again, and I had a choice.

I made my way back to street level and headed down the sidewalk. I walked fast, weaving between other pedestrians. I had only a vague sense of the direction in which I needed to go, but once I got close, I recognized the streets, walked even faster. I didn't stop until I'd reached the train station.

I stood across the street from the station, staring at the

tracks, imagining a life for myself. The same kind of life my mother had lived when she was my age. On the run. Entirely alone.

Somehow that felt safer than staying. Denise had seen me. It was unbelievable. It was cataclysmic. She had actually *seen* me.

But a small voice in the back of my head said: *Is that really so different from what she's been doing all along?*

Almost from the beginning, she had seen me as a person, not a monster or a bizarre phenomenon. Seen me as someone to get to know. To talk to, to joke with, to fight with, even. To befriend. She had seen my secrets, seen my flaws. Seen what was good about me, too.

She had always seen me.

Maybe that was why it happened. Why I'd become, for that instant, visible. I did control my power after all, but subconsciously. So maybe some part of me felt that, with Denise, it was okay to be seen. Maybe some part of me felt ready to show myself.

I watched a freight train speed past. Then I turned and walked all the way back.

By the time I got to the school, I only had to wait fifteen minutes or so before Denise came out.

"Pie?" she asked, head swiveling.

"Here," I answered softly.

"Come on," she said with a small smile, "follow me. I can't just stand here, or I'll get in trouble for cutting class."

She led me down the street, toward the bridge over the river, but she turned before we got there, headed along the underside of a big convention center. A descending path wound underneath the building. Along both sides of the path, a manmade waterfall cascaded down sheer concrete walls.

Denise stopped about halfway down the path. The rush of the water covered up the distant sound of traffic. We both just stood there for a while.

"So," said Denise finally. "Did you know that would happen? The thing, you know, earlier?"

"No," I said. It was cold here, with the wind coming off the nearby river, howling through the concrete undercarriage of the building, sending little sprays up from the waterfall. I shivered. "It's never happened before."

"Is that bad?" She didn't try to look in the direction of my voice, just stared at the water rushing down the wall. I stared at her, though.

"I don't know," I said. Someone walked past in the distance, but they wouldn't hear me over the sound of the water. Denise had been thoughtful to bring me here. "It did freak me out a little, I guess. No one except my mother has ever seen my face before."

"No one?" Denise did turn now. She was several feet off, eyes focused to my left.

"No one," I answered.

"Well, shit." She smiled. "I guess I'm lucky."

I wanted her to look at me. Just the thought embarrassed me. I glanced back at the water, watched it fall and fall and fall. "Did I look different than you thought I would?"

She considered. "You know, it's strange. I guess I hadn't

pictured you any one particular way. In my mind, your face was like a ball of light. Like the night your head fell off and the candles flared up behind you."

"Sorry to disappoint."

"It wasn't a disappointment. You have a nice face."

"A boring face."

"Don't say that. You have gorgeous eyes."

For a moment, I was too shy to speak, to look at her. I glanced up, finally, at her own eyes.

"So do you," I said.

She laughed. I felt a stab of jealousy, staring at her. She was so vivid. Her solid white teeth, her full mouth, the top lip darker, the bottom fading to pink in the middle.

I was struck with the sudden absurd urge to step forward and kiss her.

Impossible, of course. Imagine me. Kissing somebody.

"Do you want to try again?" Denise held out her hand, upturned. I remembered the first night. Her palm in the lamplight.

Her skin had been warm when I'd touched her hand. The center of her palm rough with calluses, but the pads of her fingers soft. A strange and miraculous landscape.

Now my mind was screaming at me to run. To escape.

I fought all these competing urges. Tried to focus, instead, on the moment.

My hand trembled slightly as I reached for hers. I hesitated before letting our palms touch.

"I don't know how this works," I said. "I don't know if it will turn you invisible, or if it will turn me visible, or what."

"Only one way to find out," she said.

I closed my eyes, let my hand drop. I trusted her.

"So what are you going to do now?" Denise asked.

I opened my eyes. She was transparent, the waterfall across from us streaming through her face, her chest. She was made of water, a raging river. I must have been, too.

"What do you mean?" I asked, staring at our hands, stacked one on the other, just barely touching. I could see her hand through mine.

"Well, where will you go? What will you do?"

"I don't know," I said.

"You should stay with us."

My eyes darted up to her face. She didn't look like she was joking. "I couldn't do that."

"Why not? I mean, if you don't want to, obviously that's fine. But there's plenty of room up in the attic. I'm sure Jules wouldn't mind sharing. When I first moved in, they told me they were glad I was here because they always kind of wanted an older sister anyway."

"What about your aunt and uncle?"

"Well, we'd have to tell them."

I swayed a little, almost let go of her hand.

She must have seen something in my expression— imagine that, seen something!—because she said in a rush, "I know they wouldn't mind. Larissa offered to let Neely move in when her parents kicked her out."

"If you really think it would be okay," I said, uncertain. It was too much to hope for. To have a place where I belonged. A place to stay.

"It would be cool," said Denise. "We could hang out all the time. I mean, if you wanted to. Or whatever."

I laughed. "I like hanging out with you."

"I like hanging out with you, too."

I grinned, found myself leaning toward her and then away, as if drawn with a magnet but resisting.

She tightened her grip on my hand, pulling me forward. She leaned in close. I could see her eyelashes. See one that had fallen, a black dash on the smooth brown hill of her cheek. She closed her eyes. Her face was coming toward my face. It was coming closer.

I panicked, gasped, jumped back, my hand slipping free from hers.

Her eyes shot open.

"Oh, shit." She yanked her hand back as if it had been burned, clutched it to her chest. "I'm so, so sorry. I thought we were having, like, a moment?"

I stood, frozen, reeling, invisible again.

"Shit," said Denise, her words frantic, breathless. "Pie. Are you still here? Did you run away? I'm really sorry about that, that was so wrong of me. I'm such an idiot. I totally misread the moment, but I swear I'll never try anything like that again. Please, just forgive me. I got it wrong."

My heart hammered. But I didn't want to sink away into oblivion. I didn't want to leave my body for the safety of nothingness. This was all so much. Too much. Inside my head, I was screaming. Every nerve in my body was screaming.

But it was kind of amazing.

"You didn't get it wrong," I said quietly.

"Oh," said Denise, startled. She swallowed, stared down at her feet. She almost seemed more embarrassed now.

I reached forward and took her hand again. She looked up and met my eyes.

"Is just this okay," I said, "for now?"

"Yeah." She smiled.

The world didn't literally vanish the way it had when I'd been plunged into the darkness of the shadow space.

But it might as well have been gone.

As far as I was concerned, there was nothing else in existence worth paying attention to. Just that smile.

53

Jules and Denise introduced me to Larissa and Terrance gradually. First: the idea of me. Denise mentioned a friend of hers. Told her aunt and uncle that I had recently become homeless, that I suffered from an unusual health condition.

Meanwhile, I took up temporary residence in the house with the chandelier in the elevator. In the days when I traveled with my mother, I would have considered it a perfect house, so cavernous I barely ever saw the family who lived there. I had a guest bedroom all to myself. I did enjoy the fancy food I snuck from the pantry, the luxurious high-thread-count sheets.

But I found myself missing the small dark hallway of Denise's house, with its ugly burgundy carpet. The cozy rooms. The floorboards with gaps. The couch with the stain in the shape of Texas.

I guess it wasn't the house I missed, really.

I passed the time by writing letters. Suddenly, I had quite a few pen pals.

Steve and I exchanged letters via his mailbox. My mother's letters, on the other hand, would simply appear beside me out of nowhere, regardless of where I was. To my surprise, my mother and Steve started writing letters to each other as well. At first, I acted as a go-between, but soon they bypassed me and began corresponding directly.

Most surprising of all was the letter I received one day from none other than Felix. It popped into existence the same way my mother's letters did. The two of them had been communicating, too, in the shadow place. He thanked me for finding him, for giving him the courage to reach out. He wrote about how afraid he'd been, how alone he'd felt. He wanted to know how I'd done it—how I'd gone to that place and then returned.

I wrote back immediately, left the letter sitting on the floor. Right in front of my eyes, it vanished. We wrote more over the next few days. He told me he'd sent a letter to his sister, Cynthia, as well, and she'd written back, expressing all the regret she had for not protecting him enough from their parents' harsh treatment. In fact, a whole complex network of written communication had sprung up, messages passing among Cynthia, Steve, my mother, Felix, and me.

A community of people who never touched or saw one another. But a community, nonetheless. Something my mother and I had never had before.

I told Felix that whenever he was ready to return to the world, I would be there to greet him, to help him adjust. We all would.

For a while, I kept up with the investigation into the mysteriously returned paintings, to see if my father would be implicated. I'd returned to the spot where I'd ditched the van, but it was gone. My best guess was that he'd skipped town. Maybe he'd come back once the heat died down, and if he did, I'd talk to him. But if he wanted a relationship, he would need to treat me as a daughter, not an accomplice. I'd made it clear I wasn't going to be used.

After all, he was no longer my only link to the visible world. As Denise had predicted, Terrance and Larissa were sympathetic to the idea she'd planted of a friend in need. They wanted to help. They were willing to meet me.

When the moment finally came, they took it better than I could ever have hoped. Jules and Denise had prepared them with several days' worth of hints. So there was no fainting, no screaming.

Sure, when I showed up in the living room and floated a book around, they both thought it was a prank at first. But after letting them both touch my gloved hand, after Denise touched my ungloved hand and went invisible herself, they had no choice but to believe.

And they agreed to let me stay.

I thought Jules would resent sharing their room with me. But they threw themselves into redecorating the attic with gusto, moving plants and hanging fabric from the ceiling to split up the space, to make a space for me.

A space. For me.

The week after I moved in was much less eventful than the events that had led up to it, but even the quiet normalcy of it was strange.

I woke up in a bed (well, a pile of blankets at first, but

still) that was mine. I sat at a table with other people and ate food with them. Some days, I followed Denise and Jules to school. Other days, I stayed home and did chores around the house. Larissa and Terrance hadn't specifically asked me to, but I still wanted to make myself useful. Useful in a way that didn't involve stealing and endangering them. So I scoured the countertops, scrubbed the floors. I knew Denise had said I didn't need to be useful to earn my place, but I was happy to do it. I'd never had a place to take care of before.

"Okay," Denise asked me one Saturday morning. "What state are we on?"

We were in her room. I was perched on the edge of the futon, she sat at her desk with a mirror propped in front of her. Cindy stood on tiptoes as always.

"California," I said as I watched Denise deftly remove her colorful crochet braids. The past week, I'd started telling her about all the places I'd visited. We were going through each state in the nation, one by one, alphabetically (skipping Alaska and Hawaii, since those were the only two I'd never been to). "Honestly, this one could take a while. It's a long state."

"We've got time," she said. And she was right. For now, I was staying right here in Pittsburgh. Maybe not forever. That was too long to think about.

But for once, I had a home.

"Well," I said, "you get off the train in LA, and a breeze carries the scent of the sea through the arched latticework windows of the station . . ."

While she worked from one side of her head to the other,

gently pulling the knots of the old extensions free, I told her about the places my mother and I had stayed. How big the mansions. How blue the sky.

Later, after lunch, I sat with her while she combed her freshly washed hair and I told her about the earthquake, the ocean. While she smoothed coconut oil through the strands and spun them into twists, I told her about a movie star's house we'd stayed in once, the raging parties he'd thrown. I told her about Joshua trees and shrubby juniper.

I talked until the sun went down. Until Denise was done with her hair. Until, checking the time, she announced that it was time for us to go.

A bus ride later, we met Neely outside a bar in Lawrenceville. She and Jules and Denise all had to get big black Xs markered on their hands to show they were underage. I could just ignore the guy at the door, walk right in.

Inside was dingy, cavelike. Graffitied walls, some ratty couches along one wall. Not so different from the Church, except there were pool tables, and a long bar glittering with bottles, and a real stage with a sound system. A band was up there playing.

They didn't sound that great to me, but Neely was just about out of her mind with nerves.

"Ugh, they're so much more polished than me," she said as the four of us found a corner to hang out in. "I'm going to bomb."

"Nonsense," said Denise. "You'll be great."

"And I can't even have a drink." She poked mournfully at the black X on the back of her hand.

"Really, Neely," Jules chided. "Isn't that what you fought with Tess about?"

"Well, yeah," she said. "Drinking too much turns people into jerks. But one beer? Is that too much to ask?"

Denise rolled her eyes. "Nineteen isn't twenty-one, Neels."

"If we were in England, they'd let me have a beer," Neely grumbled.

I leaned in and whispered into her ear, "Say you have to go to the bathroom."

Her eyes widened slightly before she did as I said.

About five minutes later, I met her there. She turned as the door swung open and shut on its own. I set a single tallboy down by the sink. It popped into visibility as soon as I let go.

"Don't tell the others," I said.

Okay, fine, so I was no saint. Just because I'd returned a bunch of paintings, just because I was being careful not to get my hosts in trouble, didn't mean I'd completely reformed. Besides, I'd left money for the beer and a generous tip sitting on the counter. So it wasn't stealing.

Where did I get that money?

Well, I'd returned the objects I took from those rich people's houses. I hadn't been able to remember which cash came from which house, though, so I hadn't bothered. I mean, come on, they didn't need it.

Neely grinned as she popped the can and took a sip. When I'd eventually told her the story of my heist and then my reverse-heist, she'd been more dismayed by the latter. As far as she was concerned, nobody got rich without benefiting on some level from a deeply corrupt and unfair system. In her eyes, I'd just been redistributing the wealth.

Still, I had mostly stopped taking things. I needed to be careful in a different way now. My days of running away were over. If there were consequences to my actions, I'd stay and face them.

"Thanks," said Neely in the bar bathroom. "You're a good friend."

"You too," I said.

Part of me still didn't believe it. Friends? Me?

But it was true. I had them, and I would do anything in the world for them. Maybe that was dangerous. Maybe that's what my mother worried about. But I had to live my own life. Make my own mistakes.

Neely held the beer out to me. "What about you? You nervous?"

I took the beer but only pretended to take a sip, for friendship's sake. I didn't really like beer. "So nervous I might just sink through the floor."

Literally, perhaps. I set the beer back on the sink for Neely.

"So," she said, "are you and Denise, you know . . ." She trailed off, raising her eyebrows.

I coughed, backed away. "Um, we'd better get back."

Neely was laughing behind me as I rushed out of the bathroom.

Denise and I hadn't kissed again. But we had held hands a few more times. We had spent hours talking. Had spent almost every waking hour together, in fact.

I had let her see me again, too. I mean, I'd become visible.

It wasn't something I could do on purpose, or for very long, but if it was just the two of us, and I got into the right frame of mind and touched her hand, it would happen. It was a little scary but pretty cool, too.

For now, I wasn't ready to show myself that way to anyone else, but maybe I could work up to it. Maybe one day we could walk down the street holding hands and everybody could see.

I gave Denise a gentle nudge on the elbow as I sidled up to her out in the bar. She smiled and leaned sideways so her shoulder pressed against mine. That didn't send me into a panic anymore, but it was still overwhelming. Even that. For a while, a few lovely minutes, my whole consciousness was focused solely on the world of my shoulder. The slight shifting pressure, the vibration of her laugh at something Jules said.

The band finished up, finally, and we moved away from the wall so we could get closer to the stage. Neely set up her keyboard, her hands shaking slightly.

I stood in the audience and watched while she played her "Your Head Is an Egg" song. She was unpolished, certainly, and she still shouted rather than sang—I guess that was her style—but if you asked me, she undoubtedly had those needles that got under your skin.

At the end, there was a smattering of claps, a cheer from Denise.

"Thank you. I'd like everyone in the audience to know I'm a fucking witch!" Neely shouted into the mic. "And this next song is called 'All My Friends Are Ghosts.'"

"The living ain't shit. Only ghosts can get down."

It was a short song, I knew. I ran back to the bathroom. Went into a stall, bolted the door. From my backpack, I pulled out a dress, a wig, hurriedly put them on.

"Okay," I could hear Neely saying as I exited the bathroom a minute or two later. "Thanks. You've been great. I've also been great. I have one more number for you."

She pushed the microphone away from her, toward the front of the stage. It spat and crackled.

I stood at the back of the room, frozen for a moment, watching.

Neely played a melody on her keyboard. It was delicate and beautiful, and then she broke it apart into discordant noise, and then she put it back together.

Moving as if in a dream, I made my way to the front of the room and stepped onto the stage, my heart so much a hummingbird I thought I might lift off, even with all my layers. Double gloves, double tights, skintight long-sleeved dress and over it the second dress with a hundred layers of tulle netting exploding out in rainbow extravagance.

A dress I had not stolen, for once.

Denise made this dress. Larissa had given us a ride to the craft store. I'd helped pick out the colors, but Denise was the one who had sewn them all together.

It was a chaotic dress, haphazard even, but it was without a doubt the most beautiful dress I'd ever worn in my whole life. It was mine. Denise made it for me, gave it to me.

I held up my hands, my lilac pearl-buttoned gloves gone

pinkish under the stage lights. I shook out my hair of multi-colored extensions sewn onto a cap. Denise had made that for me, too.

Every person in that room could see me. It was like the party, but this wasn't Halloween. It was like the Church, except I wasn't doing any tricks. My eyes searched the crowd.

And there she was. Right up front, next to Jules. Smiling. My eyes met hers.

She saw me. Better than anyone else. And I saw her.

I moved up to the microphone. I opened my mouth, behind the mask that Jules had painted for me.

And I screamed.

ACKNOWLEDGMENTS

Thanks to everyone who let me haunt their houses for a while: Toaster the corgi, Emily, Brenton, Heather, Brooke, Delia, Dan, Deidre, Marianne, and no doubt several others I'm forgetting.

Shout-outs to writer friends Toni Judnitch and Jenn Marie Nunes, who helped keep me going during difficult times.

Much credit to local expert Michael O'Brien for showing me around Pittsburgh when I first moved there many years ago.

Thanks to amazing agent Jim McCarthy and incisive editor Krista Marino. You both absolutely understood this book from the beginning and helped me bring it to life.

Thanks to Jasmine Walls and Nita Tyndall for their invaluable feedback on drafts. Thanks to Angela Carlino for the fabulous cover and Andrea Lau for the interior design. And thanks to everyone who worked on the editorial and marketing sides, including but not limited to Lydia Gregovic, Kris Kam, Kelly McGauley, Jenn Inzetta, and Colleen Fellingham.

Thanks to those two horses I saw from the window of a train once.

ABOUT THE AUTHOR

Mar Romasco-Moore is the author of *I Am the Ghost in Your House* and *Some Kind of Animal,* as well as *Ghostographs,* a collection of short stories paired with vintage photographs. She is an instructor at Columbus College of Art and Design.

marromascomoore.com

@MarRomasco

@marromasco